DEDICATION

To my princess, my heart, my daughter, Kameron Gabrielle.

ACKNOWLEDGEMENTS

This moment has been something that I've been waiting for, for quite some time, and it feels good to finally thank everyone who made my dream possible. I'm asking for forgiveness now if I forgot you on paper...know that I haven't forgotten you in my heart.

First, I would like to thank God for blessing me with a talent as well as with supportive people in my life to make my dreams come true. Without You nothing is possible and that's why I praise You. When I close my door every night with my family, when I wake up every morning with my family, I thank You for sheltering us from any harm and blessing me, and for this reason and many others.

To my daughter Kameron, my number one fan, I love you and I'm blessed to have an angel by my side every day. You are a true blessing and have totally changed my life for the better. I don't know what I would do without you. I appreciate your patience during this process. It was a tough, but we made it. Keep in mind that Mommy wants you to grow up and always be better than me. That's why I sacrifice and work hard, all for you. Whenever you're going through anything, always remember that no matter what- your Mommy loves you.

To my best friend, Rodney. I love you so much and I'm so blessed to have someone like you in my life. Your support and love has been a true blessing and I look forward to years of happiness and bliss with you by my side forever. It's been quite a road, but we made it through it all.

To my mother, Lita Gray, I love you dearly. You raised your children to love each other and know that when this world feels cruel, we have each other. Your struggles and sacrifices that I witnessed growing up have made me grow into an independent woman who knows what she wants in life. No matter how much it might go unsaid, know that I love and appreciate everything that you've done for me.

To my Daddy, Willis Poole. I pray for you every day. I know that life might seem hard sometimes, but know that you have love from your daughters. I will always be a Daddy's Girl no matter what.

To my siblings that I love dearly. My sister, my BFF Jawaun. Thanks for never judging me and being not only a sister, but a friend. I love you so much and don't know what I would do without you. There's something about a sister's love and you have surpassed any expectation of being a sister that I could ever expect. To my sister Mia, I love you so much and I appreciate you for being such an amazing sister to me. Through our adult years we have grown so much closer and if I don't say it enough, know that I love you. To my brother Cornell "Da Cook" I love you so much. I know I can be overprotective of my six foot something little brother, but it's all love. No matter how old you are or how tall you get, you're still my little brother. To my big brother Harold, I'm so proud of all you and Helen have accomplished. Thanks for loving your lil' sister the way you do, love you back- Eden's Lounge, B-More Stand up! To my brother Brent, thanks for being such a great support and listener, love you. Many thanks to my "step dad," Eric Bower.

To my niece and Goddaughter, Sydni Prather. Your poise and innocence makes you special. Don't ever change, know that you can do anything! To my neice Kyndall, know that we love you and I can't wait until you get older so we can spend time together. Don't forget your family in DC. To my baby, my nephew Javone Braxton, I love you so much and can't wait to see you on the big stage lil MJ.

To my Goddaughter, Ashley Sligh. I love you dearly and pray for you every day. I have tried my best with you and gave you all I had. I pray that you always know your worth as a young lady and I have always wanted you to grow up to be better than me. That's why I will never apologize for being hard on you and having high expectations. You can do anything that you set your heart out to do. Believe in yourself the way that I believe in you. When times get hard, know that I love you no matter what.

To my aunts and uncles and many cousins, the Lynch Clan and Books and Babes.

To my extended family, thanks for blessing me with your baby boy. Mema Thomas love you to death. Big Rodney and Ducie, hugs and kisses. Jordan and Doodie my babies, Eve and Jaron love you guys. To the cousin clan- Rontu, Ava, Christine, and Demetrie can't wait, it's on this summer. Delonte thanks for the love in Seattle, bring home a ring this year, Cavaliers all the way!

To John "Whitey," your friendship over the years has always been special. You've always been like a big brother to me, but over the past couple of years your friendship has been proven even more. Thanks for believing in me and helping make my dreams of becoming a writer come true.

Darb, I wanna thank you for hooking me up with my first laptop that I began writing with. The amount of money I have spent over the years on fashion and had never thought of making an investment like a computer that would help me get this much closer to my dreams. You made it possible. You're a true friend and thanks for being a Godfather to Kameron. I know I can be a crazy BFF, and know I never stay mad at you too long. Mr. Hughes, thanks for your continuous support over the years. Your support will never go unnoticed.

To all my girlz that have been true friends and I love dearly. You guys never judge me and are always there to listen to all my episodes. You truly know me and know why I can write novels for days, LOL, but through it all, again I will say y'all know me and know my heart.

My BFF Toya, I hope you really know how much you being my best friend means to me. Thanks for always being there to listen and you keep me grounded. Love you, BFF's forever!

Pam, I love you so much. Thanks for being you. Love the

new shop, shout out to Demi Mode. Gill and Demi, love you guys, too. Renee' take care of my brother and Travina thanks for keeping me laughing.

To my Godbrother Detrick. You have no idea how much you mean to me. We have been tight for almost twenty-five years and that's enough said in itself. Thanks for being you and accepting the "real me" no matter what.

Jermaine, my hairstylist, I love you to death. Many fun times up all night dancing and being silly. You keep me laughing and looking fierce. Dike, Angie, and Ty y'all know how crazy that boy is.

Toni, we've been friends for so long and I just want to thank you for always being there. Chop, Nicky, TT and Cubby love y'all too. Love you, Praya. Hurry home Kam misses you.

To my girl Poo, love you since our days Uptown. Love you to Bonton (smile). Endiah thank you for believing in me through this process and understanding I'm trying to get this paper, can't party all the time (LOL). Tanya, stop being MIA all the damn time. Love you cuz. Tiffany, I love you and I'm glad that I was able to find a friend in Hartford, CT. Des, Nicky, and Melissa, miss y'all.

Philly Times are always great times. Shana, I love you so much and I'm so blessed to have you as a friend. Peta Gaye, love you. You always are there to listen, now get outta NY and visit me! Tenidra, Tifah, Sharice, Tasha, and Niveah y'all keep the party going!

Jullette, your friendship over the past couple of years has brought me through some rough times. I love you for that and never forget it. We've had good times, Houston stand up! Fish and Tony love y'all too. Miss Ranata, love you no matter what. Kiana, Deon, Tanya, Jade and Candy all I can say is FUN TIMES!

Samantha, thanks for being a true good friend outside of work and always being there to listen. Love you too Rob. Carla, Caroline, Steph and Deb, I love my co-workers.

My childhood chums, I love you all. Shelrese (Chucky),

no matter what nobody could ever come between our friendship. Our Monroe St. days were the bomb. Hump, thanks for your support through this process and being a true friend even way past our Takoma days. To Latrease, "Baby Girl" my friend 'til the end since 7th grade, you know you started it all (LOL). To Dona and Nia, no matter how much we don't keep in contact like we should, distance could never erase our good times, love you both. Rayshawn, Tarrese, Shelvy, Janell, Markita, Tarina, Rochelle, Pam, Snookie, Joe Burnie, Donnie, Tarik, Terrance, Perry, Demi, Bernard, Jodie and the rest of my Mt. Pleasant family, GOOD TIMES!! Shawanna thanks for being a true friend.

To my homies, Mike Walker and Roy. Thanks for always being a friend no matter what, never judging, and accepting the real me. Dee, James and Big Steve, Pure Lounge all day! Big Leen, my other big sister, holding Richmond down. Pat of Paradise in Richmond, Mr. Bossman! Taz and Frank Suite 202 thanks for keeping DC Live! Abdul hold your head up, we miss you out here. From DC Live, Platinum, H20 and Lux, you kept it poppin. Good looking out Dean! Tupac D and Dominique Moxcey, K Street days were a blast. Oh Boyz much love Boobie and Chooch. George, love you brother. Love my 640 and 14th St Family. Madness for life, love you Eddie, Ty, Scotty, and Larry. Dorian, Troy and Tarik holding down the Philly parties, thanks for always looking out. Donovan and Frank, many thanks.

To my folks who are down right now- Woozie, KM, Musa, Gerald, Chop, and Julio! Sending you love in the inside. Prayer changes things, keep ya head up!

Rob Brown, thanks for believing in me. You're such a great friend and I appreciate your honesty. This is your year, can't wait to see you in your NBA jersey. Love you Stephen Andre. Malik, thanks for your friendship and opinions, and yes my cover is hot! With that being said thanks to Ms. Nessa for gracing my cover. BI, wassup? Murph Derrty, Lil bro, STL love you much. To my Wire family with much love, Hasaan Johnson and Andre Royo thanks for always believing in me and being so motivating. Idris and Oronde wassup?

Wendy Williams, thanks for being my big sister in my head. 93.9 WKYS and 95.5 WPGC thanks for keeping me jammin' in 270 traffic. Big G, love you, BYB for life! Big Tigga, wassup?

To my publisher, Azarel. I appreciate you believing in me and giving me a chance to share my dreams with the world. You're such a beautiful person and I'm thankful for the chance to join such a great team.

To Leslie Allen, my editor. Wow…we did it! Thanks for working with me and teaching me in the process. I couldn't have done it without you. The late night talks were helpful and therapeutic. The team effort is amazing, so I thank you again.

Many thanks to my Life Changing Books family- Tasha Simpson, Nakea Murray, and to my test readers, Cheryl, Tonya, Achundria, Shannon and Virginia. To the LCB authors…Danette Majette (Good Girl Gone Bad), Tonya Ridley (Talk of the Town), Tiphani Montgomery (Millionaire Mistress Series), J. Tremble (My Man Her Son), Jackie D. (Love Heist) Ericka Williams (A Woman Scorned) Capone (Marked), Mike Warren (Sweet Swagger), C.J. Hudson (Chedda Boyz), VegasClarke (Snitch), and anyone else, I left out on the LCB team. Thanks for welcoming me with open arms.

To my fans, thanks for your support. I can't wait to hear your feedback. You know part 2 will be just as good as this one, so make sure you look out for it.

With Love and Many Thanks,
Miss KP baby!!!

www.misskp.com
www.twitter.com/misskpdc
www.facebook.com/misskpdc

CHAPTER ONE

Lisa

Love is a powerful thing, I thought, climbing the stairs from the basement to the first floor living room. I took another swig from the bottle of Dasani, hoping to cool off before fainting in the middle of the floor. I'd just finished another two hour work-out in our custom designed gym that my husband built especially for me. Yet somehow, I didn't feel like myself. It was that *woman's intuition* that old people always talked about. Something just wasn't right.

Even though I knew Rich was out celebrating with our daughter, Denie, my mind couldn't stop wondering what he was doing, or who he was with whenever we were a part from each other. Over the past few years, he'd become so shady. Nothing he said was believable anymore. Countless lies and alibis were the only thing that ever came out his mouth, and I was immune to it.

When I entered the foyer and glared at the imported crystal chandelier, my heart questioned where things had gone wrong. The twenty thousand dollar chandelier was ordered when we first moved in, from my favorite furniture store in

Georgetown; that's when things were great. Whether it was a new fur, a new outfit, or diamonds, Rich always made it happen for me. Anyone could say I was a bit spoiled, but I deserved it. Besides, by me carrying the title, Mrs. Juan "Rich" Sanchez, I was entitled to the finer things in life.

Breaking from my daze, I started up the stairs to the bedroom taking two steps at a time in a hurry to get ready. It was my daughter's seventeenth birthday, so I needed to freshen up quickly, and head downtown to pick up her Chris Brown tickets and backstage passes.

As I entered our master bathroom, I couldn't wait to soak in our circular Jacuzzi tub. My daily baths had become routine and fairly therapeutic; the ultimate anti-stress treatment that allowed me to drift away from all my problems. Preparing my vanilla almond bubble bath, I was determined to make today drama free. Many years ago, my Aunt Lita told me vanilla was the scent men were mostly attracted to, so of course that stayed in my smell good collection. With a man like my husband, it was important to keep it tight and smelling right.

Lighting my vanilla candles, I took a look at the woman in the mirror. I was raised in a Christian home. My dad was a pastor, and my mother, brothers and sisters were all still active in the church, and yet I was the one who strayed and married a ruthless drug dealer. Being raised with high standards and morals, I tried hard to hold on to that by making my marriage work with whatever it took. Nowadays, I wasn't so sure if I could hold on any longer. In a daze, I began to ask myself, what type of woman had I become? I'd been doing all the good wifely duties over the years just to keep my man, but it was clear to me now that shit hadn't made a difference; crystal clear. Just like any other no good ass man, Rich was gonna do what he wanted, regardless of who he hurt in the process.

My husband was the finest thing in the city. His father was Columbian and his mother was Black, but with more of his father's features, he was just the right mix. His tall stature and his lean but muscular build gave him power when he entered any room. His warm, brown complexion and thick, curly hair had many people mistaking him for a Dominican, and women were definitely weak for his dimples. He was definitely the type of man that you had to keep interested. Rich was "The Man" in D.C., with plenty of money and clout in the eighties and nineties. An entrepreneur at heart, Rich owned t-shirt stores, Laundromats, a few small car lots, but where most of his legal money came from was his bar, Bottom's Up. Rich had old money, but his swagger still gave the young dudes a run for their money. We were definitely financially stable. He was the most wanted man in the streets by both the Feds and the chicks. That was just how it had always been. Many had tried, but none had succeeded.

After finally getting out of the tub, I wrapped myself in a towel, then waltzed to my dresser and pulled out my red lace La Perla bra and thong set. Our wedding photo on the dresser always made me smile anytime I started to feel insecure. With naughty thoughts on my mind, I figured I would give Rich a night cap after the birthday festivities. That's if he didn't reject me. He was known for doing that from time to time. His excuse, which sounded like a broken record, was that he was tired or had a stressful day. I wasn't sure why he thought I believed that shit. Every woman knows that men never turned down pussy, not unless they were gay of course. Rich definitely wasn't gay, but he was a cheater. Someone who'd been caught a countless number of times; so many times that I'd lost count.

Feeling refreshed, I put on my white terrycloth Juicy Couture robe and went back in the bathroom to do my hair. I'd been debating on cutting my hair forever because it was so long, falling past my breasts. However, the thought of how Rich would feel about me with a bob or a short pixie cut made me erase that thought immediately. He'd told me on countless occasions how women with short hair weren't attractive. The last thing I needed right now was for him to think I wasn't sexy. Pulling my hair up into a sleek ponytail with my custom-made, Tiffany diamond barrette Rich bought me years ago, I played with a few loose strands before I was finally satisfied.

Looking at myself in the mirror, my hazel eyes stared back at me. My high cheek bones and honey brown skin used to give me confidence, but now my self esteem was low. I thought my beauty and innocence was enough that Rich would never cheat on me. Boy, did I have myself fooled.

I leaned over the sink then began washing my face with my Dr. Perricone facial cleanser when suddenly I heard a strange noise. I quickly stood up even though I couldn't see anything, trying to figure out what it was. Maybe Denie and Rich came back, I thought.

"Rich!" I yelled out. When he didn't respond, I called out his name again. "Rich!" There was complete silence. "Maybe I'm tripping," I told myself.

Bending back down, I began rinsing my face with water then stood back up to grab a hand towel off the rack. After patting my face in several different areas, I finally looked in the mirror, and gasped at what I saw. My heart thumped. Chest pounded. Immediately, my brain told me it was really an extra set of eyes staring back at me. A shock of terror shot through my body. Who was this man with these big eyes filled with lust and what was he doing in my home? I didn't even have time to scream before he put his left hand over my mouth and shoved a knife toward my throat.

"I always wondered how it would feel to fuck Rich's girl. Ummm, you smell so damn good," he whispered in my ear in a seductive yet powerful tone. He smelled like a pack of Newports mixed with Armani cologne.

"What do you want from me?" I muffled through his black glove.

"Bitch, I want to destroy your husband's life like he destroyed mine, and you're gonna help me do it," the intruder replied in a forceful, yet calm tone. "Now, cooperate with me and I'll make this as easy for you as possible."

Tears immediately streamed from my face. I was paralyzed with fear and couldn't move. He pressed his body against me, squeezing my stomach against the porcelain sink. It felt as if he wanted to cut off my circulation. I began squirming, trying to get loose when he flung my body around to face him and then...he struck me...hard. So hard, I instantly fell to the floor. Hitting my head on the black and white ceramic tile was all I remembered, until I woke up in a warehouse full of goons. It was obvious that hours had gone by. The darkness seeping in from the skylight above told me so, but I couldn't remember a thing. My naked body shivered uncontrollably from the cold air, and I felt beyond sore in my vaginal area. My ribs even felt like they were broken. As my teeth chattered, I couldn't stop shaking from a combination of fear and the cool brisk air. I wondered how long I'd been unconscious.

Oh, my God they raped me, I thought to myself.

I tried to yell for help, but felt so lethargic and weak that I couldn't even raise my voice. My head ached and my vision was blurry. When I tried to move, I discovered I was handcuffed by my wrists and ankles to a rusty iron bed. The warehouse smelled like a combination of weed and funk. The room I was in had old computers on the floor and different sized file cabinets stacked against the wall. As I tried to figure out where I was, I noticed old poster advertisements of a variety of go-go bands taped on the walls. At that moment, it dawned on me that I was probably in an office of an old abandoned club. As my eyes began to focus, I saw the attacker walking up to me playing with himself. He was completely naked. At that moment, a lump formed in my throat, and before I knew it, I started to vomit all over myself.

"Damn, bitch. You gonna make my dick soft throwin' up and shit! Man-Man get in here and clean this bitch up, I'm ready to fuck her again!" the attacker yelled with authority.

"Please no, please let me go. I'm sorry for whatever my husband did. Please just let me go, I have kids," I pleaded.

"I know you sorry baby, but see, your man Rich isn't, so fuck yo kids. That nigga rides around town like he the man, fuckin' everybody's girl and shit. So, that's why I snatched you.

Your man fucked up my fam. Shit was good and he fucked it up. Now, shut up!" he demanded.

I cried as Man-Man did as he was told and the attacker spread my legs apart and rammed his dick inside of me. The harder he pumped, the more nauseous I became. From the pain of my broken ribs, I could barely breathe or cry out for help.

Feeling defeated, I laid there as he ejaculated all over my face a few minutes later. Since I was handcuffed, I couldn't even stop his cum from dripping on my bottom lip. Humiliation was an understatement for how I felt as the other guys started to file into the room. They just stared at me with lust. The tallest one kept looking at me, licking his lips at the same time. He scared me even more than the attacker, because he had that look; like a child molester.

The attacker began to put his clothes on, then took his cell phone of out the holster on his waist. For some reason, I knew he was about to call Rich. As he placed the call on speakerphone, he started singing a few lines from Chuck Brown's song, *I Need Some Money*. It was almost as if he was rehearsing for what he was about to say. Knowing Rich didn't answer calls from unknown numbers, especially if they were blocked, I prayed that he would answer. Seconds later, my prayers were answered.

"Who's this?" Rich asked.

"Is this Rich?" the attacker asked trying to disguise his voice. "It's about time you answered."

"What the fuck you think? Didn't you call my phone nigga? Who is this?" Rich sounded irritated already.

The attacker began to pace the floor. "If I were you, I wouldn't come so slick out the mouth, muthafucka."

"Oh, yeah, why?" Rich questioned.

"Because I got yo' bitch that's why. Now, if you want to see her again, you might want to stop asking so many fucking questions and start listening!"

"Who the fuck is this?" Rich demanded with authority.

"Now Richie, you don't mind me calling you Richie do

you? I need you to meet me at the old warehouses on Ritchie Road."

"Look, you punk-ass nigga. I'm not in the mood for games!"

The veins in the attacker's neck began to pop out. "Oh, it's not a game. You think I'm fucking playing? I've been beating up your wife's pussy all day, thanks to you dodging my calls. This is my third call to your ass."

"Man, what the…" Rich began to say.

"Shut the fuck up! I'm in control and you're gonna do what I say. Come alone. Don't call anyone or she dies."

"I need to speak to my wife!" Rich yelled.

"Fuck no," the attacker said with authority. "This beautiful, tender wife of yours will die right now, if you try and fuck with me. You have one hour to bring me $500,000 in cash. If you don't, I can't imagine what I'll do to this beautiful bitch here." The attacker began to laugh before finally hanging up. He then walked over to me and started playing with my hair. "I sure hope yo' husband knows how to follow instructions."

"Is it my turn yet?" one goon asked.

The attacker smiled. "Yeah, go ahead. I've had enough pussy for now."

"Nooooo. Stop it!" I screamed with terror as the tallest of the goons began to stick his skinny fingers inside of me.

He asked for the keys to the handcuffs so he could flip me over. All I could think was, this couldn't be happening to me. Any minute I thought I would wake up and it would all be a nightmare, but that never happened.

"No, please," I continued to plead. I didn't know why I thought he would have some type of sympathy.

"Shut up, bitch!" the tall goon belted.

After taking down his pants and boxers, he flipped me over and entered my ass with a forceful thrust. At that moment, I felt like I was going to die. It felt like my anal walls were on fire as he moved in and out at a rapid pace. No KY Jelly or another lubricant for him to have easier access, just completely dry. The pain was excruciating.

Despite my constant screams, the goon moaned and bragged on how tight it felt. As many times as Rich tried to get me to do it, I'd never had anal sex before and now what was so precious to me, was being taken away. My body was filled with so many emotions; fear, anger, and animosity. What did I ever do to deserve this? All I wanted was my husband to come to my rescue. Feeling so weak, I passed out…again.

CHAPTER TWO
Rich

Denie and I were on our way to Cold Stone Creamery for her favorite, cookies and cream ice cream cake; a birthday ritual we'd been doin' for the past two years when my cell phone began to ring once again. It had been ringin' non stop for the past two hours from a private number, but everyone in my circle knew that I didn't answer calls from blocked numbers. However, this time my street intuition kicked in and somethin' finally told me to answer. Denie was jammin' to T.I.'s old song, *Whatever You Like*, when I turned down the radio and pressed the button to accept the call; a call that I had no idea would change the state of my family forever. When the nigga on the other end told me he had my wife, I just sat at the traffic light in a daze… in complete shock. I started to go ballistic, bangin' on the steerin' wheel in a psychotic rage.

"Daddy, what's wrong?" Denie asked.

I shook my head. "Nothin', Denie."

"Then why did you hit the…"

"Denie, please let me think," I said, cuttin' her off. My mind began to race. *How the fuck did this happen*? I began to ask myself. *How did my day of happiness, celebratin' my daughter's birthday, turn into me havin' to rescue my wife? I'm gonna kill whoever the fuck is responsible for this.*

People were beginnin' to beep their car horns and yell obscenities when the light turned green, and I still hadn't moved. Before I could even put my foot back on the gas pedal, a police car pulled up beside us.

"Shit. I don't need this right now," I said as soon as I heard the annoyin'-ass police siren. As much as I hated the police, I had to keep my composure, especially since I had a gun under the seat. Just in case the officer wanted to get out of the car and question whether or not my brand new black Range Rover belonged to me, I quickly grabbed my registration out of the glove compartment to stay one step ahead. I watched as a young white female cop wit' dirty blonde hair rolled down her window. I quickly rolled mine down as well and tried to display a warm smile.

"Sir, is there a problem?" the officer questioned. Even though she didn't have on any makeup, I could tell she was a cutie. I loved to fuck wit' white broads since they were the freakiest in the bedroom. However, wit' my daughter in the car, I didn't want my eyes to roam too much. *That reminds me, I need to get wit' my white bitch, Brittney, from Ashburn at some point. I haven't seen her in about a month.*

"No, officer, we're fine. My daughter is asthmatic and we were lookin' for her inhaler, but we found it. She's fine now," I answered, tryin' to keep my cool. Denie quickly played along by grabbin' her chest like she couldn't breathe. She'd been taught well.

"Do you need an ambulance, sir?" the officer asked.

"No ma'am. She'll be fine, but thank you."

"Alright you folks be careful," the officer said, as she drove away.

I looked over at my daughter who had a victory look on her face. Yet she was still worried about somethin'. "You always got my back, huh?" I asked, drivin' off.

"You know it," Denie replied, soundin' like a grown woman more so than a seventeen year old.

Instead of headin' to Silver Spring, I detoured immediately and made my way to my mother's house in the Northeast part of the city. Wit' rapid speed, and a concerned look on my face, Denie knew somethin' was up.

"Are you gonna tell me what's wrong now?"

I glanced over at my daughter, who was my twin. A light skinned version of me, and more Hispanic than black, she reminded me of the actress Lauren London wit' her deep dimples and almond shaped eyes. Not to mention, her body made her look ten years older, which scared me. "Somethin' came up, so I need you to stay at your grandmother's house 'til things get settled."

Denie sighed. "Oh, no. Please don't take me over there," she said wit' so much disappointment in her eyes.

"Trust me. It's best if you stay there for a while," I answered.

"Are you coming back? Please promise that you're coming back. Suppose they kill y'all."

I couldn't believe she'd just said that. I glanced at Denie again. "What are you talkin' about?"

"The dude who called on the phone. You should've never turned down the music because I could hear what he was saying. Just give him what he wants, so you can come back and get me." Denie was a lot smarter than I gave her credit for.

My baby girl was so much like me, it was scary. She was down for whatever, and could handle whatever came her way, which made me proud. Any other kid would've probably been sheddin' a tear by now. I'd raised both of my kids to be strong. In my line of work, weakness wasn't an option.

"Don't worry, baby. I promise I'll come back and get you. I'll never leave you again. Who's Daddy's girl?"

Denie was hesitant at first. "Me, your Baby Girl," she said in a low child-like tone.

"Damn right. You're my pride and joy." That was our little thing since she was a little girl. I knew that would comfort her…for the moment.

Makin' sure we weren't bein' followed, I hit a lot of back streets to watch my back. As I pulled into my mother's drive way ten minutes later, I noticed the ice from the snow storm a few days prior hadn't been shoveled, which was another thing for me to feel guilty about. Wit' my mother sick wit' Coronary Heart Disease, there was no excuse for her yard to look like that. I made a mental note to take care of that as soon as I got out the current mess I was in.

Taking my .9mm from under my seat, I put it in my coat pocket and got out to open Denie's door. Seconds later, we walked up the hill of the driveway wit' my arm draped around her shoulder. Denie had been so quiet the past few minutes, I knew she had an attitude, but she had no other choice but to get over it.

My mother took forever to answer the door. It was cold as shit as I rang the doorbell at least ten times.

"Where's your key?" my mother asked when she finally appeared. Her body seemed more frail since the last time I'd seen her.

"Hey, Ma." I bent down and gave her a kiss on her forehead. My mind so was distraught that I'd completely forgotten to use my key. "Sorry, it's a lot on my mind right now," I said walkin' further inside. "Hey, can Denie stay here for a while? I have to make an important run."

"Boy, it don't make no sense. It's that girl's birthday, and all you can think about is running those damn streets!" my mother yelled wit' frustration. "Aren't you too old for that mess?"

Denie hated goin' to my mother's house, especially since all she did was ramble off quotes from the Bible and utter broken Spanish under her breath, and I couldn't blame her. Ever since my father died ten years ago, she hadn't been the same.

"Ma, it's not like that. This is important," I replied. "Look, I gotta go." I walked over to Denie and gave her a kiss on the cheek. "Don't worry, Baby Girl. I'll be back."

The look in Denie's eyes was pure sadness as she watched me walk out of the door. When I got in my truck, I could see her starin' out of the livin' room window like a little puppy. As bad as I didn't want to leave her on her birthday, it was about her well-bein' at this point. Not to mention, I didn't know who these fools were or what I was dealin' wit', so my mother's house was the safest place for her at the moment. I didn't want to take any chances. My son, Juan, didn't answer his cell phone as usual, so I left him a message lettin' him know to stay at one of his girlfriend's houses for a minute 'til he heard from me. Like father like son, Juan had plenty of women. Ever since I'd bought him a 750 Li BMW when he graduated from high school, he'd definitely been a bitch magnet.

My mind began racin' again and I was officially in guerilla mode. How could I let these muthafuckas catch me slippin'? I knew that the recession and the recent drought in the game had caused a lot of dudes' money to be fucked up, but I questioned who had the balls to come after me and my family. I loved my family, and everyone in the streets could attest to how much they meant to me. Now that somebody had decided to fuck wit' them had me in a rage, and they were going to pay…big time.

When Denie disappeared from the window, I zipped up my Northface coat, pulled my skull cap over my ears, and hopped back out the truck. I didn't want her to know what I was up to. Runnin' around the back of my mother's house, I had to get some doe. A good amount of my money was stashed in the bottom of the shed since I really didn't trust banks like that. Even though my mother was nosey, she never went into the shed, so it was the perfect spot. I raced through the snow in the backyard to hurry since time was not on my side. Unlockin' the padlock, I looked over my shoulder to make sure no one was watchin'. Not only was my mother nosey, but her neighbors were even worse. More importantly, I wanted to make sure the muthafuckas who were tryin' to ruin my life weren't tryin' to creep up on me either.

After walkin' inside and closing the door behind me, I quickly began removin' all the bags of soil that I'd placed over a huge wood board. Once the board was removed, I stared at the deep hole that had been covered in dirt. Grabbin' the shovel, I began diggin' as fast as I could to get to the suitcase that contained my cash. However, the more dirt I removed, the angrier I got.

"I'ma kill these muthafuckas," I said to myself. Even though my wife was worth it, I was ready for war at the thought of me havin' to fuck wit' my stash.

When I finally reached the suitcase, I quickly pulled it from the hole and placed it on my lap. Knowin' I had to act fast, I opened the plastic bag the money was in, then began to count out several stacks. I kept my money in bundles, ten thousand in each. When I reached fifty, I placed the money in one of mother's old gardenin' bags, and put the rest back. Once everything was back in it's proper place, I quickly placed the padlock back on the door, ran through the yard and jumped in my truck. The way I pulled off down the street, you would've thought I was a driver for Nascar.

After drivin' for a few minutes, I picked up my phone, realizin' that I'd left it in the car. I had five missed calls from a private number.

"Shit," I said, then banged my fist against the steerin' wheel. I didn't want those niggas to do somethin' stupid.

Before I could think any further, my phone rang again. It was from a blocked number again, so I knew exactly who it was this time. "Hello."

"You better start answering yo' phone nigga, if you want this shit to work out. You got fifteen minutes or this bitch is dead. When you pull up, blow the horn twice. Oh, and come unarmed." CLICK

I hated when muthafuckas gave me orders. No one gave me orders, but I had to bow down 'til I found out who was responsible for this. They were definitely goin' to pay though. If I had to kill their whole family so be it. I already had it in my mind that I wasn't goin' to show any mercy.

Doin' as I was told, I drove through D.C. at top speed, hopin' not to get pulled over. Lookin' at the clock on my radio every few minutes, I ran every red light I could 'til I finally made it to Ritchie Road. There was so much goin' on I didn't even have time to call my cousin, Carlos, who was my right hand man. At a time like this, I wish he didn't live on the West Coast.

Wit' only two minutes to spare, I pulled up in front of the abandoned warehouse and tapped the horn two times. Moments later, a door on the side of the buildin' opened, and an arm appeared, gesturin' me to come inside. After placin' my gun back under the seat, I hopped out of my truck to find three masked men all pointin' their heat at me as soon as I walked inside. Wit' both of my hands in the air, one of them patted me down and checked every single pocket in my coat. He then handcuffed me to a pole, and snatched the gardenin' bag out of my hand.

"Richie!" a deep voice rang out from behind a door. "I'm so glad you could make it. Now, punish that nigga!" he yelled.

The tallest of the three dudes immediately came over to me and did exactly what his boss ordered. I didn't even have a chance to look for Lisa before the muthafucka shot me. The hot metal burned through my skin and instantly tore open my knee. Blood gushed everywhere. It was evident that they weren't playin'. Seconds later, somebody hit me over the head wit' a blunt object and I hit the cold dusty floor instantly. The next thing I remembered was the feelin' of a hot liquid pourin' over my face. When I finally realized that one of the muthafuckas was pissin' on me, anger consumed by body like a rapid spreadin' disease.

"Wake the fuck up!" one of the goons yelled as he shook his little, shriveled up dick.

"Yeah, wake up Richie," the voice from behind the door said. "Since you decided to fuck my girl, now, it's time for me to fuck yours again." At that moment, I realized that this just wasn't about kidnappin' Lisa or the money; it was much deeper.

"Are you serious? All this over some bitch!" I belted. The crazy thing was, I'd fucked wit' so many women over the years, hell over the past few months, I had no idea who he was talkin' about.

"No, don't get it twisted. The money was first priority, but the fact that you been fucking my girl, just makes the shit worse," the voice replied.

"Rich…help me…please!" I finally heard Lisa cry out.

"Shut the fuck up!" the voice demanded. A few minutes later, I could hear the nigga gruntin' in the background.

I shouted to the top of my lungs. "Why…why my wife? I'm gonna kill you muthafucka!"

"You sending death threats while my man fucking yo' wife?" one of the goons asked.

"Awww shit I'm bout to bust…fuck," the voice behind the door moaned.

All I could hear was Lisa screamin' as the rest of his goons laughed.

"You're going to die!" I prayed I could make good on my threat. "Show your face, you punk-ass nigga!"

"Is that how you treat the man who just banged yo' wife? See, that's why I won't reveal to you who my girl is. You just think about all the bitches you fucked and wonder who I'm talking about," the voice replied.

The other guys laughed as I squirmed. I think this was the day my manhood was stripped. I felt worthless, especially when I heard Lisa's voice again.

"No…please...wait. What are you doing?" she asked.

I thought I was about to hear the nigga moanin' again, when suddenly the door opened. Hopin' I would see his face, I lifted my head as somethin' was tossed out the door. The more I focused in on the Tiffany diamond barrette, I knew that it was a wad of Lisa's hair.

"What the fuck? What was the point of that?" When no one answered me, all I could do was just lay there and wonder what else was about to go down. Seconds later, I watched as my wife crawled out of the room lifeless and naked. She was so badly beaten that it hurt me to even look at her.

"Crawl bitch, I love it when you crawl!" the taller goon called out as the other two laughed.

As soon as Lisa was half way across the room, one of the goons grabbed her by the leg and pulled her toward him. "Come here, bitch. Now, I want some of that ass."

"No…please. Not again," Lisa wailed as the goon began to slap her ass. I could tell he loved the way it bounced.

"Get your fuckin' hands off of her!" I demanded.

"Man get the duct tape and shut that nigga up," the taller goon instructed. "He about to make my dick go soft."

Doin' as they were told, I squirmed as the goons placed duct tape over my mouth as well as Lisa's. Seconds later, I watched in complete horror as the tall goon grabbed my wife's hips, shoved his raw dick into her ass, then began poundin' at a rapid pace. Watchin' my wife bein' sodomized was heart wrenchin' especially how her eyes cried for my help and knowin' there was nothin' I could do.

"Yeah, this shit nice and tight," the goon said as his dick plunged in and out.

"You muthafucka!" I muffled through the tape, knowin' he couldn't hear me.

I could only imagine the pain Lisa was in as tears streamed down her face. The pit of my stomach felt sour. There was nothin' I could do to save my wife and it hurt. This bitch-ass nigga had stripped me of my manhood and I wanted to kill anything in the room movin'. As the goon finally pulled out moments later, his dick dripped of blood and semen. He even had the nerve to pull on his shit so the remainin' fluids could fall on Lisa's back. It was beyond degradin'.

After the bastard zipped his pants back up, he and the other goons went into the room where the nigga was callin' the shots and closed the door. At that moment, I glanced over at my wife, who was still layin' in the same spot. She looked helpless.

It killed me not bein' able to run over to her to see if she was okay. Suddenly, I heard a lot of noise before the annoyin'-ass voice called out again.

"Richie, word on the street is you about yo' business, and I guess they're right. Since you kept yo' word and all the money is here, I'ma keep mine, but damn I hate to give yo' wife's pussy up." The more he continued to talk shit, the more it pissed me off, but it was nothin' I could do. "Come on my niggas we out!" the voice yelled as a small white box was tossed out the door.

After all the goons left, and I could hear tires screechin' away, Lisa finally turned and looked in my direction. At that moment, I motioned to her wit' my head to get the box. She continued to lay there for a few seconds before finally crawlin' to the package. Wit' barely any energy, she picked it up and opened it. It was the key to the handcuffs and a note. Finally makin' her way over to me to unlock the cuffs she handed me the note in complete silence, which read, *Thanks for the cash in the shed, you shouldn't have.*

Oh, shit! How the fuck did they find that out, I thought. Since they knew where my mother lived, I had to get her and Denie out the house before somethin' else popped off.

CHAPTER THREE
Lisa

No matter how many baths I took to meditate and clear my mind, I just couldn't forget the day that changed my life. As I continued to soak and smell the aroma of my vanilla candles, all I could think to myself was, *I should've left his ass a long time ago.* My husband, the man that meant the world to me, had turned my world upside down. Being so loyal, I was always down for Rich, but the riches, cars, big house, and furs weren't worth it anymore. For years I'd been asking Rich to leave the streets alone. He was so knee deep that he felt it was all he knew. Sometimes I wondered whether he was married to me or the game.

It was so hard for me to deal with being abducted and raped because I couldn't talk about it to anyone. Since high school, Rich had caused me to alienate my friends and family so I didn't have anyone outside of him, Carlos' wife, Marisol and my girl, Trixie. Marisol always came through for me when I needed her. Once Rich and I learned that my attackers had taken the money from the shed, we knew it was no longer safe for Denie to stay at Rich's mom's house. Carlos had Marisol fly in from California, so that Denie and his mother could stay with her at their East Coast home in Potomac, Maryland. We knew they would be safer there. Rich didn't play around when it came to his street business, and he did his best to keep me out of it.

He made it clear to me that it would ruin the children if anyone knew, so I had to stay quiet. Even though Marisol was well aware, I was even prohibited from talking to her about it. Since Trixie was known to run her mouth, she wasn't even an option. Rich warned me on more than one occasion that he would fuck me up, if I ever said anything to her. Hell, he didn't even want me talking to Trixie about the weather most of the time. I couldn't understand how Rich wanted me to stay mute about such a traumatic event; like he wanted me to forget that the shit even happened. Who could erase a pain like that?

Reaching for the prescription bottle of Ambien on the side of the tub, I took a sleeping pill in order to let my problems slip away. Faced with my nightmare, I heard the voice of the bastard who raped me every day; a voice that constantly rang in my ears. Night sweats, startled by loud noises, had me so paranoid. Lately, there was no way possible I could rest peacefully without taking sleeping pills. The pills were my only way to cope. I imagined and stared at the flames of my candles and let my problems just melt away into the wax. Three weeks had passed and I knew it would take time, but it was still hard for me to even enter my bedroom, let alone my bathroom, which used to be my sanctuary.

Meditating on my thoughts, I wondered if I would ever be able to move past this situation. I just couldn't believe how I nursed Rich back to health after he was shot, but yet I was the one who needed him. I'd been raped and sodomized for hours by my attackers but yet, on wifey duty, I catered to Rich and focused on him. Getting back to himself was his first priority as always. He never once asked me if I was okay. The anger I felt secretly toward him, made me want to leave so bad. Back in the day, he knew how to use the kids to make me stay. Now that the kids were getting older, I really didn't have a reason to still be with him. Every time I would bring up what my attacker said about Rich fucking his girl, he would say he didn't want to hear that shit. He would go on to say how I couldn't believe someone else over my husband. I knew Rich was lying. I just didn't have any proof. In my mind, Rich just couldn't face that his infidelity was the reason why our lives would never be the same.

Breaking from my deep thought, I heard Rich enter our bedroom. He'd been in the basement playing pool and meeting with his cousin, Carlos, for hours. When he limped into the bathroom and we made eye contact, I felt the sudden urge to curse his ass out. It didn't even matter to me that his knee was still messed up. At one time, I used to be afraid to express how I felt to Rich fearing that he would hit me for being disrespectful, but now all that shit had changed. I was numb, and just didn't care anymore.

"What's up, babe?" Rich asked as he leaned over and gave me a kiss on my forehead. I could smell the alcohol on his breath.

I wondered what he wanted because he hadn't called me babe in a while. "Are you drunk?"

"I just had a couple of bottles wit' Los. Why the fuck are you questionin' me anyway?" he slurred.

"Because we need to talk."

"Man, here we go. What's up, Lisa?" He sounded irritated as if he knew what I was going to say. He put his hands in the water trying to rub on my legs.

"Our love has survived many things, but Rich I don't know about this. I've always loved you and forgiven you for your lies and cheating, but this, I just can't do this anymore."

"What are you sayin', Lisa? Are you tryin' to leave or something? Bitch, you ain't leavin' me."

"Bitch! Who the hell are you calling a bitch? You're an evil, selfish bastard and I'm tired of your ass!" I quickly stood up, got out of the tub and began to dry off. "Tell me the truth, Rich. You fucked that dude's girl, didn't you? You said you were done with all of these whores in the streets and yet you're still out here sleeping around!"

Rich sighed. "Man, you need to get over that shit. The dude took your pussy, so what, life goes on." He gently patted his knee. "The doctor talkin' about I might not walk the same again since I got shot at such a close range. Did you forget about that? I told you I'ma find the niggas who did that to you. Trust me."

"Well, what about all the shit he was saying about you and his girl? You think I'm just gonna forget about that? You think I'ma keep sweeping shit under the rug?"

"That nigga was lyin' to you. What the hell Lisa, I'm the one who got shot. Do you hear me complainin' every five minutes about this shit?" When he reached out and grabbed me in his arms, I wondered if this was a bad idea, but felt a need to express myself. "This is forever. You know I love you. Those other bitches never mattered. Don't I take care of you and keep you in all the flyest shit? Don't you hit up the fuckin' mall at least once a week? I don't take care of those other bitches. You my number one!"

"Your number one? I should be your only one! I'm your wife and the mother of your children. You should always respect me, but that's not always the case. These streets have made you a gutter nigga. What would you do if someone disrespected your daughter like this? I'm somebody's daughter, Rich!" I yelled as I tried to back away from him. As soon as those words came out of my mouth, I instantly missed my father.

"Lisa, keep Denie out of this. This is about you and me." The look he gave me instantly told me that I'd struck a nerve.

He tried to kiss me as I continued to push him away. I didn't want him to touch me; after what I'd gone through I didn't want any man to touch me. Rich didn't like the way I was rejecting him and started to get rough. At that moment, he grabbed me by my hair and forced me out of the bathroom where we ended up on the bed. Lying on top of me, he kissed me all over my neck. He then started to suck on my breasts, biting each one of my nipples. Immediately, I flashed back to being raped and started screaming.

"Rich stop it! Get off of me!"

"You're gonna give me some pussy. I need to feel you, Lisa!"

I could feel Rich's hard dick pressing against my leg. At one point in my life it made me want him, but times were different now. I had no desire to ever let Rich make love to me again. Moments later, Carlos came to my rescue. He'd obviously heard me screaming all the way from the theater room in the basement.

"Rich, what the fuck are you doing man?" Carlos yelled as he pulled Rich off of me.

"My own wife won't give me any pussy that's what's wrong. It's been three weeks, and she won't even let me touch her. I can't even get her to suck my dick." Rich looked at me. "Now, you wonder why I be fuckin' them other bitches Lisa, because of shit like this!"

"Rich, I hate you! I can't believe you were gonna rape me, too!" I cried.

"Come on man, you drunk, Rich. That's your wife. Let's go back downstairs," Carlos intervened.

I was so embarrassed to be completely naked in front of Carlos. I covered myself with my towel and balled up in a fetal position as tears raced down my cheeks.

Rich continued to rant until he finally decided to go back downstairs. "Come on Los. Leave that bitch alone!" he yelled.

"Are you okay?" Carlos asked.

"What do you think, Carlos? You and Rich go out and fuck around on me and Marisol and think the shit is cool. You're the reason why Rich doesn't make it home some nights." I often wondered if Rich had a problem with Carlos using the shit he was supposed to be selling. Over the past two years, Carlos had become a heavy cocaine user, who was high most of the time when he came around. He even had Marisol indulging in it now.

"Look, don't blame the shit Rich does on me," Carlos shot back.

"I was raped because of some woman Rich fucked, and now I'm supposed to want to have sex with him!"

"You don't know that this happened because of a bitch, Lisa. All these young niggas have been going hard since the streets been light. That could've been a way for him to throw us off."

"That's bullshit and you know it. I need to call my son. It's time for him to come home."

"No, don't call Juan. It'll only cause more problems," Carlos replied.

The kids hadn't been home since the incident, and the more I thought about it, Carlos was right. Not only was I was glad that they didn't have to witness any of this dysfunctional shit, but Juan hated Rich ever since he went to jail a couple of years ago, so him being home would've definitely caused more confusion.

"Just get out!" I yelled.

"Sorry about all of this, Lisa," Carlos said before he walked out and shut the bedroom door.

As more tears began to flow, the more I began to ask myself questions? What happened to that man that I loved? The Juan Sanchez Sr. I fell in love with would've never been this disrespectful. Now, he'd become Rich, the thoughtless, cruel cheating asshole who I couldn't stand to be around. He didn't even like for me to call him Juan anymore. I had to call him by the stupid-ass nickname his boys had given him years ago. Our lives were not supposed to be like this.

After crying for what seemed liked forever, I finally walked back into the bathroom and put on my pineapple Body Shop lotion. I took a deep breath as I opened the medicine cabinet. Feeling helpless, I couldn't believe that I even considered downing the entire bottle of Rich's pain killers. I just needed to get away. However, the more my son crossed my mind, I knew that I could never leave him. Walking to my customized walk-in closet, I slipped into one of my cashmere Juicy Couture sweat suits to get comfortable. Normally, I would've put on something a little sexier, but the last thing I wanted was for Rich to see me partially naked. After hopping on the bed, I turned to VH-1 to catch up on my reality shows until I passed out.

The next morning, the sun peaked through my bedroom window waking me up extra early. I also woke up in the bed alone, which wasn't surprising. I was so used to Rich staying out all night it didn't even bother me anymore. Going into the bathroom, I washed my face and brushed my teeth before going downstairs to fix some breakfast. After deciding to skip dinner, my stomach was definitely on "E", and I needed something to control my nausea, which I was sure came from me taking too many pills.

When I walked down stairs, I could hear Rich and Carlos in a deep conversation, obviously plotting something. I was surprised to even see them. I just knew they would still be out getting into some trouble. Whenever Carlos came to my house, it usually meant bad news. Carlos was in the game deep and ran shit on the West Coast, from L.A. to Arizona. With them being first cousins they'd been close since they were young. Rich's father cared for Carlos most of his life due to Carlos' father, Lorenzo, being in and out of jail. With jet black hair and thick eyebrows, Carlos' Columbian heritage was very distinctive. Everyone always thought they were brothers because he and Rich looked so much alike, but they were complete opposite. Carlos had this rugged side to him. He dressed in jeans and sweats all the time and wore long cornrows that touched his shoulders. He also had tattoos everywhere, and even had tears tatted on his face under his eye. Rich on the other hand, switched his look up more often. He had more variety in his style. He would wear anything from a button up and loafers, to a hoody and jeans. He dressed for the occasion and was classy, while Carlos was hood.

When I walked past the family room Carlos said, "Good morning," while Rich said nothing.

"Why are you still here? Don't you have somewhere to be?" I asked irritated. "Does Marisol know where you are?"

"Lisa, mind your fuckin' business and stay in a woman's place," Rich responded with an old-school authority.

Ignoring him, I went in the kitchen, opened the refrigerator and decided to make breakfast for the guys despite all the drama the night before. As soon as I put the finishing touches on the eggs, French toast, and turkey bacon, Rich came into the kitchen and just stood in the doorway. Since I knew he was on edge, I decided not to say a word and just fixed my plate.

"Damn, where's my plate?" he asked.

"Fix your own plate!" I snapped.

As I walked past him, Rich instantly smacked my plate onto the floor. The plate along with the food splattered everywhere.

"Are you crazy? Why the hell did you do that?"

"Because you're tryin' to be cute. You know better than to talk to me like that," Rich scolded.

As bad as I wanted to tell him to clean up the mess, I didn't have the energy to fight with him. Instead, I got down on my knees and began picking up several pieces of food. Moments later, the front door opened and I heard my son's, voice. Dropping the bacon back on the floor, I immediately jumped up and went to the foyer to greet my son.

"What's up, Ma? What's wrong?" Juan asked.

"I missed you," I cried uncontrollably as he held me.

Rich walked into the room with a frown. "Didn't I tell you to stay away from here 'til I gave you the okay to come back?"

"Man, I was tired of staying at that chick's house. She was starting to get on my nerves," Juan answered.

"You need to obey me when I tell you not to come home. That's what's wrong with you Juan. Your ass never listens," Rich continued.

"Look, I've been gone for three weeks. How long did you expect me to stay away? I'm not a lil' kid anymore." Juan looked around the room. "You told me not to handle any business, and to stay off the street. What's going on around here?" he questioned.

I took a step back and looked at my son, who obviously had been working out. His arms were becoming extremely buff. "Did you have enough money to get you through these past few weeks? You know…to buy a few outfits and necessities." I kept telling Rich to make sure he got some money to Juan instead of just being worried about Denie, but he always had the same response, "He'll be a'ight."

"Yeah, I was straight." Juan stared at me. "Ma, why are you crying, and what happened to your hair?" He then looked at Rich. "Did you put your hands on her again?"

Rich chuckled. "This is my wife, boy. Don't question me about what I do wit' her. I told you that shit before. Stay out of our business."

"Ma, I don't see how you deal with this shit. Call me when he leaves again," Juan said. He turned around and started out the door.

"No, don't leave," I pleaded, even though Juan never turned around. I knew he wanted to avoid a fight with Rich.

"I'm tired of that lil' nigga being disrespectful. How does he think he's gonna eat if I don't supply him wit' shit," Rich said. "Now, take your ass in the kitchen and fix me and Carlos a plate." Rich didn't even wait for me to respond before he walked away.

That's it. I got something for his ass, I thought as I power walked to the kitchen. After warming everything back up, I fixed Carlos' plate, before starting on Rich's. Once the French toast was in place, I scooped up the last bit of scrambled eggs and sat them next to the bacon. However, instead of sprinkling a dash of salt, I opened my mouth and let a wad of spit garnish his food. All I could do was smile as I took a fork and mixed the clear salvia into the eggs, instantly losing my appetite.

"Lisa, hurry up, we hungry!" Rich called out.

I grabbed Rich's plate along with Carlos' and walked back into the family room. "Here you go, I said handing each of them their food." Moments later, I looked at Rich who was already digging in. "Enjoy," I said with a devious smile before going back upstairs.

Laying back down on the bed, I hit the button on the remote for the DVD player, and decided to watch Tyler Perry's movie, *Why Did I Get Married* for the umpteenth time. However, this time I started to ask myself that same damn question.

CHAPTER FOUR

Lisa

Since Rich was still in search of my attacker he'd been extra protective over me, so I had to let him know my every move or take one of his boys with me when I had something to do, which was annoying. It made me wonder if Rich had that many affairs that he couldn't pin point who was behind this. It was taking way too long to catch those fools. Rich was fast asleep on the couch as I walked into the living room to explain to him that I was going to the hairdresser. He immediately woke up.

"Where you goin'?" he asked. "What time is it?"

I looked down at my iced out Chopard watch. "It's 3:00 in the afternoon. You been sleep since Carlos left. I'm going to get my hair done. I can't take this anymore," I said, pulling on my raggedy edges. I still couldn't figure out why those dudes had cut off my ponytail or what they got out of it.

Rich looked at me sideways. "Is Jermaine doin' it?"

"No, I'm going to Trixie. Jermaine was booked."

"Didn't I tell you I didn't want you goin' to that bitches shop? Do you need me to call so Jermaine can fit you in?"

"No, Rich. I just didn't feel like sitting in Jermaine's shop all day since I didn't make an appointment earlier."

"Well, that's too bad. Either go to Jermaine or take your ass back upstairs."

"Why do you have to act like that, Rich? Trixie has never done anything to you. Why do you hate her so much? Not only is she my hairdresser, but she's been my friend for years."

"I just don't want my wife hangin' around whores. That's all. Besides, that shit might rub off on you."

I really wasn't in the mood to play tug of war with his ass at the moment. "Alright Rich, go back to sleep. I'll call Jermaine and see if he can squeeze me in," I lied.

"Good. I'm tired of tellin' you to stay away from Trixie's hot-ass." Rich was about to turn over, but quickly continued. "Oh, by the way, I'm ready for Denie to come back home. After you call Jermaine, make sure you call Marisol and tell her to meet you at the salon."

"So, what about Juan? Can I call him, so he can feel comfortable about being home this time?"

"I guess. If that muthafucka don't stop comin' slick out his mouth, he's gonna be out for good."

I was happy that Rich agreed for them to come back, but I wasn't sure if Juan would even want to come back since him and Rich were always bumping heads. Denie, I knew was dying to get home to her father. I knew that I was a Daddy's girl growing up, but Denie was a special case. She acted as if she was Rich's wife sometimes, and was always up under him every five minutes; asking him about his whereabouts. It was a bit frustrating at times how Rich showed his favoritism, but I had to admit...I did the exact same thing with Juan.

After walking back upstairs, I called Marisol and told her to meet me at Trixie's hair salon with Denie. I also told her not to let Carlos know I was getting my hair done there and she agreed. Slipping on my D&G long sleeve t-shirt, J Brand jeans, and one of Rich's W fitted baseball caps to cover my chopped up hair, I prepared for my interrogation at the hair dresser. Before leaving out the door, I snuck back into the living room, and grabbed a wad of cash out of Rich's jean pockets that were lying on the floor. It was definitely more than what I needed for my hair, but I damn sure wasn't about to put any of it back. After all I'd gone through, I deserved whatever I wanted. Besides, he should've been used to me peeling off his money, something I'd been doing for years.

Entering the family room, I looked up at the huge twelve foot Christmas tree. The smell of pine was so refreshing, but still it didn't feel quite like the holidays, even though Christmas was in a few days. Grabbing my shearling Storm Louis Vuitton bag, I threw my I-pod and one of my new novels inside and headed out the door.

As soon as I jumped in my X6 BMW, my paranoia kicked in. I checked my surroundings before pulling completely out of the garage and turned on my radio. There were a variety of different CD's in my six disc changer, but I was trying to find the right song for my mood. After pushing number two, Stephanie Mills blasted through my speakers. Singing to the top of my lungs, it wasn't long before I broke down crying.

"Damn Rich, how did we get here?" I yelled out.

My physical aches were healed, but I couldn't see my mental pain ever going away. I was scarred for life. All I wanted was the truth from him and maybe it would help us both heal. I hated when he lied to me. He swore that he hadn't been unfaithful, but I found that hard to believe. I continued to cry all the way to Georgia Avenue, but knew I had to get myself together because I could never let those bitches in the hair salon think Rich and I were having problems. They all wished they were his wife, but little did they know being Mrs. Juan Sanchez Sr. carried a hefty price tag.

Pulling up at Trixie's salon, I was in complete awe. I knew I hadn't been there in a while, and she'd definitely upgraded her shit in a major way. She went from having a hole in the wall with customers barely wanting to park on the pot holed lot to valet service. I was still in shock as I stepped out of the car and handed one of the valet drivers my keys. I couldn't wait to see what she'd done to the shop. Putting on my, *I'm okay face* I walked in with a huge smile even though I was already feeling a little nervous about being out and lying to Rich about which salon I was really going to. I wondered if this was a bad idea.

"What's up, Lisa?" Trixie yelled before I could even get in the door good. "You can go ahead to my station."

"Hey, Trixie."

"Bitch, that Louie is hot. Is that an early Christmas present, cause I saw that shit behind the glass showcase at the Louie store. That bag had to be about four or five stacks," Trixie said. She was always on my wardrobe. "Damn, and you got on those Dior Snowboots, too. I hate your ass."

I shook my head. "No, it was one of Rich's "baby I love you, I'm sorry" type of gift. You know how men are. I've been saying the same shit over and over."

"Shit, girl I know that's right. I wouldn't ever trip off what that nigga, Rich did if I was you, especially if you get gifts like that. Every time you come in here you got some new shit on. Rich that nigga," she said with a little hate in her voice. She then picked up her phone and started texting.

Yeah, he's that nigga alright, I thought. Although Trixie was loud, ghetto, and known to be out there with lots of men, she was still a good friend with a heart of gold. Ever since meeting her ten years ago, I knew I could count on her whenever I needed anything.

"You're crazy." I began to look around. "Damn, the shop looks like you ran into some major dough. Tell me all about it," I said sitting in her chair.

I tried to focus on Trixie's life because I never liked to talk about Rich at the salon. I would share things with her privately, but didn't go there in public too much. Besides, Trixie loved attention, so I let her get her shine on. She told me about Mike, her latest boyfriend and how he hit the number and surprised her with an early Christmas present, remodeling her salon. The shop looked amazing. The décor was very modern with cherry wood stations and black and white paintings of various female artists hanging throughout. The waiting area was comfortable with plasma T.V.'s and plush brown leather sofas and chairs. There was even a dining area with vending machines and café style pedestal tables with bar stools.

"What the hell? Did you let Jermaine from Hairsport do your hair? When you were ready to cut off those locks, you should've let me do it," Trixie said pulling off my baseball cap.

"Girl, no. It's a long story, and something I don't want to talk about."

There had always been competition between Trixie's shop, Natural Potions, and Hairsport. I'd been going to Hairsport ever since we moved to Upper North West four years ago. Not only was it easier to get to, but Jermaine did such a great job. Trixie knew damn well that Jermaine wouldn't have cut my hair like that, so I felt like she was trying to come at me with an insult. Then again, I didn't know if it was just my insecurities of being used to long hair. My jet black hair always fell down my back and I just didn't feel like myself. Searching through the December Edition of Black Hair magazine, I was undecided on how I wanted it cut.

Staring out into thin air, I began to notice how much the salon had been upgraded since the last time I was there. Christmas decorations laced the place inside and out, with a Bose sound system blasting Christmas carols. A shop that was once a hole in the wall; somewhere you went because you were dedicated to your stylist, now felt like a palace. With the complimentary champagne and chocolate covered strawberries being passed around, it was obvious Trixie had a come up. Her new man, Mike, must've thought he had him a good girl, and I wasn't mad at her game. He never came around, but she spoke of him often. I probably would've thought he didn't exist if I hadn't seen her ass pregnant. At the moment, I saw her youngest daughter running past us. She had to be around three years old.

"Oh my gosh, Trixie that's the baby. Look how big she is now. Come here, cutie," I said holding my arms out. "She's so pretty."

"Thanks. Come here Nita, and say hi to Miss Lisa," Trixie instructed.

I smiled. "Hi, Miss Nita. How old are you?" When I placed her on my lap, she put three fingers up.

"You're not three silly, you just turned two," Trixie answered for her.

"She must look just like her father Trixie, because she looks nothing like you. I mean she has your eyes, and your complexion but that's it." I figured the guy Mike was the father, but didn't want to say his name just in case he wasn't. Trixie definitely had a lot of men.

"Yeah, she does, but it's okay because her father is fine." Trixie looked at her daughter. "That's Mama's baby." She looked at her oldest daughter, then pointed across the room. "Toya, come get your lil' sister and take her in the lounge." Once they finally walked away, she turned her attention back to my hair. "Speaking of daughters, how's Denie?"

"A handful. She acts just like her damn father," I replied. "Actually she's supposed to be on her way up here."

"I haven't seen her in so long. You never bring her up here to get her hair done."

I was too embarrassed to tell her the real reason why Denie and I weren't allowed in the salon. Before I could continue, I saw Marisol and Denie walk into the shop. "Speak of the devil, there she is right there. Marisol, Denie, I'm over here." I motioned for them to come toward us.

"Well damn, if that girl don't look just like her father. She's growing into a little woman," Trixie complimented. "She got those deep dimples like him and everything."

I looked at Denie's light cinnamon complexion. "Yeah, she's definitely Rich's daughter. He can't deny that," I replied. "Hey, Denie," I said. Denie of course didn't acknowledge me at all. Instead, she sat down and immediately began watching television.

"So, I haven't seen you in weeks, and you can't even say

hi?" I asked. Denie and I had a rocky relationship. It had been that way ever since Rich got locked up a few years ago.

"Is there a problem, Denie?" Marisol finally asked. She didn't tolerate Denie's disrespectful ways.

"Hi," Denie responded in a nonchalant tone.

"What's up, Marisol? Are you getting your hair done?" Trixie asked.

Trixie looked Marisol up and down. Of course Marisol walked in the shop like she'd just stepped right off of Rodeo Drive. She had on a chinchilla fur bomber with some Robin's jeans and Alexaner McQueen boots. Her makeup was flawless and her hair was highlighted with blonde streaks. She never removed her oversized Chanel sunglasses.

"Trixie, why the hell do you always look at me up and down every time I come in here?" Marisol questioned. "And no…you know I get my hair done in Cali." Marisol gave Trixie much attitude, which she did every time they saw each other. They could never get along for some reason. Even though Marisol lived on the West Coast most of the time, when she was in town, she stayed far away from Trixie.

I tried to smooth over the situation and asked Marisol how I should get my hair done. Before Marisol could answer, Trixie interrupted.

"Girl, we need to get some weave in this head." Trixie held my hair up as if it was some type of bad experiment, then ran her fingers through her own untamed weave. Although she was a hairdresser, her own hair never seemed to be in place.

"Please, Rich doesn't like weave girl. He would have a fit if I came home with that," I responded.

"Lisa, why didn't you just go to Jermaine? If Trixie has been doing your hair this long, she should know that Rich doesn't like that shit," Marisol interjected. "Especially if it's gonna end up looking like hers."

"Marisol, I don't know what your problem is, but this is my shop and you will respect me. I ain't never done shit to you. Not yet, anyway," Trixie added.

"Sweetheart, stay in your lane, because you don't know who you're fucking with," Marisol countered.

All I could do was shake my head. This was the normal back and forth cattiness that took place between the two women.

"Denie, let's go to the nail salon. We can come back to meet your mother." Marisol looked toward me. "Lisa, call me when you're done," she said in a very calm, but chilling tone.

Females would test Marisol all the time because she was a pretty woman. Thick in all the right places, she had 36D breasts, a small waist, and a beautiful smile to match, but she could be cold and would blast somebody in a minute. She was definitely a ride or die chick and had no problem with pulling a trigger. Even with three kids all under the age of five, that still didn't stop her from being ruthless. She definitely wasn't a soccer mom.

To avoid anymore drama, I got up and immediately asked Marisol if we could talk outside, and she agreed.

"Marisol, what's wrong. Stop acting like that before Trixie fucks up my hair on purpose. What's your issue with her anyway? You all have never gotten along."

"Lisa, I love you and you know you're my girl, but I just don't trust that bitch. Never have."

"But you've never even tried to get to know her. Trixie's cool. We've been friends for years. I mean she's got a lot of issues, but who doesn't."

"Whatever. I'll never forget what that bitch did when we were in Vegas for All-Star a few years ago. Remember I told you about when me and Carlos were at a party at the club Pure and she kept being disrespectful trying to come at him right in front of me."

"Refresh my memory, what happened?" I tried to play along even though I remembered Marisol telling me about the entire incident. I just didn't want her to think that I'd written the whole situation off.

"Remember, I said we were at the party doing our thing; sipping champagne, partying, and that bitch came up to the table and started trying to come at Carlos right in front of me. After he told her he was good, the bitch told him that she bet her pussy was better than mine." Marisol bit down on her bottom lip. "If it wasn't for Carlos pulling me away that night, I would've wiped the floor with her ass."

"Yeah, now I remember. Girl, you're still tripping about that. When you pulled her card the next day, she told you she was drunk."

Marisol swung her long cinnamon brown hair over her shoulder. "Trust me…it wasn't the liquor. I can tell in her eyes that she meant that shit. The only reason why I haven't beat her ass by now is not only because of you, but I'm really trying to watch my temper. Besides, I don't need no bitches pressing charges on me and fucking up my bread, so I'm trying to avoid the bullshit." Marisol was definitely a go-hard type of chick; straight from the Bronx with thick Spanish roots.

"Well, try and let it go…for me. Maybe she really was drunk. Otherwise, I don't think she would've disrespected you." I hated to make up excuses for Trixie, but I just wasn't in the mood for anymore drama. I had enough of that shit going on with Rich.

"I can't stand to be around her. That's why me and Denie are going to the nail salon across the street. Hit me on my cell when you're done."

At that moment, Denie walked outside. "How long are we gonna be here, because I need to see my Dad?"

"I'm not sure Denie, but it will be a while," I answered as pleasant as I could.

"Well, Aunt Marisol can you drop me off at home, because I don't have time to wait while she gets her hair done. I got things to do," Denie replied.

"Denie, didn't we talk about you showing your mother some respect," Marisol interjected before I could respond.

Instead of creating a scene in front of the salon, I told Marisol after she and Denie finished at the nail salon, she could take Denie home.

"Are you sure because you know Denie don't run shit around here?" Marisol gave Denie a look that said, *I dare your ass to say something else.*

"Yeah, I'm sure. I'm not in the mood for Denie today," I said folding my arms. The chill in the air gave me an indication that it was time to go back inside.

A few seconds later, I sat back down in Trixie's chair.

"Girl, I was giving you three more minutes before I moved on to another client," Trixie said popping some gum.

"I'm sorry. I had to get some things straight with Marisol. I apologize the way she came off."

Trixie rolled her eyes. "Please…I'm used to it. Chicks hate on me all the time girl, so it's all good."

It took everything I had to hold my laugh in. Although Trixie had what most men would call a video vixen body, her eyebrows were entirely too thick and the fake gray contacts she wore were completely over the top. However, the girl could put together an outfit. Speaking from someone who had Neiman Marcus on speed dial, we had the same expensive taste.

"Now, what kind of weave do you want? Trixie questioned. "We can do it straight and maybe cut some bangs or I could layer it."

"No, I don't know how Rich will feel about weave. I mean he loves long hair, but a weave Trixie." The moment I mentioned Rich's name, all eyes in the salon were on me for some reason.

"Girl, you need to get a Beyonce look for the holidays. I know you used to having long hair, so how you gonna go home with a short cut, knowing your man was obsessed with that hair. Besides, you never told me what happened," Trixie pried again.

"It doesn't matter what happened. Okay go ahead and do your thing, but don't make me un-beweavable." We both laughed.

I finally let Trixie convince me in to getting a complete weave. I needed a new look anyway so I figured it probably wasn't such a bad thing. Since my husband was obsessed with

Beyonce anyway, Trixie figured he'd like the look she was going for. Little did she know, it was no longer about what Rich liked. I was finally living for me and *I* needed a change.

This new process of a hairdo was never what I expected. I had no idea that a weave took as long as it did. From the main wash and conditioning treatment, back and forth sitting under the dryer for color processing, then getting a trim, braiding, sewing the weave in, cutting and styling, the process was well over four hours. This wasn't the norm for me and I was beyond restless. Not to mention, I had to constantly listen to Trixie talk about how her baby's father had just bought her the new 2009 Mercedes convertible SL 500 and how I had to come out to their new house in Ft. Washington for her holiday party. Needing to see what her new man looked like before she kicked him to the curb like all the rest, I gladly accepted her invitation. Hell, I needed to get out of the house for a drink anyway. I knew Rich wasn't going to tag along and that was fine with me.

Leaving the shop, I felt better and my new hairdo looked fabulous. It was very different for me, so I knew it would take some getting used to. The braids from the weave were so tight that it made my head ache, but I loved the long layers, and loose curls. With its jet black color, I looked like one of those Kardashian sisters instead of a mother, but anything beat that chopped up hair style I had before. After the valet brought my BMW around, I jumped in feeling confident. Fumbling through the radio stations I landed on 93.9. They were playing Keyshia Cole's song, *Should've Let You Go*. Listening to the lyrics of the song made me really feel that what Rich and I had was gone, and that it was really over. I just needed to find a way out of my dead end marriage.

Since I couldn't talk to anyone else, I could only express the way I felt about Rich, during my karaoke moment, alone in my car. Trying to snap out of it and focus my energy elsewhere was so hard because he was all I'd known. After a few tears made their appearance, I dried my eyes and faced the reality that it was too hard for me to leave Rich. I thought back a few years.

The perfect time to leave had been when he gave me Chlamydia when Denie was two years old. He claimed he didn't know where I got it from and slapped me for my accusations, even accused me of cheating. When I threatened to leave, Rich told me he would kill me if I ever left him. He was ruthless and I never wanted to be on his bad side. Maybe that's why I stayed for so long. I knew I was weak, but after all this time, I didn't know any other way to be.

CHAPTER FIVE
Rich

An infuriatin' feelin' came over me so strong that I felt the urge to go to war. It was a must that I caught up wit' the niggas responsible for the recent turmoil in my life. Carlos and I had spoken about me joinin' him on the West Coast to take over more territory, but that shit had to wait 'til I made an example of my unknown enemies. Puttin' my family through so much had taken a toll on my mind and I just needed to get to the bottom of this as soon as possible. Here I was, thinkin' my family was safe from these niggas out on the street, and some dumb muthafucka wit' a death threat had obviously been followin' me. I couldn't wait 'til I caught up wit' that fool because the shit wasn't gonna be pretty. Nobody fucked wit' Rich Sanchez and got away wit' it. Feelin' like Scrooge, I wasn't in the holiday spirit. I was ready to make any and every one pay for violatin' my family.

Turnin' on the flat screen T.V. on the master bathroom wall, I began to watch ESPN to catch the highlights of the Cleveland game so I could see what Lebron and D. West gave the people the night before. As the highlights began to play, my cell phone started to vibrate, which instantly irritated me. Due to my hectic lifestyle, there never seemed to be a quiet moment for me without someone needin' my attention. When I looked at the phone and saw Lisa's number, I quickly hit the ignore button. I wasn't in the mood to listen to her whinin' ass either. Tryin' to get back into the show, I turned the volume up ready to see who scored the most points, but my phone began to vibrate again. It was Lisa.

"What?" I asked in a harsh tone.

"What's wrong with you?"

"I'm busy, and you're disturbin' me, that's what's wrong."

"Oh, sorry. I was just trying to tell you that Marisol is gonna bring Denie home."

"Is that it?"

"Look, why are you being short with me? You're the one who demanded that I tell you what's going on with us, especially when it comes to Denie."

"Is that it?" I repeated.

Lisa was quiet for a few seconds. "I also wanted to tell you about my hair, but from the way you're acting, I'm sure you don't wanna hear about that."

"You're right." CLICK

I knew she hated when I hung up on her, but I didn't give a shit. Nobody told her to call me twice. If I didn't answer the first time, that should've been a hint. Turnin' my attention back toward my sixty-inch plasma, I was just about to get settled when the phone vibrated again. This time I didn't even look to see who it was.

"Lisa, if you call me one more fuckin' time, it's gonna be a problem when you get in this house!" I belted.

"Hey, Daddy. It's not Lisa," a sexy voice spoke.

A smile instantly spread across my face. "Hey, baby." It was my favorite side chick.

"What are you doing tonight?"

"You, if possible. I miss you."

"Why haven't you called then?" she asked.

"I've been tied up, but I'm tryin' to see you tonight, so what's up."

"You ain't called me in a month. What's going on with you Rich?" Her sweet tone had faded.

"Man, I don't have time for that naggin' shit. You either gonna give up some ass, or I can call somebody else."

"Damn baby, I just miss you that's all. Look, I have a flight to catch to North Carolina in the morning to make sure my mother's new condo is straight, so I'm free tonight."

"Cool. What airport you flyin' out of?"

"National, so can we stay in Crystal City?"

"That's cool, but make sure you don't have nobody fol-lowin' you and shit. You know how messy you can be. I don't have time for shit gettin' back to my wife. By the way, I want a treat tonight."

"Well, you must be giving up extra funds for that."

Any woman I dealt wit' knew that I would always look out and take care of them. Money wasn't an issue. "I'll hook you up, but don't be demandin' shit. Go ahead and get the room. Text me when everything is in order."

After hangin' up, thoughts of me not comin' home to Lisa once again popped in my mind. Bein' the man that I was, I still had needs and since my wife wasn't givin' me pussy on a regular, I needed my side sex kitten. Throughout the years, I often asked myself why I even cheated on Lisa in the first place. I mean…she was the full package; beautiful, loyal, and an over-all good girl, but for some reason that just wasn't good enough. Up 'til now, I couldn't answer the famous question of, *Why Do Men Cheat*? Shit, maybe it was a sickness, and if it was I had no plans on tryin' to get well anytime soon. I'd fucked so many women, I had no idea who could've possibly made me and my family a target. But regardless of my infidelity, I was determined they were goin' to pay.

After watchin' what was left of the highlights, I looked forward to rubbin' in Carlos' face that my team had won and King James got his man hittin' forty-eight points. I turned on the shower, feelin' good about my plans for the night, but at the same time I was frustrated wit' my wife and my current situation. *Lisa needs to step her fuckin' game up*, I thought. A man like me needed special attention on a regular, and she was definitely slackin' in all areas, especially below my waist.

Ten minutes later, I limped out the shower and got dressed. I had no idea of when and if my knee had any plans on gettin' better, but I damn sure hoped so. This temporary handicap shit was wearin' me out. To finish off my outfit, I went to my secret compartment in the back of my closet where I kept my guns. Once I scanned the selection, I decided on my .45 then placed it in the holster that I kept strapped under my sweatshirt. Just when I was on my way down to the kitchen to grab a Red Bull, Marisol and Denie came in through the front door.

"Daddy, I missed you. Are you okay?" Denie dropped her house keys on the floor then ran up and hugged me, damn near knockin' me down.

"Yes, I'm fine. I missed you too, Baby Girl. I missed you too." I kissed my daughter on her forehead and felt a sudden calmness.

"I'll let you guys catch up. I have something to take care of for Carlos. Bye Denie and remember what we talked about," Marisol said.

"What did you all talk about?" I asked.

Marisol smiled. "Girl stuff. Besides, it's none of your business, Rich."

"Was Lisa still at Jermaine's when you left?" I inquired.

Marisol looked at Denie at first, then back at me. "Yep, she sure was." Marisol turned to leave. "Well, I'ma get out of here. I'll see y'all later."

My daughter was excited to see me. Besides my mother, Denie was the only person in my life who I was weak for. I used to be weak for Lisa, but those days were over. Denie could get anything from me and could do no wrong. When I got locked up a couple of years ago, I felt bad that I wasn't around to teach her the things a father was supposed to teach their teenage daughter.

It was but so much I could tell her over the phone or durin' an hour visit in prison. It was rough and my absence caused my daughter to reach out to a little boy for love. She got pregnant at the age of fourteen, but locked up or not she wasn't goin' down like that. I demanded that she get an abortion, which ultimately she did. I didn't want my daughter to go through what Lisa and I did wit' Juan. I always wanted better for both my children, and was determined to see that happen.

"So, Daddy what happened? What did they do to you?" Denie asked wit' a wide eyed expression.

"Baby Girl, it doesn't matter. I'm okay." I patted my knee. "I got banged up a little bit, but nothin' I can't handle. Now, I really don't want to talk about that."

Denie nodded her head. "Okay."

"You didn't tell anyone what you heard did you?"

"Of course not, Dad. I was just worried about you."

"Aww, my baby love's me," I teased.

"Be quiet." Denie smiled and gave me a shove on the shoulder. "So, Daddy can we go grab some lunch or dinner today? I wanna spend some time with you. "

"I'm sorry, Baby Girl. I have some important business to take care of today, but can I get a rain check for tomorrow."

"No, today. I haven't been home for almost a month and you're putting your business before spending time with me."

"Come on Denie, it's not like that." She was spoiled as shit, but I didn't have anyone to blame but myself.

"Then how is it? All I'm asking for is a little time."

Before I could answer, Denie stormed off and headed into the family room. She knew that I would eventually give in just so she wasn't upset. After shaking my head, I agreed to take her to The Cheesecake Factory in Rockville, MD. Since I had to meet up wit' one of my dudes out that way before I hooked up wit' Carlos anyway, it all worked out. I was down wit' anything to keep my Baby Girl happy.

My day was quite busy, but I got a lot accomplished. I met wit' Carlos after my date wit' my daughter to see if he had any leads on the mysterious nigga, and even though the streets still weren't talkin', I didn't let that ruin the rest of my night. It was time for my night cap wit' my side chick, who I'd been dealin' wit' off and on for a few years now. She was always down for whatever and since I hadn't seen her in a while, I knew the sex was about to be unexplainable. Unlike my other bitches, she knew her place and rarely asked questions, which was another reason why I kept her around. The minute she started comin' out of her mouth wrong, it was a wrap. I picked up my cell phone and dialed her number.

"Hello, baby," she answered seductively.

"Wassup, you ready for me? I see from your text that you got a room at the Ritz Carlton. Your ghetto-ass needs to stop actin' like you're used to shit."

"Shut up. We're in the room. The key is at the front desk."

"We? What the fuck do you mean, we? I ain't in the mood for games. Who's wit' you?"

"Baby, calm down! You said you wanted a treat, and trust me, you're gonna love it. Now, hurry your sexy-ass up, cause I'm ready to take care of you. You been away too long and I'm wet just thinking about what's about to go down tonight."

I calmed down instantly. "A'ight cool. I'll be there in like a half." After hangin' up, I pressed my foot on the accelerator even harder. Maybe I shouldn't have been so paranoid, but in my line of work you had to be.

Thirty minutes later, I walked up to the front desk, got the key then limped toward the elevator. *Damn, I hope my leg doesn't act up too bad tonight*, I thought when I pressed the number twenty-two for the top floor. My chick had obviously gotten the

Presidential Suite. *That bitch loves to spend money.*

When I entered the room, the lights were dim and there were candles and rose petals spread throughout. I could smell sweet perfume in the air, and could also hear the sound of Maxwell's voice oozing out of some speakers. Once I made my way to the bedroom, Trixie rushed toward me wearin' a sexy red lace teddy. She knew how red made me weak.

"You missed me, baby?" she said in a seductive voice.

I was glad to see her. "Did you miss me?" I asked wit' a huge smile. She loved my dimples so I had to show them off. I knew it was wrong to fuck Lisa's hairstylist and friend, but what could I say. I was weak for a phat ass.

"Yes," she said getting on her knees.

Damn why can't Lisa do shit like this? I thought. "Well, show me."

Trixie didn't waste time unzippin' my pants and placin' my entire dick in her mouth, and I didn't have a miniature dick either…nine inches to be exact. She made love to me wit' her mouth as if she was suckin' on a popsicle. It felt like I could feel her tonsils on the tip of my dick. Not wantin' to leave the warm pocket in her mouth, I tried my best to think of stupid shit to keep from cummin', but it was hard. I was ready to handle my business, but as aggressive as Trixie was, she wanted to take control. Standin' back up, she grabbed my hand and led me to the bed. Pushin' me back, she climbed on my lap and began to take my shirt off. Lookin' at myself in the floor length cherry wood mirror, I loved every minute of bein' seduced by this fine woman.

"Trixie, show me how much you missed this. Get on top," I instructed.

"I'm ready to fuck your brains out Rich, I missed you," she responded while taking off my pants.

Just like the good side chick she was, it wasn't long before Trixie climbed on top of my dick; ridin' me like a stallion. She put so much effort in her love makin'. It was like an art to her. Her pussy was so good, and the way she threw it on me, always made me want to scream out her name, but I wasn't about to go that punk-ass route.

I began to suck on her grapefruit sized breasts, when Trixie said she had a surprise for me a few moments later. I loved it when she took control in the bedroom, especially when this girl who was phat as shit walked from out of the bathroom and started kissin' me on my neck. She was beautiful wit' stack house measurements just the way I liked my shit. Before I could even part my lips, Trixie started kissin' the girl like they were long lost lovers. I just watched them have their way wit' each other. Trixie swore up and down she wasn't gay, but she enjoyed women way too much not to be. This wasn't the first time we'd had a threesome.

After climbin' off my manhood, Trixie began suckin' on the woman's pussy as if her life depended on it. Trixie was gentle, but aggressive. The woman moaned and screamed like someone was killin' her. Moments later, the woman began to shake a little before her body went completely numb. It was obvious that she'd cum for the first time of the night, but not the last. At that moment, I turned the chick around and started fucking her doggy style. I loved the way she felt as her ass bounced up against my stomach. I smacked it a few times then continued to pound her pussy like a jackhammer 'til the base of my dick began to tingle.

"Oh, shit I'm about to cum!" I yelled.

"Go ahead. Cum Daddy," Trixie replied.

Seconds later, I quickly pulled my dick out and squirted warm cum all over the chick's back. It wasn't long before Trixie came over and placed her mouth back over my tool to suck the rest of the juices out. Trixie was a real freak, and I loved that shit.

After the last round of sex, Trixie dismissed the chick after she got dressed and I gave her a stack for her services. As good as the girl's pussy was I definitely had to have her back for another one of our little rendezvous. As soon as we were alone, Trixie laid on the bed and put her arms around me.

"So, did you get my text today? I saw your wife and I want that Louie bag she got, so you owe me."

I frowned instantly. "Where did you see Lisa at?"

"She came to the shop to get her hair done. Somebody fucked her hair up, so I had to nurse that shit back to health. Maybe one day you'll let me and Lisa fuck you together so that way we don't have to keep sneaking around."

Suddenly, I smacked the shit out of Trixie. Even though she was always sayin' somethin' slick out of her mouth, this time she was way out of line.

"Why the fuck did you hit me?" Trixie asked, holdin' her cheek.

"Learn what the fuck to say out your dumb-ass mouth. I don't play when it comes to my wife. You've known me long enough. Don't play wit' me like that. We just fuck. That's my wife."

"So, I'm just a fuck, Rich? I've been fucking with you for over two years and I still don't mean anything to you? Do you know how hard it is to play dumb in front of your wife?"

I shook my head. "Trixie, how am I supposed to feel anything for you when you go around town givin' up your pussy to every man you meet? Not to mention, you got a dude at home. You just fuck wit' me because your man is broke. You think I'm stupid, but I know the game."

"For your information, my man ain't broke. He just came up on some bread and I've been doing just fine. If your ass had been around and not ducking my calls for the past month you would know that he upgraded my shop and bought me the new SL Benz. I fuck you because I love you Rich, not because of what you can do for me. I…"

I had to stop her. "What the fuck did you just say?"

"I said I love you. It started off with you being just a fuck for me, too. I had sex with you because you were looking out for me, but now it's bigger than that. If that wasn't the case then I wouldn't be here. Mike has been doing everything possible to make me happy, but for some reason I can't shake you. Rich, I love you!"

"I wasn't talkin' about that stupid love shit. I'm talkin' about your so called man. How did he come up on some money?"

"Him and his boys robbed some dude and came up in a major way. He said he did it for me. He said he wanted to make me happy and give me the world. I told you it's not always about money. Rich, you have no idea how I feel about you."

As Trixie began to vent and cry, I immediately tuned her out. So many mixed emotions started runnin' through my mind. I knew for a fact that the nigga she fucked wit' was the same dude who'd robbed me. It wasn't a doubt in my mind. He had to die tonight. As anger consumed my body, I looked at Trixie and placed my hand around her neck.

"Did you have anythin' to do wit' that shit?" It took everything I had not to kill her ass right on the spot. Trixie had this thing where she would make her boyfriend jealous and talk about all I did for Lisa, just to get him on his game. Trixie loved drama and kept shit goin'. Luckily, nothin' ever got back to Lisa. This was the main reason why I kept my wife away from her shop.

"Get off of me! What are you doing?" Trixie asked as her eyes bulged.

"Answer me! Did you have anything to do wit' that nigga robbin' somebody?" For some reason, I didn't want Trixie to know I was the person her boyfriend had robbed just in case she wasn't involved.

"No...I didn't," Trixie pleaded. "What's wrong with you?"

Somethin' in her eyes told me she was tellin' the truth so I let her go. I just hoped my gut instinct was right.

Trixie grabbed her neck then began to cough for a few seconds, before finally looking back at me. "Are you fucking crazy? What the hell was that all about?"

"Nothin'. I just wanted to make sure you weren't in-volved. I don't want my girl to be participatin' in shit like that."

Trixie was no where near my girl, but I had to put that out there to make sure she wouldn't know what I was up to.

"So, that's the way you had to show me?" Trixie asked as she coughed again.

"I'm sorry," I replied, turnin' on the charm.

Trixie finally forced a smile. "I'm glad you finally called me your girl. That sounded nice."

After calmin' her down a bit more, I let Trixie know that I had some things to take care of and I would be back even though I had no plans on comin' back at all. Wit' revenge on my mind, I quickly left the hotel, jumped in my car and called Carlos to let him know what was up. He knew what time it was and was ready for us to handle our business. As I drove down Route 1 in Alexandria, thoughts of me fuckin' Trixie in the first place, started to consume my mind. If I'd just kept my dick in my pants, none of this would've probably ever happened. Trixie threw it at me and I fell for it, but I guess I had finally learned the hard way that good pussy had a hefty price tag.

CHAPTER SIX

Rich

Carlos and I headed down Indian Head Highway three hours later to make sure Mike paid for what he did to me and my wife. I had one of my other soldiers, Rico, casin' Trixie's crib to see if the nigga was home, and luckily he was. Trixie had made the caper easy by givin' up all the information I needed for my revenge. She'd told me months ago exactly where they lived and what kind of car the nigga drove which ultimately worked in my favor. The bitch loved to pillow talk, which was probably the reason I was caught up in this shit to begin wit'. As I listened to Lil Wayne's song, *Shoot Me Down*, my rage began to rise and my blood boiled. Thinkin' about all the shit the nigga had done, I was ready for war. Mike was gonna pay for what he did. I was ready to settle the score.

Once we pulled up on Trixie's street, we parked behind Rico who was sittin' several yards away. After quickly turnin' off the car and the headlights, I made sure to call Trixie one last time to make sure she was still at the hotel. I didn't need her to make any surprise visits, and we definitely didn't need any witnesses. When Trixie confirmed that she was still in Crystal City, and would stay there 'til her flight the next mornin', I quickly hung up then gave Carlos a head nod lettin' him know it was time.

Dressed in all black, all three of us made our way to the back of the house like trained ninjas makin' sure no one spotted us. Our plan was to go in through the basement door, hopin' that his punk ass hadn't activated the alarm. However, even if he had, that shit still wasn't gonna stop me from draggin' his ass out. If the alarm was on, I would just snatch his ass up and continue the job somewhere else. Either way, this was his last day breathin'. My anger was so built up. I wanted to just blast his ass, but I had to remember how much he'd hurt my family, so his death had to be slow and painful. There wasn't even a need for maskin' up because I wanted the punk muthafucka to see my face. This nigga was going to pay.

When we reached the basement door, I looked at Rico. "Have you seen any activity in the house since you been posted up?" I asked in a low tone.

"Yeah, his niggas left about an hour ago, so he should be alone if his bitch not in there," Rico replied. It was hard for him to speak in a low voice since his shit was so deep.

"No, she's not here. I just called her," I replied.

"Then we're straight," Rico said just before Carlos pulled out a mini flashlight, along wit' a tension wrench and began to pick the lock. Luckily, Trixie didn't have one of those slidin' glass doors because we would've had to break the window, which was the plan if all else failed. However, Carlos was a beast when it came to locks. Not only had he started stealin' cars at the age of twelve, but he also had been caught as a juvenile on several breakin' and enterin' charges. All that changed when Carlos got into the drug game, but he still had his skills.

A few moments later, we heard a click, and Carlos immediately spoke up. "Bingo." It didn't take long for him to slowly turn the doorknob and open the door. To our surprise, an alarm didn't go off, which made shit even smoother.

We started up the steps from the basement and ended up
in the kitchen. You could smell the aroma of weed and cheap-ass
dollar store air freshers throughout the house, which was so disrespectful for a crib in the suburbs. *You can take the nigga out
the hood, but can't take the hood out the nigga*, I thought to myself as Rico, Carlos, and I moved through the kitchen to the
foyer. We listened closely before we approached the carpeted
stairs that led to the top floor.

Glancin' to my left on the wall was a nearly nude photo
of Trixie that all three of us stared at. *Damn, why does Trixie's
dumb-ass have a picture like that downstairs instead of in her
bedroom? I could never make a bitch like that my girl. How did
I let her stay around for so long anyway*? I thought. No matter
how good her pussy was, I vowed to never fuck that hot-ass
bitch again. It was time to move on.

Hearin' the loud music from upstairs, we had a feelin'
that's where the nigga was, so we didn't waste time headin' that
way. Wit' all of our guns drawn, we went straight into the master
bedroom then stopped when we heard Mike on the phone in the
bathroom orderin' tickets to Jay-Z's show at the Verizon Center.

"Yeah, Nikki, I need you to order me two tickets on the
front row, ya dig. My bitch gotta be front in center, she love that
nigga Jay." I could tell he was takin' a pull from his blunt because his voice got extremely hoarse like he was about to choke.
"Put it on yo' credit card and I'll bring you the money later on.
Man, that's my wifey. I'll give you some extra money, damn!"

We stood in position in case he was about to make his
way downstairs. However, the more we waited for the right time
to get at his ass the more pissed off I got, but Carlos shot me a
look, that said be easy, so I did. A few seconds later, we heard
the shower runnin' and then he started to sing, so at that point I
knew we had to go in after him. As we all moved upstairs, Carlos adjusted the backpack on his shoulder that contained all the
shit we needed to torture Mike's ass as the music and singin' got
even louder.

Mike blasted Young Jeezy. "Let's talk about money cuz I

get a lot of it, I get a lot of it," he sung as I heard the shower curtain close. "Twist my fingas tho up my hood. Let's get this money, I know I would, I know that's right, but still I do wrong." All of a sudden, Mike started laughin'. "Damn I need to call my niggas back over here, so we can test out my new studio downstairs!"

As Mike sung Jeezy songs like he was about to get a record deal, my blood began to boil. Little did he know, we were two seconds away from puttin' him six feet under.

I didn't even wait to see if Carlos and Rico were ready before I slowly opened the bathroom door, then quietly walked inside.

"I need to call up Trixie so she can give up some of that ass before she leaves for N.C.," Mike said out loud.

"You know what nigga, I still got your bitch's pussy on my dick right now," I boasted as I snatched the curtain back to expose his bitch-ass.

Before he could respond, Carlos immediately smacked the shit out of him wit' the butt of his .9mm.

Even though Mike seemed scared, he didn't show it. "Fuck you, Rich!" he boldly stated. He leaned against the shower wall holdin' his head.

"No, muthafucka...fuck you. Did you think that I wasn't gonna find out about what you did? I mean did you forget that the streets are always watchin' and always talkin'?" When he didn't answer, I continued. "So, all of this over Trixie, huh? Who the fuck makes a hoe a housewife?" I looked over at my soldier. "Rico, grab that nigga so we can get this shit poppin'," I ordered. It felt good. I was on top and now this nigga was my bitch. My prisoner.

Rico immediately grabbed Mike and drug him out of the shower. Although Mike tried to put up a fight, he didn't succeed up against Rico's massive 6'2, two hundred and fifty pound frame. This had been somethin' I dreamed of every night since Denie's birthday a month ago. How I was going to make the muthafucka who ruined my wife pay.

I contemplated fuckin' him up to the point that he would live a miserable ass life, like sawin' off his legs and arms, but then I decided he didn't need to live. We ended up draggin' him to the basement completely naked. Since he wanted to lay down some tracks so bad, I thought it was best for me to do him right in his studio.

I laughed when Rico threw his ass on the floor. "Get up Mikey, you don't mind me callin' you Mikey do you? Does that shit sound familiar?" I yelled then kicked him in his stomach.

Carlos was treacherous and I knew he was the one for this job when he pushed Mike down on his stomach and stepped on his head wit' his Nike Boots while he taped Mike's mouth, hands, and feet. He then grabbed the hammer out of the backpack and began to sodomize Mike wit' the handle. The shit was gross, but I wanted him to feel Lisa's pain. Carlos then took the hammer out of his ass and smacked him straight in his mouth wit' it. It must've instantly loosened some of Mike's teeth because he began to choke.

"Fuck y'all!" Mike managed to say.

I bent down and leaned over him. "So, is this the same dick you stuck in my wife?" When Mike didn't respond, I looked over at Rico. "Oh, I think this muthafucka must have some type of memory lost!" I yelled before punchin' him in his face.

When Mike began to squirm, it didn't take long for the bitch to definitely come out. The look in his eyes gave me satisfaction that the war was soon to be over. The look of fear in his eyes made me bend down again to hear what he had to say.

"Man, you were fucking my girl. All I wanted was for Trixie to love me, and all she talked about is how much money you had. I got tired of hearing your name in our fucking conversations."

"You kidnapped and raped my damn wife all because of some speculation in the streets. She's a whore! Why the fuck you think they call that slut Trixie? You fell in love wit' a trick!" I yelled.

"It wasn't speculation. I've been following y'all for a while now. I even followed y'all to Atlantic City. I knew you were fucking her."

"I take all my bitches out of town. Your bitch wasn't special. You the only nigga out here who loves that hoe!"

"So, what. She was my girl, not yours," Mike replied.

I laughed. "You sound like a real bitch right now. Are you that pussy whipped?" At that moment, Carlos and Rico started laughin', too. "Was Trixie involved?" I asked Mike. I had to know if she was tellin' the truth.

"Why?" Mike inquired.

"Did I tell you to ask me any questions, nigga? Answer me! Did Trixie have anythin' to do wit' that shit?"

I guess Mike could tell from my expression that I wasn't playin' around because he answered wit' a weak, "No."

"Good because I can't even begin to tell you what I was gonna do to her if she was," I answered. "Where them other niggas at?" I wasn't sure if Mike was gonna snitch on his boys, but it was worth a shot. He never responded.

"Enough talking. Let's punish this nigga," Carlos added. I could tell by the look in his eyes that he was ready to do some damage.

"Yeah," Rico co-signed.

All of a sudden, Mike got extremely bold. "You should've stayed away from her then I wouldn't have had a reason to do what I did. You fucked my girl, so it was only right that I fuck yours."

The veins in my neck began to throb. I was so pissed off. "That was the wrong answer." I turned to Rico. "Since this muthafucka decided to stick his dick in my wife without permission, cut that shit off. I'm tired of hearin' him talk!"

Luckily we were in the soundproof studio because when Rico grabbed a pair of hedge clippers out the backpack and cut Mike's dick off, he let out a horrific scream that could be heard from miles away. Blood shot out from everywhere.

Carlos shot me a look. "This is how we do it on the West

side!" he blurted out wit' his Columbian accent.

I had to admit, Carlos was definitely better at killin' niggas than I was. He'd learned it from the best; his father, my Uncle Lorenzo, who was our Columbian connect and had street cred that I would die for. I handled my business when I had to, but I just popped niggas, never any demented shit like we were doin' now, but Mike deserved it. I had a message to relay to all the young niggas in the street who didn't know who the fuck I was.

Not wantin' to be at the scene too much longer, I decided to hurry up and finish Mike off. Not to mention, the stench of his fresh wound was damn near unbearable. It was time to go. When I gave Carlos a quick head nod, he handed me the silencer that I quickly placed on my gun. Moments later, I put the .45 caliber to Mike's temple and smiled.

"Lights out, nigga."

CHAPTER SEVEN
Rich

Instead of goin' back to the hotel wit' Trixie, I called her just to cover my tracks so there wouldn't be any suspicions later. Not to mention, bein' wit' her right after I'd popped her man wasn't the best idea. I told her Denie was sick and that I had to rush home to be wit' my baby. I started to use Lisa as an excuse, but Trixie would've caught on to that lie instantly. She knew Lisa didn't come between me and my infidelity most of the time, so I had to switch up my story. As I turned on Military Road, I thought back to Trixie tellin' me that she saw Lisa today, which pissed me off. I hated when Lisa lied to me. Regardless of the fact that it was in the wee hours of the mornin', I was gonna let her ass have it once I got home.

After I pulled into my driveway a few minutes later, for the first time in weeks I felt a sigh of relief. Now that I'd taken care of Mike, all I had to do was pop them other two niggas so my family could be safe again. I needed to know that my family was no longer a target so I could focus on my business ventures in L.A. 'Til then, I couldn't get too comfortable. I knew how niggas were when it came to revenge, and even though no one knew I'd killed Mike, I still couldn't get too relaxed. I had to stay two steps ahead of these muthafuckas at all times.

When I walked into the house Lisa had fallen asleep on the couch in the family room. Before I woke her up, I stood over her and stared at her honey toned skin for a bit. She was such a beautiful woman and despite all the other bitches I had, I still loved Lisa. It upset me sometimes because she didn't see how much I loved her. I tried to give her the world even though I felt like nothin' I did was ever enough. My anger set in all of a sudden when I looked at her hair and thought back to her goin' to Trixie's shop and how she had lied to me.

"Lisa, wake up!" When she didn't move, I shoved her. "Wake your ass up!"

"Huh, Rich I'm tired. Let me go back to sleep," she replied incoherently.

I pulled on her arm. "Man, get the fuck up. You know I can't carry your ass up the stairs."

"Leave me alone!" she yelled then pulled away.

"Where you go today, Lisa?"

"What? Rich leave me alone," she said as she dozed back to sleep.

I glanced over at the leather ottoman and saw her prescription bottle of sleepin' pills, which explained why she was so out of it. At first I agreed for her to take them after the rape incident, but now that she was obviously becomin' addicted, I had to put an end to that shit. I slapped Lisa's face a little to wake her, but she still didn't budge. At that point I started to wonder how many sleepin' pills she'd actually taken.

"Fuck it. She'll just have to stay down here," I said to myself as I made my way toward the stairs. I left her in the family room and decided to take a shower, go to bed, and deal wit' her lyin' ass later.

When I woke up the next afternoon, Denie was layin' in bed next to me, sound asleep. Whenever she came into my room and climbed on my bed like a toddler was an indication that she wanted somethin', so I had to be prepared. After doin' a few much needed stretches, I leaned over and kissed her on her forehead.

"Hey, Baby Girl."

Denie opened her eyes and smiled. "Hey, Daddy, did you get enough rest?"

I looked at the clock which read 12:18 p.m. "I guess. I got in pretty late, so I'm still a little tired. What's up wit' you? What are you doin' in here?"

"Well, I came in here early this morning, but you were still sleep."

"I'm glad you didn't bother me."

"Daddy, I know how you are about your rest. I kept coming back every thirty minutes, but you would never wake up, so I just decided to wait. I guess I fell asleep waiting," Denie replied. "It feels good to be back at home with you."

"I know you're glad, Baby Girl, but let's just cut right to the chase. What do you have to ask me?"

Denie smiled again showin' her deep dimples and guilty expression. "Can we go shopping today?"

I shook my head because I knew she wanted somethin'. "Denie, tomorrow is Christmas. What would be the point of going shoppin' today?"

"Daddy, there's always a reason to shop, but mainly because I want to pick out my own stuff for Christmas this year. I'm seventeen years old, why can't you just take me to buy my stuff?"

"Because you're still my baby and I like surprisin' you wit' gifts. If you pick everything out, that'll take the fun out of it Denie. Besides, I'm sure your mother has already picked out your gifts."

"So…I don't care. We don't have the same taste, so I doubt if she gets me the stuff I really want. I wanna go to

Neiman's to get me a new bag. My salesperson, Quincy, called and said they just got a new shipment of Gucci and Chanel bags in. Let's ride out to Tyson's Corner before they close."

"Denie, baby, I don't really have time to take you shoppin' today."

"Please Daddy, you bought Ma a new Louie bag before Christmas." She poked her lips out like a spoiled brat.

I hesitated for a few seconds, then caved in. It was hard to say no to my Baby Girl. "A'ight Denie, hurry up and get dressed because I don't have a lot of time."

"Thanks, Daddy. I love you!"

As Denie left my room, Lisa walked in. She looked out of it...as usual.

"What is she so happy about?"

"I'm about to take her to the mall."

"The mall? Rich don't spend anymore money on Denie. I already told you what I bought her. That girl is too fucking spoiled as it is."

The last thing I wanted to talk about was the mall. "Where did you go yesterday?" I made sure my tone was serious.

"I told you I was going to get my hair done. Where were you? What time did you get in here last night? Or should I say this morning?" Lisa asked.

"Don't play wit' me, Lisa. Where did you go and get your hair done and what the fuck did you do to it? Is that weave? You know I hate that shit."

"I went to Jermaine. Damn, why are you interrogating me? Do you want to know what time I took a piss, too?" she asked walking to her closet.

I couldn't take her smart-ass mouth any longer. Before she even had a chance to figure out what was wrong, I was already out of the bed and right behind her. "You know the one thing in this world that I can't stand is an ungrateful, lyin' bitch!" When I smacked her, Lisa fell into the jewelry cabinet and hit her head.

Her mouth was full of blood. "I'm tired of your ass, Rich! Hit me again and I'm calling the po.." before she could get it out I smacked her ass again.

"Don't you ever threaten me again about no fuckin' police! Bitch, are you crazy? You have no idea what I just did for your dumb-ass and you want to lie to me about stupid shit. I told your ass not to go to that bitch, Trixie's shop, didn't I?"

Denie walked in and ran over toward us as soon as I slapped Lisa for the third time. "Daddy, stop hitting her like that!" she yelled.

Not wantin' my daughter to see my violent streak any further, I quickly stepped back. However, my eyes told Lisa that this shit wasn't over.

"Denie, did you tell your father where I was yesterday? I should whoop your ass!" Without a seconds notice, Lisa jumped up and lunged at Denie like a professional wrestler. It wasn't long before they started fightin' like two girls on the street.

"Lisa, stop! Denie didn't tell me anything," I said.

I tried my best to break them apart, but every time I would pull Lisa away, she found a way to make it back in Denie's face. If it wasn't for Juan comin' in a few minutes later, I would've never been able to stop them. I knew they'd both had a bit of anger toward each other lately, but I never knew shit was this bad. I began to wonder what went down when I was locked up.

Juan immediately ran to Lisa's defense. "Denie, what are you doing? Get the fuck off of her!"

"Fuck her, I hate that bitch!" Denie yelled.

"Who are you calling a bitch?" Lisa asked. She tried to break free from Juan's tight grip, but couldn't.

"I didn't tell Daddy anything about you. Maybe if your sneaky-ass didn't lie so much he wouldn't have smacked you," Denie countered.

Denie tried to hit Lisa again, but I grabbed Denie in time and took her back to her room.

"I'm gonna get your ass back for disrespecting me!" Lisa

belted.

There were red scratches all over Denie's face as she paced back and forth. "I can't believe she attacked me," she said. "Daddy, you can't let her get away with that."

As mad as I was wit' Lisa, I couldn't allow Denie to think what she'd done was cool. "Denie, you can't go around talkin' to your mother any kind of way. And I'm not even gonna touch the fightin' issue."

"But she started it." I could tell by the tears in her eyes that she was mad because I was takin' Lisa's side.

"I know Baby Girl, but you still can't do that."

After calmin' Denie down, I told her to get dressed so we could leave. I knew at this point, it was best to separate the two before things got any further out of hand. When I walked back toward my bedroom door, I could hear Lisa and Juan in a deep conversation.

"I told you to leave his ass. You don't deserve this shit, Ma," Juan lectured.

"But you don't understand. It's not that easy," Lisa replied. It sounded as if she'd been cryin'.

"Look, don't worry about it. Whatever you need to do, I'll help. All…" Juan stopped in mid sentence when I walked in.

"Don't stop talkin' shit on my account," I said then looked at Juan. It was my first time noticin' that he'd cut down his mustache really low…too damn low. Now, he looked like the rapper, Nelly or a fuckin' State Trooper. "What were you just sayin'…that she should leave me?" When a few uncomfortable seconds passed, I continued. "This is the last time I'm goin' to say this Juan. You need to stay the fuck out of me and your mother's business, son. Shit just got out of hand that's all." I then looked at Lisa. "But I know one thing, if you ever lie or put your hands on Denie like that again, you're gonna have me to deal wit'. My man saw you at Trixie's shop when he was picking up his girl, so you need to go and apologize to her." I didn't care about stretchin' the truth.

"I'm not apologizing to her. Since both of y'all are always up each other ass why don't the both of y'all just get the fuck out!" Lisa screamed.

"This my fuckin' house. Did you forget?" I asked. "You got shit twisted. You and Juan would be put the fuck out before my daughter. Juan's twenty-two. He shouldn't be livin' here anyway."

"I can roll, that's not a problem," Juan added.

Lisa shook her head. "I can't believe you always take her side. Didn't you hear the way she disrespected me?"

"Come on Ma, get dressed so we can go," Juan suggested. "I'll be downstairs waiting," he said before walkin' out of the room. He knew I would knock his ass out if he jumped out there and said somethin' smart.

Followin' Juan's lead, I left out of the house to start and waited for Denie in the car. Minutes later, it hit me that my daughter was growin' into a woman, as I watched her walk to the car. She was such a pretty girl wit' long beautiful hair that she wore pulled back in a ponytail most of the time. She was beginnin' to really fill out and that shit scared me. Wit' a body like her mother's, I knew that was goin' to be a problem for me soon enough. Now I understood why Lisa's family always hated me because I couldn't imagine my daughter bein' a mother at her age. When Denie got pregnant the lil' nigga who knocked her up would've been dead if I'd been out on the street. I wondered all the time if Denie had a boyfriend, but she would never tell me. She said she'd learned her lesson and wouldn't date again 'til she got out of high school, but somethin' told me that was complete bullshit.

As we rode down the highway Denie didn't say much. I knew she was still mad at what happened between her and Lisa. I thought I would break the ice and see what was on her mind.

"Baby Girl, why are you so quiet?"

"Daddy, I hate Ma so much. She treats me so messed up. Every time she's mad at you, she takes it out on me."

"Denie, you can't hate your mother. How did y'all get to this point? It seems like ever since you've become a teenager things are different wit' y'all."

"When you were locked up she treated me like I wasn't even related to her."

"Why didn't you tell me that back then? I thought shit was straight."

"I mean she would buy me stuff and come to my games to watch me cheer, things like that, but it was like she was always on edge starting arguments with me all the time. You know she loves Juan more than me."

"Don't say that because it's not true. Your mother loves you very much. Maybe you all just need to go through counseling or somethin'. I'll even pay for it. I mean you're gonna have to learn how to get along. I'm not gonna always be here, especially since I have some business to take care of in Cali, and I'll be back and forth a lot. I don't need y'all to be at war while I'm gone. If she upsets you Denie, just ignore her, or call me."

Denie sucked her teeth. "That's if you answer your phone."

"I'm sorry Baby Girl, but sometimes I might be in the middle of somethin' important, it's never intentional. You know you're my number one and I love you, right?"

Denie was hesitant for a moment. "Yes, Daddy. I love you, too."

It made me feel good to see her smile again. I wanted to ask her if she'd been datin' anyone, but I decided to save that conversation for a later date. For now, I wanted to make all her worries go away. She was my princess and it was important to me that I made her feel that way.

One thing about Baby Girl, she knew how to shop. After four hours of shoppin' in Tyson's Corner, she talked me into buying her everything from a new I-Phone, one of the latest Gucci bags wit' the shoes to match as well as several new outfits from various stores. Ten thousand is what I ended up droppin' on this last minute shoppin' spree. I felt sorry for any guy who my daughter ended up datin' because she already had expensive taste; a trait passed down to her from Lisa. When we finally left the mall, I quickly drove back home knowin' the time I'd spent wit' Denie had pushed me back. I had plans to fly out later on in the evenin', which no one knew about, especially Denie. I hadn't told her that I wasn't goin' to be home for Christmas because I knew she would be upset so I left her another gift under the tree right along wit' Lisa and Juan's, hopin' it would be a substitute for my absence. No matter how upset I got wit' my wife and son, I still would never deprive them on Christmas.

As soon as Denie put her new stuff up that we'd bought, she walked in my room and gave me a kiss, lettin' me know that she was goin' over her friend's house, which worked out perfect. Now, wit' no one home, it was effortless for me to leave unnoticed. Openin' up my closet I pulled out my Louis Vuitton duffle bag and threw in a couple of things for my trip. I was only flyin' to L.A. for a couple of days and since it was goin' to be a short trip I packed light. Now, with Mike taken care of, I had some catchin' up to do wit' expandin' my new empire on the West Coast. I was ready to get some real money at any cost, even if that meant spendin' Christmas without my family.

CHAPTER EIGHT
Lisa

After Rich and Denie left, I immediately went to the garage and keyed the entire passenger side of Rich's fully restored 1981 Corvette. A car he'd nicknamed, Snow White because of the customized paint. As if that wasn't enough, I took a steak knife from the kitchen and stabbed the soft convertible top several times. He'd just invested $60,000 into his precious old-school car last summer. Besides Denie, I knew it was one of his prized possessions, but didn't give a fuck. I wanted his ass to pay this time for hitting me, and destroying his car made me feel so much better. After stabbing the hood one last time, I walked around to all four tires and poked holes in those as well. As air slowly made it's way out, I began to think about how Rich was going to react when he saw what I'd done. I knew it was going to be a battle, but after all the stress he'd put me through over the years, I was ready for whatever.

After giving the car my own little makeover, I decided to do one last thing to piss Rich off. Knowing he hated when anybody fucked with his money, I decided to treat myself to a little shopping with one of his many stashes; money that he had no clue

I even knew about. Opening the glove compartment, I pulled back a small lever that had been installed, which automatically popped open the stash spot under the passenger's floor board. Moving the stupid, *Corvette's Rule* floor mat, I opened the entrance to the square shaped hole, reached inside and pulled out several stacks of money. Normally, this spot had about a hundred thousand tucked away, but for some reason the stash was light this time. However, it didn't matter. Regardless of the amount, I had plans to blow it all.

Shopping had always been therapy for me, so I knew I would feel much better about Rich putting his hands on me once I spent all his shit. Juan and I ended up going to Mazza Gallerie to avoid bumping into Rich and Denie since I knew Tyson's was her favorite mall. It was hard for me to believe that my daughter and I had actually gone to blows with one another. My mother would always tell me, she couldn't wait for me to have a child of my own, because I would get back everything I ever did to her. I guess she was right because my feelings were crushed, especially at the fact that Rich sided with her all the time.

When we would get into it in the past, I would grab or shake her, but it had never been like this. I guess I was just fed up and frustrated. Since Denie had become a teenager it had gotten much harder trying to raise her, especially with Rich in and out of her life. I wonder if he ever realized how his constant absence had affected Denie's behavior. It seemed as if she had so much anger built up inside of her; anger that was always directed toward me.

Rich's absence also affected Juan, who ended up turning to the streets since I wasn't able to buy him the material things he was used to having once Rich got locked up. With most of Rich's money tied up in expensive legal fees, and me struggling to pay a $5,500 mortgage, three car payments and a stack of other bills, Juan decided to use his advantage as Rich's son to make his own money. I hated the fact that my son decided to go that route. I never wanted that lifestyle for him, and prayed constantly that he would someday be college bound. Until my prayers were answered, I had no plans to give up hope.

After hours of shopping and spending the entire twenty g's on everything Juan and I put our hands on, we finally made our way back home. Even though I was mad at Denie, I even ended up buying her a necklace from Tiffany. Since Rich wanted to put his hands on me, I was determined not to come back home with a dime. It felt good spending his hard earned money…always had. He would learn sooner or later to stop fucking with me.

When we pulled up to the house, Juan didn't waste anytime jumping out and running around to open my door, like a true gentleman, which immediately made me smile. My son was always there for me when I felt Rich wasn't and I really needed him right now. I was still suffering from so much mentally and Rich just wasn't sympathetic at all about my needs or feelings. It was hard dealing with being raped, abducted, and having to watch my back every five minutes. I always felt on edge, so Juan and my pills were truly my safe havens away from reality.

"Juan, are you going to church with us tonight?" I asked as he grabbed a hand full of bags.

"As long as your husband doesn't go, I'm there."

"He's supposed to. Regardless, just please go for me."

"Okay Ma, for you. I have to go make a run first, but I'll meet you there."

I shook my head. "Juan, it's Christmas Eve. Do you have to do that on a day like this?"

Juan smiled, showing his perfect set of teeth. A charming characteristic he'd gotten from my side of the family. "Ma, my line of work is open twenty-four seven. Feins don't take off for vacation."

I shook my head again. *I really need to find a way to get you out of that line of work,* I thought before walking into the house. It didn't take long for me to realize that Rich and Denie were still not at home. "Your father and sister must still be out. Maybe they're so pissed off that they're not even going tonight."

"Don't worry about them, Ma," Juan said, putting all the bags down.

"You're right. I'm not going to worry about it. They both

know that we go to church on Christmas Eve as a family, so I'm going to get dressed. If they're here when I leave then fine, if not…oh well."

"Exactly. Do you want me to take the bags upstairs?"

"No, I'll do it."

Juan kissed me on the cheek. "Okay. I'll see you tonight. Love you."

"Love you, too."

When Juan left, I started up the stairs to my room with a couple of bags. I had so many, I knew it would take me at least three trips. Entering my room, I was on my way to my closet when I realized the light inside Rich's closet was on. Flashing back to when the attackers invaded my home, I instantly stopped in my tracks. Since I wasn't sure if someone was in the house again, I stood frozen for a few minutes, waiting to see if I heard someone moving around. After standing in the same spot for at least two minutes and not hearing anything, I slowly walked toward the closet. I knew I should've been walking in the other direction, but something told me that I was overreacting. Once I reached the closet door, and realized that Rich had obviously left the light on, I breathed a sigh of relief.

"Damn, maybe I should carry the gun Rich bought me," I said to myself. Right before I went to turn off the light, the fact that Rich's luggage was gone immediately caught my attention. "He left?" I asked out loud like someone was there to respond. After staring in the empty space for a few more seconds, I picked up my house phone and called Rich on his cell.

"What?" he answered on the first ring.

"Rich, where are you?"

"After the shit you pulled earlier, don't ask me anything right now."

"It's Christmas Eve. Why would you leave without saying anything?"

"Look, I've got some things to take care of."

"So, those things couldn't wait until after the holidays? Denie will be crushed if you're not here tomorrow."

He paused for a moment. "I know, but I'll just have to make it up to her later."

"You know we all were supposed to go to church tonight. My family is gonna be wondering where you are. I don't feel like dealing with that tonight."

"And I don't really give a fuck about your family right now. I got more important things to do than to sit up in another one of your father's borin'-ass Christmas Eve sermons. Just put some money in the offerin' bucket from me tonight. That should satisfy him. Look, I gotta go. Tell Denie, I love her." CLICK

I dreaded hearing my mother and father asking questions about where Rich was. My parents had been waiting since the day I got married, for me to run back home and let them know how much they were right about Rich. My father and Rich hated each other with a passion. They got into a huge fight when I was about to deliver Juan because Rich was nowhere to be found when I was going into labor. One of the elders at the church called my dad to let him know she saw Rich at the movies with some girl, and my father has never gotten past that.

The fights between them caused Rich to forbid me to bring his kids anywhere near my parent's house. I could hear his disrespectful ass voice in my head, *"If your father's bitch ass can't respect me, I don't want my kids anywhere near him."* To keep the peace, I just stayed away. He was only cordial during the holidays, and we were only allowed to go to church, which hurt my dad.

My father and I were so close before Rich and I got together and I regretted everyday that I'd allowed Rich to come between us. No matter how jealous my mother was of our bond, she knew my dad loved me and there was nothing she could do to destroy what we shared. Sometimes I felt guilty that I wasn't that strong when it came to Rich, but I would always be a daddy's girl. I just didn't want to disappoint him and not be there for Christmas. That was a time where he looked forward to seeing us, me and the kids that is.

I spent the rest of the evening wrapping gifts before it was time for me to get ready for church. It was 6:00 p.m. and Denie had just gotten home.

"Denie, we have to leave by 7:00 p.m. to get to church on time."

I repeated myself twice before she snapped. "I heard you!"

I didn't feel like any drama, so I just ignored her funky-ass attitude...for now.

It really made me upset that Rich was going to miss my father's sermon. Since the relationship with Rich and my parents was so strained, the kids rarely interacted with my family, but Christmas Eve was the exception. The only time Rich wasn't with us in church on this special occasion was when he was in jail. *I wonder what the hell could be keeping him away this time*, I thought. *He's never let business interfere before*. I continued to think. *Business, I doubt it. It's probably some bitch.*

After wrapping the last of the gifts, I went straight to one of the Saks bags from my shopping spree and pulled out my brand new black taffeta Roberto Cavalli dress. To finish off the look, I put on my new leopard print Christian Louboutins shoes. Once I sprayed on my Tom Ford Black Orchid perfume, I felt refreshed and was ready to go to church and give praise. I definitely needed prayer.

It was a quiet car ride to the church, but I knew Denie was still mad at me for hitting her earlier. I started thinking about Rich not coming with us and got upset myself. The last thing I was in the mood for was my mother and father asking a lot of questions about his whereabouts; questions that I couldn't even answer. Rich knew I hated when my family was in our business, but just like everything else, I guess he didn't give a fuck.

When we pulled into the parking lot several minutes later, I dropped Denie off at the front door and went to find a parking space. It wasn't long before I noticed Juan's car. He'd parked in two spaces to save me a spot, which was completely thoughtful. My son was always doing kind and considerate things for me, which was much more than I could say about that sorry ass husband of mine. After parking my car, my sadness for Rich's absence was immediately overshadowed when I stepped outside the car and saw Juan waiting for me with a huge smile. My black fur wrap coat was able to combat the blistering cold as Juan and I walked inside the church at a fast pace. The air smelled as if snow was in our forecast. *A white Christmas would be beautiful*, I thought to myself.

As we walked into the sanctuary the service had already began. My father and I made eye contact and he gave me a nod as he continued thanking the new visitors. We filed into the second row and it felt good that our reserved seats were still free even though we were thirty minutes late. My mother looked back at me, gave me a half smile, and turned back around. With all of the whispers and stares, I felt as if the whole sanctuary was watching my every move. Not to mention, the sermon my father preached, I felt, was geared directly toward me.

His message was about not forgetting why we celebrate Christmas. He said it wasn't about the cars, the furs, the toys, or the material things man had given, but it was about celebrating the birth of Jesus Christ. Love your family and be thankful, were the last words my father said as he looked at me with tears in his eyes and smiled. My brother, Brent, was the lead male singer in the choir and had a way of moving me with his voice. When the keyboard began to play my favorite gospel song, *Never Would've Made It*, by Marvin Sapp, I knew it was a matter of time before the flood gates opened and I began to cry. My father walked down the steps of the pulpit with so much power and began to speak to his audience.

"If you need prayer today, if you never would've made it without him, join me right here, right now…it doesn't matter what your neighbor thinks, it doesn't matter what someone is going to say about you…come and lay your sorrows down with Jesus."

At that moment, something came over me and before I knew it, I was on my feet walking toward my father.

As soon as I made it to the front, he held me and cried. "I

love you baby, I love you. Please don't be a stranger," he whispered in my ear.

If my father had turned his back on me before, it didn't matter, because I needed him. Even if it was only for this moment, I appreciated my father holding me like he used to. I didn't expect my mother to join us since she always envied me and my dad's relationship.

After the service, it was nice to see Juan and Denie interacting with their cousins and catching up on the latest family gossip, but I still decided not to mingle as much to avoid being asked where Rich was. We stayed at the church for dinner, which of course was amazing since my Aunt Pam's catering service always served at any church function. As soon as I thought I was in the clear, my mother approached me.

"I know you weren't about to leave without saying something to your mother," she said.

I gave her a kiss on her cheek, "Hi, mother," I said fake as ever.

"So, where's that sorry son-in-law of mine? Somewhere off making a deal?" she said sarcastically.

"Dad did such a great job tonight, and church was wonderful, but we need to get going. It was nice seeing you, Ma." Ignoring her question, I motioned to Denie and Juan. It was time to go so we left immediately without giving her a moment to respond.

The car ride home was just as quiet. As I listened to the soothing Christmas carols on 96.3 WHUR, I glanced over, noticing how precious Denie looked asleep. It reminded me of how sweet she was as a child before she began to endure so much heartbreak. I just imagined what she was dreaming of. We probably had the same thoughts. No matter how much I hated Rich right now, he was still my husband and the father of my children. I wished for him to be home when we arrived, not only for me, but more importantly for Denie.

When I hit the remote for the garage, there was no sign of Rich's Range Rover on the opposite side. Thoughts of him possibly changing his mind and coming back home flashed through my mind periodically while we were driving home, but I guess I was wrong. Moments later, Denie woke up with excitement, but instantly fell into a somber mood after not seeing any signs of Rich. She went straight to her room once we got in the house. Juan, however, stayed up with me while I placed all the gifts under the tree. No matter how old my children were, they still wanted to be treated as if they were three years old when it came to Christmas. Rich and I had always spoiled them that way.

Puzzled, I came across a gift that I hadn't noticed before that was made out to me. It read, *"To My Wife, with Much Love, Rich."* I didn't even know he'd decided to get me anything. Deciding to wait until the next day to open it, I placed the gift on the ottoman in the family room then quickly turned my attention toward the 11 o'clock news. After curling up on the sectional, Juan came over and patted my leg.

"Ma, what's wrong? Are you sad because your husband's not here?"

"No, I'm fine baby. You're here with me, and that's all I need."

"Weren't you supposed to go to Trixie's party tonight after church?"

"Yeah, but I'm so drained. With all the drama today, I just want to watch T.V. and chill."

Flipping back and forth between several news channels, I immediately stopped on channel five when I spotted a familiar face. She was completely distraught. It was Trixie. I quickly turned up the television.

"There was another murder last night that we regret to report on this Christmas Eve. Michael Johnson father of three, was found by his girlfriend, Theresa Elliot, in the basement of their home earlier this evening. You know Brian, it's sad that his children have to deal with this during the holidays, my goodness, it's Christmas Eve. Such a heart wrenching story. My prayers go out to their family," one of the news anchors announced.

Just when I reached for my cell phone to call Trixie, the photo of Michael Johnson appeared on the television. He was in a family photo with two twin boys and Trixie's youngest daughter. It was my attacker. It felt like I was about to throw up.

"Ma, ain't that Trixie? Man, that's fucked up," Juan stated.

"Where the fuck is your father? Get him on the phone now!" I demanded.

"What's wrong?" Juan asked.

Realizing that he was taking too long, I reached for my cell phone and dialed Rich's number. When he didn't answer, I called right back. This process went on for at least five minutes, with Rich never answering my call. I decided it was best if I left a message; a fake one.

"Rich, I really need you to call me. I think someone was following us on our way home from church tonight. I'm scared that somebody is still after us. Please come home or call me back!"

Juan looked at me funny. "Why did you do that? Tell me what's going on."

"I just need to talk to your father. He only calls back half of the time when he thinks something is wrong."

"Is it something I can do?"

I shook my head. "No."

It was evident that Rich killed the guy, but why? Was he having an affair with Trixie? Why would Trixie's boyfriend do those things to me if Rich wasn't fucking her? I was furious and needed answers. The longer I waited for Rich to call me back, something inside of me just snapped.

Immediately, I went downstairs to the laundry room and grabbed the bleach. Passing Juan in the kitchen, I tried to keep my cool, but as soon as I was out of his sight I ran up the steps and went straight to my bathroom and turned on the water in the tub. I was so upset that I wanted to kill Rich. *I know he's fucking Trixie! The guy said that he was getting Rich back for fucking his girl*, I thought. At that moment, I went straight to his dresser and grabbed all of his watches. Cartier, Breitling, and even his diamond encrusted presidential Rolex, all went straight into the bleach bath. Next, I power walked to his closet and grabbed as many of his clothes that I could and dumped them all in the tub. I just kept going until I was stopped in my tracks by Juan.

"Ma, what the hell is going on? What are you doing?"

"Juan, I'm so sick and tired of your father's shit. I just can't take it anymore!" I yelled with tears streaming down my face.

"Constantly destroying his things isn't gonna solve anything or make him change. Come sit down and let me know what's wrong. You've been acting really weird over these past few weeks. I need to know what the hell is going on."

"Everything's wrong Juan. I just can't do this anymore!"

"Be real with me, Ma. After you saw Trixie on the news you just snapped."

"I can't, Juan."

"Ma, I'm leaving if you don't tell me what's up."

"Nooo, Juan, please don't leave me. Okay, I'll tell you what happened." Right then and there, I poured my heart out to my son and gave him details from start to finish about how I was abducted and raped. Surprisingly, along with my tears, Juan also began to cry. Something I hadn't seen since he was in fifth grade.

"Ma, why do you keep putting up with this shit from him? If it's money that you're worried about then I'll take care of you," Juan replied. "Man, I wanna kill that nigga. I can't believe this!" With all the emotional anger that was going on, Denie entered the bathroom in complete shock.

"Oh my God. What have you done to my father's stuff? He's going to kill you!"

"Denie, go back to your room, and mind your business," Juan said in a calm tone, but with a serious stare. Denie did exactly what she was told when she saw the look on Juan's face. Seconds later, she left.

"Ma, are you gonna be okay?" Juan asked.

"Yeah, but I need you to help me be strong. Don't hate your father. Learn from this and be better than him."

"I just don't get it. What the hell is it going to take for you to leave him? What is it going to take? He fucked around on you and caused you all this pain, and you still don't see he ain't shit!"

"Juan, stop it. I don't need to hear all that right now. Just be there for me. That's all I need," I replied.

"I'm sorry, Ma. I'll do whatever you need me to do."

"Don't worry, I'll be alright. Can you just get me a bottle of water from the kitchen? I'm gonna go to bed and get some rest."

When Juan brought my water upstairs, I downed three sleeping pills to help me escape my problems…once again.

On Christmas morning I woke up to breakfast in bed. I guess this was Juan's way of cheering me up.

"Merry Christmas my Queen. How are you feeling?" My son greeted me with a kiss on my cheek then placed the tray at the edge of the bed.

"Baby, I'm fine, what you got over there?"

"I made eggs, turkey bacon, fruit salad, and fried pota-toes."

"Wow, it looks good. I'm so glad I taught your ass how to cook," I replied with a smile. However, Juan didn't return the expression.

"For real Ma. What are you gonna do about Rich?" he asked wanting answers already.

"Baby, it's really over this time, I promise you that. I just have to come up with a plan."

"I got you, Ma. Whatever happens, I'll be by your side."

"In due time, but for now I need you guys to be strong for

me. I need you kids more than ever. No arguing, no drama, just love, that's all. It's Christmas."

I tried hard to hold it all in, but I got emotional and my eyes begun to tear up. I also tried to enjoy my breakfast, but it wasn't long before my appetite disappeared. I needed Rich to come home. He had some explaining to do. At that moment, it was as if Rich was listening to me because the house phone started to ring. Quickly glancing at the caller ID, I noticed that it was Rich.

"Juan, this is your father. Let me talk to him in private," I requested.

I could tell Juan was uneasy, but didn't hesitate to leave the room. My hands began to shake as I pressed the talk button. "Hello."

"Where's my daughter? Let me speak to her," Rich said. "Her cell phone is off, and you know I don't really do messages."

He couldn't even say Merry Christmas. "So, I left you an important fucking message last night, and you're just calling me back?" I yelled. "What if something had happened? Do you care about anything other than fucking other women?"

He let out a huge sigh. "You don't need me. You have Juan there." His tone was cold and unconcerned. "Besides, that's why I'm callin' to check on my daughter."

"I need to talk to you about something."

"Lisa, I'm gettin' ready to lose my fuckin' patience. Can you tell Denie to get on the phone? I'm not really interested in talkin' to you about anything right now. It's Christmas, shit. Can I get one day with no damn naggin'?"

I was so mad, that I instantly threw the phone across the room causing it to hit the wall and shatter in several pieces. "Fuck him!" I belted as I jumped out of bed. At that moment, I told myself I wasn't going to allow Rich to fuck up my day.

Walking downstairs, I attempted to enjoy the holiday with Denie and put aside our differences. She was on the floor opening her presents, so to break the ice I gave her a kiss and sat on the floor beside her.

"Thanks for my Tiffany necklace, Ma."

"You're welcome, Denie. You know I love you, right?"

"Yes, I do. Who were you upstairs yelling at? My dad? Did he call?"

I shook my head. "No." I knew it was wrong to lie, but I just didn't care. If Rich wanted to play hardball then so could I.

CHAPTER NINE
Lisa

A week passed, and I still hadn't heard back from Rich. He hadn't even tried to call Denie back, which was odd. My emotions ran wild and the thought of Trixie and Rich sleeping together had me ill. With Juan devastated, I prayed that the bad news I told him wouldn't start a war under my own roof. The anger that Juan felt for Rich had turned from disappointment to hate. His words rang over and over in my head.

"Ma, how could you stay with him? I hate that nigga! I don't have a father anymore!" How Juan broke down right before my eyes hurt me…bad.

My long days turned into long nights of tears and emotion, but at least Juan was there every step of the way. When I woke up the morning of New Years Eve and still no calls from Rich, Juan decided to take me to an early brunch at Crème on U Street to help get my mind off of things. Not feeling like myself or the need to get dolled up, I put on a pair of Rock & Republic jeans for comfort and a long sleeve embellished top. Normally, I would've added my Gucci peep toe thigh high boots to the mix, but I decided to put on some flat Dior riding boots instead. We invited Denie to come, but of course she passed. Most of the time, she sat around the house hoping Rich would call or finally show up, and probably thought she would miss him if she left. After telling her we would bring her something back, Juan and I left. Luckily, we took his car and he decided to drive because I needed to lay back and collect my thoughts.

When we pulled up at Crème, the wait was so long, I instantly refused to eat there. As hungry as I was, I needed to eat quickly while I had an appetite. We stopped by a couple of other spots who had long waiting periods as well, then finally ended up at Oohs and Ahhs on 10th and U Street. Juan actually knew the owners so we didn't have to wait. We even had our own private table upstairs.

"Do you guys know what you want to order?" the waitress asked.

"Yeah, we'll both take the chicken and waffles, with cheese eggs and two sweet teas," Juan replied. "Endiah, when did y'all start opening on Sundays?" He looked at the women's thick body up and down, then smiled. "By the way, you look good as always."

Juan was such a flirt; a trait he'd obviously picked up from his father. However, I knew he was going to make a good husband to some lucky girl one day.

"For a couple of months now. If you weren't such a stranger you'd know that, Juan." The waitress looked at me. "Who's this beautiful lady?"

"Oh, this is my mom Lisa. Ma this Endiah one of the owners."

"Your mom! Wow, I thought you were his sister. It's a pleasure to meet you. This meal is on me, Juan. Just take care of the waitress." She looked back at me. "Lisa, let me know how you like your food and make sure you come back and see us," Endiah said.

"I sure will, nice meeting you, too."

"So, Ma, how are you feeling today?"

"I don't know. Mixed emotions I guess. Please don't tell

anyone about what I told you, especially your father."

"Ma, I can't promise you that. I want Rich to pay for this shit. Fuck that!" he yelled.

"Your father will kill me Juan, you can't say anything, please."

"Fuck that nigga! When are you gonna stop protecting him? If he wasn't my father man I'd…"

"Don't say it, Juan. He's still your father. Rich just can't help his womanizing ways. I hate that shit, but I would never want to see harm come his way."

"Whatever. Speak for yourself."

"Can we have a peaceful meal without mention of Rich?"

"I'm sorry. You're right," Juan agreed.

After waffles that melted in our mouths and eggs that were cooked just right, we left the restaurant and headed back home. Our twenty minute ride back up 16th Street went by slower than usual. Every slow song on the radio just made me sink more into my already somber mood. Hopefully at some point, I would snap out of it.

When we pulled up to the house, surprisingly Rich's truck was parked back in his spot. As Juan pulled behind my car, we both gave each other concerned looks. With both of us beyond pissed, we didn't know what to expect from each other.

"Juan, please promise me that you're gonna control your temper, and I'll do the same."

He sighed. "Okay Ma, but the minute that nigga gets out of line, I don't think I'ma be able to keep that promise."

"Fair enough."

When Juan got out of the car and opened my door, I could tell he was trying his best to keep everything inside. Hell, I was, too. I even said a silent prayer before we walked inside the house. As soon as I placed my foot on our brand new hardwood floors, it was like everything was in slow motion. I didn't know how to react. I was so upset with Rich, but at the same time I didn't have the energy to fight. Denie was the only one in heaven. She had the biggest smile on her face as she and Rich played a bowling game on the Wii.

"Why the fuck did you do that shit to my car Lisa?" Rich asked. No Hi, how are you? How was your Christmas…nothing.

"Nigga, fuck you and that car. Don't come up in here with that bullshit disrespecting my mother. You've done enough!" Juan snapped.

So much for Juan controlling his temper, I thought.

Rich quickly turned his head. "Who the fuck you talkin' to, boy? I'll whoop your ass for disrespectin' me!" At that moment, Rich threw the Wii remote and lunged toward Juan.

I quickly stood in between them and placed both hands on Rich's chest. "Stop it, Rich! I'll be damned if you're gonna put your hands on my son. I can't believe you waltzed your ass back in here like nothing's wrong. We haven't heard from you in a damn week!"

"And it's gonna be another week, if you don't watch who you're talkin' to," Rich quickly shot back.

"Denie obviously doesn't care how you treat her, but you're not gonna treat me like shit anymore," I added.

"Stop it Ma, before you make him leave again!" Denie interjected.

"If it wasn't for these kids, I would've left your ass a long time ago. I don't know how much of this bullshit I can take, Rich. You're mad at me about a fucking car, but not once have you said you were sorry for what you did. You hit me after you promised that you would never put your hands on me again!" I didn't even bother mentioning the money. I continued ignoring Denie's pleas, as I looked Rich right in his eyes. I had to keep him from hitting my son. "Juan and Denie, please go upstairs. I need a moment with your father."

"Are you sure, Ma?" Juan asked.

I nodded my head. "Yes…I'll be fine."

"Yes, she'll be fine," Rich repeated. "Juan take your ass upstairs before you get hurt."

When Juan and Denie both walked upstairs with attitudes, Rich turned to me. "I'm really not in the mood for any questionin'."

"You know what, Rich? This is not the fucking 80's and 90's. You're not gonna treat me like an afterthought. I'm tired of this shit!"

At that moment, Rich reached on the coffee table and threw the Christmas gift that I still hadn't opened across the room. "You ungrateful bitch. You didn't even bother to open up your Christmas gift."

"Fuck that gift. You think gifts are gonna keep patching up this sorry-ass marriage? That's real classic, Rich. That's exactly the type of shit I'm talking about. All you do is fuck up, then buy me gifts like that shit is supposed to patch things up!"

"Yeah, I left that shit before I went in the garage and saw what you did to my car. Trust me, you're not gettin' shit else from me. As a matter of fact, you better go out and get a fuckin' job because I'ma make your ass pay for that shit!" He obviously hadn't been upstairs to see what I'd done to his clothes.

"And it is obvious I never pleased you with all the fucking you've been doing."

"Lisa, what the hell are you talkin' about? I just told you that I wasn't in the mood for this!"

"Are you finally gonna come clean on why that dude raped me?"

Rich threw up his hands. "Man, here you go."

I cut right to the chase. "Did you fuck Trixie?"

Rich finally gave me eye contact. "What?" he responded with a dumb look.

"You heard me. Did you fuck Trixie?" When he didn't answer fast enough, I went off. "Don't lie to me! You fucking her, got me kidnapped and raped. That bastard told me you fucked his woman. Why wont you just admit it? Be a man…for once!"

"I don't wanna hear this shit. I told you he lied!"

"So, the news lied, too? I saw Trixie on the news, crying and screaming. She found my attacker's body in her basement,

Rich. You're the one who's lying, so just stop it. I don't know why you can't face the truth. He was getting back at you for fucking Trixie!" For once, Rich was quiet for a moment, so I took the opportunity to continue ranting while I had the chance. "They showed Trixie on television the next morning talking about how Michael Johnson was such a great man."

"How did you know it was the same guy?" Rich had the nerve to say.

"Because I saw his face!"

Rich started at me again. "Look, Lisa I…"

I cut him off. "I'll never love you the same. I hate you…just leave. Get out!" I yelled.

"Lisa, did you forget that my daughter is upstairs listenin' to everything you're sayin'? Do you know what I've been through over this last month? How the fuck you think I felt knowin' that my wife had been raped right in front of my face and I couldn't do anythin' about it?" Suddenly his voice got extremely low. "But I did it. I took care of him. He's never gonna hurt you again."

"So, you can admit to taking care of him, but you can't seem to admit that you fucked Trixie. She was my friend, Rich. How could you?" I was so furious I couldn't even wait for a response. "Rich, go to hell!" I went straight upstairs and grabbed all his bleached clothes and jewelry and started hurling his shit at him from the top of the stairs.

"Get your shit and leave…now!"

His eyes became enlarged. "What the fuck did you do to my clothes?" Rich began to look around on the floor at each item. "And my watches! Have you lost your fuckin' mind?"

"Yes, I have!"

"Damn Trixie, what do you want from me?"

I stopped and looked at him like he was crazy. "What the fuck did you call me? Did you just call me Trixie? So, is that the reason why you didn't want me going to her salon, you bastard. Get your shit and get the fuck out!" I yelled to the top of my lungs.

"This my house and I'm not leavin'! Bitch, you think it's gonna be that easy to get rid of me wit' all the shit you know. You must be fuckin' crazy. Consider yourself stuck wit' me for life. You know what comes wit' the territory wit' fuckin' a nigga like me. You know how many bitches would love to be in your shoes."

"Let 'em have your ass. I don't want you anymore. What is it gonna take for you to go? You need me to go out here and start fucking, too. Maybe I will so you can hate me like I hate you!" I took off my five carat wedding ring, and threw it at him. I used to love showing off the canary yellow diamond, but now none of that shit matter anymore. "Fuck you and this marriage!"

At that moment, Rich ran up the stairs toward me skipping two and three steps at a time. However, by the time he made it to the top, I ran to our bedroom, locked the door, and immediately went to my nightstand. It wasn't long before Rich knocked down the door, but when he did my .25 was pointing right at his head.

"Get the fuck out or I swear to God I'll shoot you in your other fucked up knee!" By this time, Juan and Denie were standing behind him.

"Ma, please put the gun down," Denie said. "He didn't do anything wrong."

"Denie, fuck him," Juan said.

"Fuck this," Rich said as he lunged at Juan. This time he didn't miss. He sat on top of my son and took all his anger out and punched him in his face as if he was a stranger.

I screamed then began firing several shots in the air. It was the only thing that stopped Rich from pounding on Juan. Drywall fell from the ceiling all over my head.

"Get off of him!" I screamed.

When Rich quickly did as he was told, Denie ran up and threw her arms around his neck. She was crying uncontrollably.

"Look, I think all this shit has just gotten completely out of hand, so I'm gone for now, but I'll be back when shit calms down," Rich said. He removed Denie's hands.

"No, don't go," Denie pleaded. She sounded like a little girl.

"Don't worry, Baby Girl. I'll be back. Your mother and I just need some space." Moments later, he finally left with a defeated look.

What a way to start off the fucking New Year, I thought. Never having the courage to stand up to Rich before, I was proud of myself as I ran over to Juan to see if he was okay. No matter how much pain I was in mentally, I was done with Rich once and for all. There was no way I could forgive him for this shit. He was sadly mistaken if he thought that all we needed was some space or time apart. I needed more than that. It was time for a divorce, and I knew things were about to get dirty.

CHAPTER TEN

Rich

Lookin' into my wife's eyes, it was the first time she looked as if she had no soul. A cold, blank expression, that I'd never witnessed in the seventeen years we'd been together. I knew she was serious this time and it concerned me. She was tired of me hurtin' her and I couldn't even blame her for feelin' that way. When I pulled out of the garage, I could see Denie lookin' out of the window in her room cryin' and tryin' to get my attention. Pretendin' not to see her, I just drove off. It was hard to leave that way, but I put my pride aside and decided to give Lisa the space that she needed. The space I hope she needed. Hopefully when I got back, I could turn things around.

As I drove down I-95, I began to think. *Maybe I should meet up wit' Carlos in New York, and fly back to California wit' him. A four hour drive is what I need right about now to get my mind right*, I thought. *I'll call Los later and tell him what's up.* However, by the time I hit Baltimore, Carlos was callin' me.

"What up?

"Rich, what happened? Lisa called Marisol all upset

talking about she put you out. She also said she knew about you and Trixie. What the hell happened?"

"Man, Lisa saw ole girl on the news cryin' about her man, and put everything together." I couldn't go into so much detail over the phone, but Carlos knew what that meant. "I'm just gonna roll back out for a while and let Lisa get her mind right."

"She told Marisol that she was gonna divorce you. What's up with that?"

"She just trippin' right now, cuz. Man on everything I love, I'll never smash that whore Trixie ever again. Hot-ass bitch fucked my home up."

"No doubt, she's bad news. I told you to stop fucking with her a long time ago."

"Shit, don't front. You've had a whore or two like that before, but you're so scared of Marisol catchin' your ass you can't concentrate," I laughed.

"Naw, it's not that, I'm just more discreet with my shit that's all," Carlos bragged. "Anyway, so what's up with you now that you're homeless?"

"I see you got jokes. Man, I needed some time to think so I just started drivin' and ended up on I-95. I'm in B-More right now. I'll probably go holler at Honey, to get some head real quick, then meet you up top."

"So, your ass just got caught up in some shit with Lisa, and you're thinking about hooking up with another broad already?"

"Well, I'm stressed, so I need some good head to relieve that shit." I laughed right along wit' Carlos.

"Your ass got a problem. Okay, call me when you get here. You know Marisol wants to stay in New York until after the New Year."

"That's cool. I need to holla at some people in Brooklyn anyway."

"Are you gonna fly out of JFK with us?"

"Yeah. I'ma get Nelson to meet me in B-More so he can

ride wit' me up there, and drive my truck back. I don't know how long I'ma be in L.A. this time, and I don't want my shit just sittin' at the airport."

"You like that lil dude, huh?" Carlos asked.

"Yeah, he cool peoples. He reminds me of myself when I was his age."

"Well, hit me when you get up here."

"A'ight, cuz."

After I hung up wit' Carlos, I called my man Nelson and told him to meet me in B-More at the strip club I'd invested in, called Lace. Nelson was my young dude from Montgomery County. He was pumpin' good and was really makin' shit happen in the D.C. area for me. Nelson reminded me so much of myself when I was his age. He had that swagger like 'I'm that nigga' and had been loyal thus far, so puttin' the young soldier down on my team was a no brainer. He handled business so good that I put him in a crib out in Wheaton. It was a good location for him to still be able to shoot out to Frederick and Gaithersburg, and still get to D.C. Not to mention, it was low key.

Nelson usually just followed my lead and didn't ask questions, which I loved, because I didn't like talkin' over the phone too much. Wit' the type of day I had, it was a must to make sure I saw my stripper chick. Honey was phat as shit and had some bomb head. I usually would smash her in one of my private rooms before I hit the road to go to New York every couple of months. This time, her services were desperately needed.

When Nelson met me in the parkin' lot, forty-five minutes later, we gave each other a quick pound then walked in together. The spot was packed since it was New Years Eve, and the strippers were dressed in all types of sparkles and shit. The club was decorated for the festivities and it appeared to be a lot goin' on. As we moved through the crowd, I spotted Honey on stage in the VIP section in the back. She looked good as usual.

Honey had that caramel complexion wit' a long weave that fell to her ass. Known for her purple costumes, tonight she wore a purple feather and rhinestone dress that barely covered her ass. I guess wearin' purple was her tactic of gettin' more money from the Ravens players. They were in the back makin' it rain, while Honey shook her ass to *Arab Money* by Busta Rhymes. Nelson and I posted up against the wall as we watched Honey make her way up the pole. As she spun herself upside down and began to make her way down, we finally caught eye contact. When I nodded, she knew what time it was. After landing in a split, the crowd roared and money flew everywhere. I had to give it to her, Honey was definitely about makin' her bread. Once her act was complete, I sent one of my security guards to help clean her money off the stage, as Nelson and I went to our private room. My day so far had been rough, so I really needed Honey to earn her money tonight.

"Hey sexy, who's your fine-ass friend you got here," Honey flirted while she gave Nelson a wink.

Wit' Nelson bein' my man and all, he was entitled to smash Honey too. "Nelson, this is Honey, Honey, this is Nelson. Now, time for business because we gotta hit the road. I don't wanna be bringin' in the New Year in the car."

"So, what do you want a threesome, Rich?" Honey asked confused.

"Naw, you gonna hit me off first, then whatever my man wants you can give to him afterwards. And don't worry, the pay is good."

"Since you're in such a hurry, how bout I go get Cream and let her hit him off while I take care of you?" Honey suggested.

"A'ight, cool."

Minutes later, Nelson was greeted by Cream and before they left the room I threw Nelson ten one hundred dollar bills rolled up in a rubber band. However, I was surprised when he threw it back.

"I got this," he said smilin' as Cream grabbed his hand and led him out of the door.

"Un, un Rich, don't be looking at Cream like you wanna

fuck her. She can't put it down like me, baby. Let me show you," Honey whispered in my ear. All I could do was smell her sweet perfume and lay back so she could handle her business.

Honey got right on her knees, unzipped my jeans and put my tool in her mouth. She sucked me like a champ…always did. She definitely gave the best head that I'd ever had in my life. She could make me cum in less than two minutes, while most women couldn't make me bust like that at all. She was a beautiful woman wit' a sexy body, which was probably why I just didn't understand how she could be such a whore. I wasn't sure how she would ever get a man to wife her. Beyond the sex, what did she have to offer? I knew a lot of dudes down south wifed strippers, but that was some shit D.C. dudes just didn't do.

"Oh, shit," I said as Honey's soft lips moved up and down my shaft.

It didn't even matter that I grabbed the back of her head and pushed my dick deeper inside her mouth because she took every inch like a true professional. Even when I could feel her tonsils, she never gagged. The only time she stopped her stroke was when she licked the tip of my head or sucked on my balls, which always sent me to another level. As soon as Honey's snake like tongue did a few more of her famous moves, I couldn't take any more. My entire body began to shake as I unloaded a large amount of thick cum into Honey's mouth. I could tell she swallowed every ounce.

After round one and two, I paid Honey for her services, waited for Nelson to bust his nut wit' Cream and headed for New York. Nelson drove while I fell back and I listened to my Raheem DeVaughn CD. When the song, *Marathon,* came on I started to think about Lisa. I wished I could vent to Nelson about what was goin' on wit' my family, but I kept that part of my life separate from my business. He knew nothin' about my family and I planned to keep it that way. However, that didn't stop his ass from tellin' me his shit. By the time we got to Delaware, Nelson began to open up to me about how he was caught up in a love triangle.

He seemed to really be in love wit' this young chick and was tryin' to get rid of his old girl who was tryin' to put a baby on him. He said he felt bad for fuckin' Cream because he was tryin' to do right by his girl. It was funny to see Mr. Casanova have hearts in his eyes. I got satisfaction out of teasin' him. One little girl had left her boyfriend for him, so he didn't trust her, and the other one he really liked, but she was so private it drove him crazy. I laughed and told him that could be a good thing, but just continue fuckin' both of them. He was still young. Nelson made me laugh the whole ride to New York. Bein' wit' him made me miss Juan. It also made me long for a closer relationship wit' him. Hopefully, one day when all this nonsense wit' me and Lisa died down, we could work on that.

Nelson and I met up wit' Carlos and handled some business in Brooklyn, before tryin' to figure out how we would bring in the New Year. Carlos got a call from Marisol askin' him to meet her and her friend who lived in New York in Times Square to watch the ball drop. However, I guess Marisol wasn't happy wit' his response because she hung up on him once Carlos said that shit was corny, and that we were bringin' in the New Year at the 40-40 Club. Nelson and Carlos knew I rarely partied in D.C., but when we traveled out of town, we did it big.

When we pulled up to the club, the line was wrapped around the block. Luckily, Carlos had already called our New York connect so we were good. They knew that I wasn't about to stand in a line, even if we were out of town. It wasn't long before our waitress came to the door to get us and had security escort us through the crowd to VIP. Ace of Spade bottles and Ciroc were already on ice as soon as we arrived. Wit' the day I had, a drink was a definite. We weren't even in the club twenty minutes when I glanced over at Nelson, who was on his I-phone textin'.

"Damn, nigga. You shoulda brought her wit' us!" I yelled. "I would've even got y'all a suite."

"I'm cool!" Nelson yelled over the music as he sipped his champagne like he wasn't missin' his girl.

"A'ight, mister tough guy," I joked.

When the security guard moved the red stanchion back moments later, Marisol walked in wit' some hot Puerto Rican chick. They both were wearin' black sequin dresses wit' glittery Happy New Years hats. Tootin' their horns in our faces, they stumbled like they were already tipsy. Marisol greeted Carlos wit' a kiss first, and then came over to give me a hug.

"Hey Rich, where's Lisa!" she said wit' excitement as if she expected me to say she went to the bathroom or somethin'.

"Don't fuckin' play wit' me right now, Marisol. You know what she told you over the phone," I snapped.

"Yeah, but I honestly thought y'all would've worked that shit out by now. She's mad at you all the time," Marisol responded. Her breath definitely smelled like vodka.

"Well, she's a little more than mad this time, but fuck that shit. Let her trip. I really don't care right now." I looked at the fine Puerto Rican honey. Who's that wit' you?" I gave her friend the eye, but Marisol wasn't havin' it.

"Don't fuck with me Rich, that's my friend Jade and she's off limits. I love Lisa, she's like my sister. I would never hurt her!"

"Look, Lisa put me out and told me she wants a divorce, so I'm doin' me right now, so fuck her! She fucked my car up, bleached my fuckin' clothes, and ruined all my watches. She lucky she ain't bringin' in the New Year at Washington Hospital Center. I'ma give her the space that she wants, but I know she'll be back in my face in no time!" I yelled over the music.

"You fucked up Rich. You've been *doing you* for a long time, not just tonight. If Carlos did the shit that you do, he would be dead. Real talk, I don't fuck around with my feelings." When Marisol saw that I wasn't interested in what she had to say, she changed the subject. "Well, anyway let's enjoy the New

Year, but you better go home to your wife, sir."

"Man, who knows, my new future wife might be bringin' in 2010 wit' me tonight!" Again, I looked over at her friend, who had thick legs like Alicia Keys.

"Fuck off, Rich!" Marisol rolled her eyes at me and walked over to Carlos.

During their deep conversation, I'm sure she was ventin' to him about how I wasn't shit, but little did she know, I was goin' to have that fine Puerto Rican mami's legs in the air by the end of the night. I was definitely droppin' balls tonight, and it wasn't gonna be in Times Square.

We popped Ace of Spade most of the night as DJ Biz Markie killed it. When I filled Jade's glass of champagne back up for the third time, she thanked me and gave me a look that let me know it was on. When Marisol and Carlos went out on the dance floor, it was time to make my move. I had no idea where Nelson was. He'd vanished a while ago.

"So, Jade where are you from?"

"I'm originally from Puerto Rico, but I've been living here in New York since I was fifteen."

"How old are you?"

"Twenty-seven, why?"

"I just wanted to make sure you're legal. You look young." One side of her long Cassie inspired haircut was completely shaved, while the other side fell to her shoulders. Wit' thick eyeliner and smoky shadow over her eyes, she definitely gave off an edgy vibe, which I liked.

"How old are you?" she asked.

"Thirty-eight."

"What difference would it make how old I was anyway? You're a married man, right?"

"Baby, I can change your life. Don't worry about things that don't matter," I replied.

"Well, it matters to me, I'm not about to play second. I'm wifey material."

I smiled. She was feisty, and I liked that. "So, you're just gonna throw away a winnin' lottery ticket, or you gonna give me a chance to show you how a man is really supposed to treat a woman."

"Marisol will be mad. She already told me not to talk to you before we even got here. She must know that you're a flirt, huh?"

"Look, put my number in your phone. I'll let you make the call if you're ready for a real man."

I didn't even have to press the issue before she grabbed my phone, and entered her seven digits. It was easy. All I had to do was kick game and she was all in. I knew that I would be inside her tonight. It didn't matter to me if she had a man or not. As fine as she was, she was gonna be my new side chick. She was good as in my room for the night. Minutes later, Marisol and Carlos raced back to the table as the countdown began.

"Ten, nine, eight, seven, six, five, four, three, two, one…Happy New Year!" the entire club roared wit' excitement.

Watchin' Carlos and Marisol made me reminisce on what Lisa and I once had. Tempted to call, I grabbed my phone and quickly realized that I had three missed calls all from Denie. I decided instead of callin' Lisa, I would send a text to my baby girl instead.

Happy New Year Baby G! Daddy loves you!! 2010 is here! I wrote.

Yeah, but you're not," she hit me back.

I knew I'd let my Baby Girl down once again, but when I looked over and saw Jade lickin' her full lips, any concerns other than me gettin' my dick sucked quickly faded away.

CHAPTER ELEVEN

Lisa

This was the first time that I'd brought in the New Year alone without Rich, besides when he was in prison. After a long hot bath, I took a couple of sleeping pills and watched the Dick Clark Special on T.V. For some reason it was hard for me to get any rest without taking at least one pill or two each night. Rich and I always spent New Year's Eve together, but I had no regrets on asking him to leave. Though the emptiness and quietness in the house made me feel lonely, I felt it was time I started my year off right. As I stared in a daze at the Christmas tree, I thought of all the meanings and memories of each one of my ornaments. We always exchanged ornaments as a tradition during Christmas, but with the drama going on, that shit never even crossed our minds this year.

How did we get to this, I wondered? One of my favorite ornaments was from Juan. It was a beautiful Swarvoski crystal angel that he'd gotten custom made for me the year before. I missed the holidays when we were all together as one big happy family. I missed them even more now that I knew our family would never be the same.

Snapping out of my daze, I heard Denie still upstairs cry-ing. She'd been in tears for hours. Now, I had a new enemy in my daughter because she blamed me for putting Rich out.

The next morning I was awakened by Juan, who came into the family room to congratulate me on finally standing up to Rich. Since he was my first born, he'd witnessed much more than Denie. Juan always had been there to comfort me, since the late night fights that began when he was only five years old. I was grateful that despite what he'd witnessed growing up, he'd still turned out to be a respectful young man, which made me proud. Juan was like the man of the house in a way.

"Ma, I'll be back to get you around six o'clock, so make sure you're ready. We're going out to eat to celebrate you being single and to get 2010 started off right."

I smiled when he mentioned me being single. "It sounds nice, but I don't really feel up to it."

"Listen, I'm not taking no for an answer, so make sure you're ready."

Seeing my husband in my sons' eyes was scary. He had this boss swagger to him and I knew it was a matter of time be-fore he would be a full-fledged spitting image of Rich. He looked just like me, but the way he spoke and carried himself was Rich all the way.

"Okay, fine. I'll be ready."

At exactly 6:15 p.m., Juan and I headed downtown to Ruth's Chris on 9th Street. This was the hangout spot for the guys who were getting it and the girls who were trying to score a dude with some cash. Since we rode in Juan's car, I had to listen to rap and go-go music for the entire ride, which had gotten on my last nerve by the time we pulled up in front of the restaurant. It wasn't long before an Ethiopian gentleman greeted Juan and opened his door. Juan let him know to keep his car out front to earn an extra tip and the man quickly complied.

Even though it was still early, there was a forty-five minute wait on a table, so Juan suggested that we eat in the bar area. He seemed to be quite friendly with all of the bartenders and waitresses, so we got a bar table expeditiously.

"What's up Steve?" Juan greeted our bartender.

"What's up man, who's the beautiful lady?" Steve flirted.

"Slow down man, this is my mother, *Mrs*. Lisa to you," Juan emphasized Mrs.

"Hello, Mrs. Beautiful Lisa."

"Hello Steve, what's your chef's special today?" I asked, keeping the conversation strictly about the meal. I was in no mood for flirtation.

Steve must've gotten my drift and proceeded to tell us about the specials and what he suggested we order. Juan and I both went with filet mignons and two sweet potato casseroles. Steve approached the table again within minutes with our drinks and some warm bread and butter. The lemon drop with Ciroc he'd made was the best I'd ever tasted.

"Mrs. Lisa, how do you like the lemon drop? It's my specialty," Steve asked.

"It's really good Steve, great job. I mean no…amazing job. Damn, this is so good," I over exaggerated and it worked because he walked off embarrassed. He was a nice guy, but I just wasn't in the mood for the flirting or the attention. I just wanted to enjoy my dinner with my son.

"Ma, you're so nice- nasty."

I frowned. "What is that suppose to mean?"

"You be shooting dudes down. I mean I don't wanna see my moms' with no dudes or nothing don't get me wrong, but if you and Rich gonna get a divorce, how you gonna plan to date if you don't even know how to talk to a man."

"Juan, do you realize your father is the only man I've ever dated in my life. I've been with him since I was sixteen. I don't plan on dating anyone in this decade. Do you know what it feels like to be sick and tired of being sick and tired? I just want to focus on living for me and being happy. I'm just taking one day at a time."

"You're such a strong woman and I love you." When Juan reached over and gave me a hug, I began to tear up a little until we were interrupted by some little hoochie.

"Who the fuck is this bitch, Juan? I just had to beat a bitch ass last week cuz you want to be a hoe, I don't mind...."

"Nicole, I should beat your ass for disrespecting my mother like that. You're the hoe! Get the fuck away from this table before I smack the shit out of you!" Juan said as he grabbed Nicole by her neck.

Her mouth was open so wide, she could've caught a fly. "I'm so sorry, Mrs. Sanchez. It's just that Juan is always cheating on....," Nicole tried to say.

"What the fuck did I tell you?" Juan interjected.

"Well, if you learned to call me back then I wouldn't be tripping out on you," Nicole said as she walked away feeling and looking stupid. I remembered her calling our house a few times a while back, but Juan never brought her around. I actually have never met any of Juan's girlfriends since his first love, Ciara, who now had a baby by some other guy. She'd definitely hurt my son.

"Juan, I'm afraid for you. You're becoming your father more and more everyday and I don't like it. I always wanted more for you. You're my first born and I love you so much. I never wanted you to turn to the streets. You have so much potential to be successful in life. It would crush me if anything ever happened to you."

Before Juan could respond, a busty young waitress named, Lauren, approached the table with our food. "The plates are very hot, so careful please," she warned with a smile directed at Juan. I knew there was something between the two of them from the look Lauren gave him right before she left. With Juan just like his father, I wouldn't put it past the fact that my son had fucked her already.

"Ma, I want this evening to be special. I'm sorry that you had to witness so much disrespect at the start of our dinner."

"It's okay. I know how these young women can get, but you always need to remain respectful. I don't ever want to hear that you're putting your hands on a young lady. It's just sad because these girls are getting all wrapped up so young, when they really need to be focusing on their futures. I just pray that your sister stays on the right track. It's so easy to get wrapped up in a man and lose yourself. I just don't want my daughter to experience the life I've lived," I said as it dawned on me that I should've taken my own damn advice.

"Ma, I'm worried about Denie. She seems very withdrawn and I blame Rich." Juan had stopped calling him Dad about two years ago and it still seemed weird to me. Juan was still very angry ever since Rich went to jail and would always blame him for everything that went wrong in our family. The exact same shit that Denie did to me.

"I know, she worries me, too. All she docs is just stay in her room, either painting or writing. Every time I try to reach out to her she just clams up and I don't know what to do. I feel like I don't know my daughter. She doesn't bring friends over anymore, I mean I don't even know any of her friends, and the ones that call the house are rude as hell!"

"That's why I get so mad at Rich. When he got locked up, she got pregnant because he wasn't there to hold us down. Man, he messed Denie up, and now with the stunts he's pulling it ain't gonna do nothing but make her worse."

"Your father ain't shit and I don't want you to be like him. That's why I keep telling you I don't want you messing around in them streets. Suppose something happens to you? Do you know how that will tear my world apart?" My eyes began to tear up at the thought of my life without my son.

"Okay Ma, we said this would be a peaceful night and you're working yourself up. Let's talk about something else," Juan suggested in a calming tone.

As soon as I was about to take my son's advice, I laid eyes on that bitch Trixie coming in the restaurant with some dude. As if she knew we were there, she made a b-line straight to the bar area with the dude in tow.

"Damn, your boyfriend hasn't been dead a month and you've got a new victim already," I taunted as soon as she was within earshot.

Trixie swung her nappy weave over her shoulder. "What? Who the fuck you talking to, Lisa?"

"You. You're full of shit, Trixie. Faking like you're my friend, and the whole time, you were fucking my husband. You home wrecking bitch!" By now, everyone was looking at us.

Juan interjected as I got up to get in swinging range. "Hold up, Ma." He then looked at Trixie's date. "Man, don't let your bitch get outta pocket."

"Slim, you don't' wanna any of this," the guy with Trixie replied.

"Don't fucking talk to my son like that! Trixie, tell your pimp he outta his league," I shot back. "You want him and your bitch-ass baby father to be side by side six feet deep, then try me!"

Trixie laughed. "Wow, fly-ass Lisa Sanchez in Ruth's Chris making a damn fool out of her self. You got so much anger and animosity, all over some dick that every bitch in the city has had. If you think you're the only one who Rich loves, then you're tripping. You have no clue."

"I should've listened to Marisol and never trusted your ass."

"Marisol lucky I ain't fuck Carlos' fine-ass anyway. Maybe he'll be next."

At that moment, I grabbed my steak knife and lunged toward her, but was quickly stopped by Juan. By that time, even Steve along with two other men who looked liked management had joined the party. They immediately asked Trixie and her guest to leave.

"Why make us leave? She started it," Trixie said pointing at me.

When the men told her it was best, she shook her head, then headed toward the door.

"This shit ain't over!" I yelled out. By the time I sat back down, Juan was shaking his head.

"Damn Ma, I didn't know you had all that fire in you. Look, try and calm down. Remember, this dinner is about us, not your loser ass husband. It's crazy how Rich can ruin anything without even being present."

"Juan, I don't wanna talk about your father, or anything that just happened. I wanna get past all that. I just made a spectacle of myself so just let it go." Regaining my composure and skipping the subject, I thought of something else to get Rich and Trixie off my mind. "So son, who's the lucky lady in your life, is it Miss Lauren?"

Juan laughed. "Ma, you think you know me. I just have friends. I let it be known that I'm not looking to get serious with anyone. I don't know why Ma, but since Ciara, I have a hard time trusting anyone."

"Baby, you have all of your life to get serious with someone, but for now just be careful. Make sure you don't bring no babies home. Be respectful to women. Make sure you treat women the way you would want a man to treat me and your sister."

Just when I was beginning to lecture Juan, his phone rang.

"Yeah wassup, Black," he answered. "Ain't shit. Them people cool or they need something else?"

After dealing with Rich all these years, I knew exactly what type of phone call that was.

"Well, I gotta drop my moms off then I'll be around the way. Okay, cool," Juan said before hanging up.

I wanted to say to him so bad, *please leave the streets*

alone, get your life together and go to college. You're too smart for this shit. You don't have to be like Rich, but I had to keep the night positive and stress free.

We ate and before leaving I apologized to Steve for being so rude. He accepted my apology and I gave him an extra tip on top of the generous one Juan had already given him for my rudeness. It was great that Juan had the valet keep his car out front because it was freezing outside. It was amazing to see how my son was so well respected in the city. On the flip side it also scared me to see history repeat itself. He was the spitting image of me, but was his father all day long. The way he walked, talked, his mannerisms, he was becoming Rich more every day. This is probably one of the reasons why Juan hated Rich, no matter how much he tried not to be him, he was becoming his father and it scared me.

Juan and I left Ruth's Chris and headed home. We didn't say much during the ride. Juan finally gave me a break from the rap and go-go music and put in his Ne-Yo CD. As Ne-Yo's smooth voice began to sing, I couldn't help but to think about Rich. *Damn, why am I missing Rich like this,* I had to ask myself. I just wanted to be done with him, but it was so hard. He's all I'd known besides the little meaningless relationships I had in junior high school. I'd made him my life and now I felt like I had nothing.

"Ma, you good, what's wrong?" Juan asked.

"I just have a lot on my mind," I answered.

As I continued to look out the window so my son couldn't see that I was crying, tears ran down my face like they were in a race. I was embarrassed to let him see me cry. There was no way I could admit to my son how much I missed his father. He was so proud of me for standing up to him, so I just had to hold it in until I found a way to let it all out.

When we pulled up to the house and Juan let me know he had to handle some business, but would stay if I needed him. I quickly shook my head. I already felt guilty for occupying his whole day, so I let him go on with the rest of his evening.

As I walked in the house I took a deep sigh then walked into the kitchen to put away the left over food that I didn't finish. Denie was sitting in the family room watching *The Game* re-runs, but as soon as I walked in she turned off the television and started to get up to leave. I didn't want my great evening to be ruined with her attitude, so I tried to approach her with a calm tone.

"Denie, what is the problem sweetie?"

"I'm not your sweetie, and you're the problem," she replied.

All my niceness went out the door instantly. "Who the hell do you think you're talking to? I will not start 2010 off with any level of disrespect from you. Two grown women can't live in this house and only one is paying the bills!"

"My father pays your bills," she mumbled as she walked off and stomped up the steps.

Before she could make it to the third step, I snatched her ass back down the stairs, pulled her close and looked her right in the eye.

"As long as you live under my fucking roof you will respect me. If you want to be grown, I'll show your ass grown, so try me Denie." As I looked into my daughter's eyes there was absolutely no emotion.

"You're such a bitch," she said and snatched away.

"That's it. Get out of my house!" I demanded.

"This is my father's house! The house is not even in your name. It's in my grandmother's!"

Denie knew entirely too much fucking information some times. I got close...real close. Up in her face. "As long as I'm here this is my home!" I could tell by Denie's expression that she knew I meant every word. "Now, I'm about to go upstairs to my room, but when I come back down here, your ass better be gone!"

"Where am I gonna go?"

"I don't know and don't care. You figure it out since you wanna talk shit."

"I hate you!" she said stomping away.

Denie's words stung. My heart hurt, my body hurt, I just wanted to take a bath and get away from reality. As I entered my bathroom I heard my front door slam, but that shit didn't matter to me. I was sick of Denie, and needed a peaceful night. My stomach felt a little upset. I knew I shouldn't have drunk that lemon drop while still on sleeping medication, but I needed a drink and it was worth it.

CHAPTER TWELVE

Rich

New Year's wit' Jade, Carlos, Marisol, and Nelson was a lot of fun and for one day I was able to escape my hell of a life. Nelson went back home to his girl and Los, Marisol, Jade, and I stayed in New York for a couple of days and went to a couple of exclusive parties. It was all for business purposes. Marisol had no intentions on me hookin' up wit' Jade and we kept it on the low for the first couple of days. After a while Marisol figured it out, but there was nothin' she could do. Jade was fine, and I needed female companionship. She was convenient, but the best convenience I had in a long time. Jade was sexy as shit, but wasn't the type of girl I usually fooled around wit'. She was in the streets heavy like Marisol, and that was just somethin' I wasn't down wit'. I didn't really like mixin' business wit' pleasure. I'd seen too many dudes get caught up wit' the Feds behind females like her. However, she was too good in bed to let that go that easily, so I made an exception.

After two weeks in New York we flew to L.A. where I'd been chillin' wit' Jade for the past month. However, now it was time to put in some work. Business meetings were lined up for me and Carlos in Cali and I was ready to start the month of February off right wit' my new business ventures. The weather was addictive. It was great to leave thirty-five degree weather back in New York to the warm seventy degree weather in L.A. Carlos and I were off to a new start and it felt good to have been away from Lisa all this time.

Although we'd been kickin' it all day, Carlos and I left the girls and went straight to meet wit' Uncle Renzo. It was still always in the back of my mind that things could go wrong bein' in Los' territory on the West Coast. I was a little uncomfortable since I'd always been the big brother and was the lead on every business venture we had. We were raised as brothers since my father really helped raise him. My Uncle Renzo stayed in and out of jail so Carlos' mom felt my father could keep Carlos on the right track.

Every time Uncle Renzo was released, he demanded my father return Carlos back to him. I knew that Uncle Renzo resented my dad for takin' his place in Carlos' life. I wondered if when he looked at me, if he saw my father. It really hurt me because when my father passed away, he didn't even come to the funeral. I knew that there was more to the story wit' them but opted to stay out of it.

Uncle Renzo didn't live far from LAX at all and we got to his hillside mansion in less than thirty minutes. When we pulled up to the big iron gate, Carlos gave a nod to his guards and they let us in. After pullin' the car around the circular driveway, we quickly hopped out. I was motivated to make some real money. It was time for me to start livin' life to the fullest. I wanted to be like my Uncle Renzo one day.

Maria, his housekeeper, led us through the marble foyer to the back of the house. There were all types of paintings and statues throughout his home. It looked like a museum. It gave the feelin' that if you touched anything, you would fear breakin' somethin'. We followed Maria to the boardroom. We only met there when it was somethin' major about to go down. When we walked in, Uncle Renzo instantly motioned his hand for us to sit down. He wasn't into affection, so hugs or even pounds weren't necessary.

"So, Rich, how's Lisa and the family doing?" Uncle Renzo inquired.

It seemed as if he'd aged the last time I saw him. His prior salt and pepper hair, now just seemed to be salt, and the skin under his neck was startin' to sag. However, regardless of his new looks, Uncle Renzo was not to be fucked wit'. Known to have an outrageous violent streak, he was definitely from the old school, wit' major street cred all over the West Coast.

"She's okay, and the family is cool," I replied. I didn't feel comfortable with tellin' him the truth yet.

"How is Lisa handling you being on the West Coast so much? You know home has got to be right for you to think you're going to be successful out here."

I couldn't hold it in any longer. "Actually Uncle Renzo, Lisa's threatenin' me wit' a divorce, but I'm sure she's just talkin'. I'm gonna give her some space for a while. She'll be a'ight by the time I get back."

Uncle Renzo played wit' the mole on his left hand. "Listen to me, Rich. Lisa is one of the good ones, and good women are hard to come by. She knows too much for you to keep fucking up with her. Besides, you don't want her to become scorned. Trust me, a woman scorned will ruin your fucking life. They're the worst kind, especially if they turn on you. I'm not trying to run your life, but just be careful. Lisa knows too much. Go home, make up with your wife, and leave all those other whores alone. All pussy ain't good pussy and it ain't worth your life."

I shook my head. "Thanks Unc, I appreciate your advice."

"Anyway, are you all ready to come up with a game plan for L.A. and Arizona?" Uncle Renzo asked. I let Carlos take the lead on this one since I was in unfamiliar territory.

"Well Dad, Nelson is handling business in the D.C. area and Julio is handling New York and Jersey. Rich is gonna do L.A. and Arizona. I'll be back and forth from here and Atlanta along with checking up on Nelson with things in Maryland and VA."

"He doesn't trust Nelson," I blurted out.

"I don't get it. Why will you be on the East Coast more than out here?" Uncle Renzo asked.

"It's best. Rich needs to get his feet wet out here. It's cool Dad. We worked it all out," Carlos replied.

Uncle Renzo gave us both a look that said he didn't like the idea, but decided to let us handle ourselves.

Our meetin' was a little longer than expected, but overall it went well. I still felt I lacked control, which was goin' to take some gettin' used to. As me and Carlos rode off from his father's gated mansion, I thought about the fact that I hadn't spoken to my family in several weeks. I knew that Denie was probably upset wit' me, and even though Lisa wanted her space, I knew she missed me, too. However, she hadn't called so maybe she was done wit' me after all. *She better not have no niggas in my house where I pay the damn bills,* I thought.

My guilt had kicked in and I felt bad that I didn't spend time wit' Denie before I left. It hurt me that I never kept my promises to my daughter, but time was money and I'm sure that she understood. She always understood me, when no one else did. It's weird now that I think about it. I haven't gotten any calls from any of them since the New Year.

When Carlos and I pulled up to my new L.A. spot, my phone rang. After lettin' Carlos know that I would hit him up later, I got out the car and answered.

"What's up?"

"Rich, you need to come home, Juan got locked up last night!" Lisa screamed hysterically.

"What? What happened?" I turned around to see if Carlos was still around, but he'd already left.

"He got pulled over for drinking and driving, and when they checked his car, they found some shit and a gun."

I shook my head. "Well, I can't leave right now, but I'll send Carlos."

As I walked through the foyer of my condo, Jade was layin' on the newly delivered couch in some black lingerie. She distracted me from my conversation wit' Lisa for a nano second 'til Lisa began yellin' hysterically in my ear. I directed my attention back to my call.

"What the fuck do you mean, you're gonna send Carlos? He's not Juan's father, you are. You didn't even call me back when I called you earlier!"

"Lisa I've been in a meetin' all day, I didn't even know you called."

"Well, I called you, Carlos, and Marisol. None of y'all answered your phones this morning. You need to come home. This is not for Carlos to deal with, Juan is your son!"

Jade interrupted my argument wit' Lisa and began kissin' me to try and direct my attention toward her. "Baby, let me make you feel better, hang up the phone," she whispered in my ear.

I quickly pushed her away fearin' Lisa would hear her, but she wouldn't stop. "Come on Papi,' hang up the phone," Jade raised her voice irritated.

"Muthafucka, are you with some bitch right now? Is that why you can't come to see what's going on with your son? You know what Rich fuck you!" Seconds later the phone went dead.

As I stared into space wit' my cell phone still in my hand, I sat on the edge of the couch, not knowin' what to do. The last thing I needed right now was for Lisa to hear me wit' another woman. There was already enough beef between us. Suddenly, I felt Jade massagin' my shoulders from behind. She then began to kiss me on my ear, but at the moment I wasn't feelin' her affection. Pissed off, I turned around and grabbed Jade by her neck.

"Let me tell you somethin' Jade, when my wife calls, you need to shut the fuck up." I quickly let her go.

Her eyes widened. "Don't you ever put your hands on me again. You know what, I'm outta here!" she yelled as she hopped off the couch and went to the bedroom.

"Bitch, you can leave when I give you permission." I jumped up and grabbed Jade by her arm. At that moment, I saw the same fear in her eyes that I would see in Lisa's, whenever I man handled her, which quickly made me release my grip.

"You're crazy! What the fuck have I gotten myself into? I should've listened to Marisol. You're bad news." Jade backed away from me like a frightened puppy.

"Stop trippin'. I'm not gonna hurt you. You just need to respect my wife when she calls." Walkin' up to her, I pulled Jade closer to me and kissed her in the mouth. I just knew she would resist, but didn't.

After our embrace, she looked up at me. "I thought you said you were getting a divorce."

"I am, but she's still the mother of my children. I'm not wit' her anymore, but somethin' is goin' on wit' my son, so I had to take that call."

"What happened, is he okay?"

"I'm not sure. All I know is he got locked up and she hung up on me when she heard your voice."

"Rich, I'm sorry I didn't know."

"It's cool, now come here and give me some of that good stuff."

"Okay Papi, make love to me," she moaned.

As Jade made her way toward me, I could tell she was prepared to give me a night full of pleasure. I was so wrapped up in the news I received about Juan, I didn't notice the candles spread throughout the room. I then directed my attention back to the black, lace Victoria Secret outfit that I'd bought her while we were in New York. She looked so damn sexy. When I couldn't take it anymore, I grabbed the back her long wavy hair and put her face right in my lap. She knew what I liked and showed me she was ready to go to work to please her new man. As she sucked and spit all over my dick, I reached over and grabbed her ass, spankin' it every so often. Feelin' like I was about to bust, I made Jade stop then told her to get on my lap and make me proud. She did just that.

"Oooh Papi' you make me feel so good, te hago sentir bien?"

"Yes, Mami you make me feel good, too. Papi' loves this Puerto Rican punani!"

"Quiero sentir que todos ustedes."

I had no idea what the fuck she was sayin', but it sounded good. "Baby, I'm gonna make sure you feel all of me, turn over."

When Jade followed my orders, I started to make love to her in my favorite position…doggy style. She felt so good as I grabbed her waist and pushed deep inside of her, long strokin' of course. When it felt like I was about to cum, I pulled out, and bust all over her pretty tanned ass. I would've loved to stay in her warm pussy, but I was done wit' being a father.

"Damn girl," I said as I fell back on the bed.

No matter how good Jade made me feel, she would never be Lisa. Despite all the drama between Lisa and I, we still had history and children together. We shared somethin' that just couldn't be replaced. No woman could fill those shoes right now. However, there was somethin' about Jade that was different though, and I liked it. Jade was nasty and adventurous in the bedroom, not like that borin'-ass sex wit' Lisa. She was a down ass chick like Marisol who knew how to stay in her place when it came to my business and that was a plus.

I wondered why Jade said that she should've listened to Marisol and not dealt wit' me. Didn't she know that once she got a taste of this dick it was gonna be hard to let go? All I could think of was the fact that Marisol and Lisa were so close. If Lisa knew that Marisol and my new side chick were friends, she would cut Marisol off completely. I really wasn't sure what state my marriage was in, but I still loved Lisa. I just wasn't sure if we had outgrown each other or maybe it was just too much pain in our relationship that it no longer could survive on love and history.

When I opened my eyes and reality set in, I moved Jade off of me. I had to call Carlos to have him go back to D.C. to see what was up wit' Juan. It was no way I could leave after all I had to do on my end to get business goin'. Not to mention, I just didn't want to leave Jade yet. I picked up my cell phone and hit the speed dial for my cousin's number.

"What's up, Los I need you to do me a favor?" I asked.

"Sure, what's going on?"

"Juan got locked up last night and I need you to go see what's goin' on. I can't leave right now."

"What? What happened?"

"I don't know all the details yet. Couldn't get all the details out of Lisa."

"Alright, man. I'll see what type of flight I can get out."

"In the meantime, I'm gonna make a couple of phone calls to see what I can find out."

"Cool, just keep me posted, and I'll call you when I get there," Carlos replied.

"Thanks, Los. I don't know what I would do without you."

"I got you, man."

If it was one nigga who was in my corner, it was Carlos. Ever since we were young, he always had my back. There was no betrayal between us, no lies, just pure loyalty. To show my appreciation, I always tried to hook him up wit' doe, but he would never take it. Even after the hit on Mike, I tried to give him and Rico twenty gee's a piece as a way of sayin', "Thank You." Rico took his share, but Carlos didn't. To me, that was a nigga who was down.

When I hung up wit' Carlos, my next call was to Denie. However, after callin' her cell phone twice and not gettin' an answer, I left her a message.

"Baby Girl, it's your father. Call me back and let me know what happened wit' your brother. Carlos is gonna come see what's goin' on in my absence. I need to know what happened ASAP, so please call me back."

Next, I called Lisa back to try and get some answers. I had to call at least four times before she finally decided to answer.

"What?" she yelled.

"What happened to Juan, Lisa?"

"Oh, so you care now? You didn't seem to care earlier when that bitch was around."

"Lisa, can you please put your personal feelings to the side for a moment, and just tell me what the fuck happened wit' my son. What time did all this shit go down?"

"I don't know all the details because when Juan called, he could only talk to me for a quick second. All he said was that he was leaving the club upset about some shit that went down then the next thing he knew the police had pulled him over for swerving the car. I guess they suspected that he'd been drinking and driving."

"Shit. I told that nigga about bein' sloppy! Have you tried to go see him yet?"

"Yeah, but the police wouldn't let me. They're obviously being petty because I waited around for at least three hours before I came back home. Now, I'm just sitting around waiting for Juan to call back."

"D.C. cops are the fuckin' worst. Where's Denie?"

"I don't know. She wasn't allowed back in my house last night, and right now my concern is getting Juan out of jail. It's obvious I'm all he's got."

"What the fuck do you mean, she wasn't allowed back in your house and you don't know where she is?"

"I didn't stutter. She disrespected me last night, so I told her to get out."

I was enraged. "What? Are you serious?"

"Yes, I am. Oh, and this isn't the first time. I put her out about a month ago, too."

"Who would do somethin' like that? What kind of fuckin' mother are you?"

"The kind who's tired of her daughter's shit. But don't worry, I let her come back home the very next day the last time this happened. I didn't even take her keys. I had plans on letting her come back this morning too, but I haven't heard from her."

"You're the one who needs to be out on the street, not her!" I yelled.

"Whatever Rich. Every time she disrespects me , I'm gonna put her ass out again. Denie is gonna learn sooner or later to stop fucking with me.

"I can't believe this. You need to find my daughter Lisa! What about school? Today is Monday."

"Hold up, so now that your grown-ass daughter is out running the street you wanna get all hype? You didn't act like this when I told you about your son!"

"Man, go ahead wit' that shit, Lisa. You don't understand. It's different wit' them," I responded. "Hell, she's only seventeen."

"You're right, I don't understand. This shit is nothing new. That girl has been out of control since you got locked up a few years ago. Both of y'all need to see each other for what you truly are. You know what Rich, you're a sorry-ass excuse for a father."

I hung up on Lisa after that comment. I wasn't racin' to the other side of the country when I had to get this bread, especially when I told Juan to keep shit out of his car. It was money that needed to be made and I wasn't lettin' anything stop me for takin' over the West Coast.

CHAPTER THIRTEEN

Lisa

After countless hours of sitting in the family room in silence by the phone, Juan finally called.

You have a collect call from JUAN. To accept charges dial one.

I pressed one so many times that I didn't let the rest of the recording play.

"Juan, baby are you okay? What happened?"

"Ma, just like the last time, I can't talk long. I need you to come up here. I don't want to say much over the phone."

"What are your charges?"

"Possession of a fire arm, and a controlled substance. Where's Denie?"

"She hasn't come home yet. Oh my gosh Juan, what the hell happened?"

"When you come see me, I'll tell you everything. Find your daughter in the meantime."

"Juan, tell me what's going on," I pleaded. Suddenly, I began to cry.

"Ma, just get over here as soon as you can. I gotta get off

the phone. I got a visit this afternoon, so come up here. I love you Ma, and stop crying I'll be alright."

"I love you, too, son!"

I hung up the phone and really cried like a baby. This was the day I never wanted to see happen. The day I constantly warned my son about. I jumped up and slipped on the first Twisted Heart sweatsuit that I could find, and my black snaked skin Uggs and jumped in my car. I cried so much and couldn't get myself together. This is when I needed Rich most. I headed on I-295 to southeast toward the D.C. jail so I could see what was going on with my son.

I pulled into the parking lot and instantly flashed back to the last time I was there visiting Rich. The line was so long, I just wanted to cut and get to Juan as soon as possible, especially since this was the last visit of the day. I knew he needed me. Once I was checked in at the window it was time for me to go through security. The same security was there from back when Rich was locked up, which proved either they loved their job or just couldn't find another company to hire them. I hated the female security officers. They went out of their way to make it difficult for me every damn time.

"You can't come in here with sweatpants on, Mrs. Sanchez, you should know that. Next in line please," one over-weight officer stated. I couldn't believe she remembered me.

"I need to see my son, can you please let me through?"

You need to find some pants or something. I gotta process this entire line and visits are over in thirty minutes. If I let you in then I gotta let everybody else in here with tight pants on. You already know what you're not supposed to wear. Now, move out my line."

Needing to see Juan, I ran back to my truck and found a pair of jeans I'd bought Rich but never gave him and changed right outside. Even though the jeans were a size thirty-six and I wore a size twenty-eight, I didn't care. Slipping the jeans over my sweatpants, I folded them over in the waist three times, then finally ran back through the parking lot. Finally, they let me in fifteen minutes before the visits were over. I'd learned years ago not to argue with the officers after being escorted out several times before. Now, I just sucked it up when they were complete assholes.

I tried my best to ignore the smart comments that were said behind my back, and continued toward the elevator; an elevator that smelled like fuck and urine. I couldn't wait to get out of there. With only twelve minutes left, I prayed Juan came out as soon as possible, so we would have a little bit of time to spend with each other. Babies were crying, young girls were arguing with their boyfriends, and the guards were staring at me like I was the criminal. It was the same scene as when I visited Rich years ago, nothing had changed. After waiting for five excruciating minutes, Juan finally came out. The orange jumpsuit he wore immediately made me think of Rich and his incarcerated days, which destroyed me. History was definitely repeating itself. Walking up toward the glass, I cried as Juan picked up the phone.

"Ma, don't cry. I'm alright," he said.

"What happened?"

"Well, I went past that club right off New York Avenue last night, to meet a buddy of mine. That's when I saw Denie arguing with this dude outside the club. He was pulling on her like he owned her or some shit, so I just reacted. I didn't know what was going on, so I pulled out my gun and told the dude to give me a reason to kill him and to get the fuck off my sister."

"I can't believe this. What happened after that?" I inquired.

"Denie started taking up for the nigga. I was so mad because first of all she's too damn young to be at the club, and the dude she taking up for is a street nigga. Anyway, I pulled off so I wouldn't get caught up. I was trying to put the gun under my seat when the police pulled me over, and said I was swerving."

"So, were you?"

"I had a few drinks, but nothing major. I blew a .11 and the police decided to search the car. I'd just made a move, so they found 500 grams of heroine and a gun."

"Juan! My goodness, how much time are you looking at?"

"I don't know yet. Need to talk to a lawyer, but the worst is twenty to life. Shit ain't looking good though, cause I've had gun charges before."

My tears continued to flow. The thought of my son not in my life had never been an option for me. I would do anything to make this all go away.

"Why did you have drugs in your car anyway? You know better than that? Besides, you know Rich is gonna be curious about what kind it was."

"Well, I can't go into all that right now, but let's just say, I didn't have plans to work for him forever. Why do you think I kept telling you to leave him and that I would take care of you?"

"Oh my God this is too much. I wondered why I haven't heard from your sister. I'm sure she knows what the hell is going on," I said. "This shit it all her fault."

"She's probably too scared to come home. She might even still be with that nigga."

"Visits are now over. I repeat visits are now over!" a fat female officer yelled.

It seemed like I'd just gotten there. "Don't worry, I'm gonna get you out of here. Carlos is on his way from L.A. to help me figure all this out."

Juan nodded his head. "What about Rich?"

"It's a long story." At that moment, the fat officer gave me an evil look, so I stood up. "I love you, baby."

"I love you, too Ma, and stop crying."

I hung up the phone and quickly made my way back outside to my truck. Even though it may have seemed like I was rushing, I wasn't. I was in no rush to drive to my big, lonely house. With Juan not around, I had no idea what I was going to do. On my way home, I called around trying to find Denie, but I still had no luck. Now, that she'd been missing for some time, I was really worried about her. While my life was in shambles,

Rich was in L.A. fucking around. Shit like this was starting to make me hate his ass even more.

When I walked in the house, thirty minutes later, I decided to take a couple of pills and get some rest. Once the pills were in effect, I slept for a while, but was soon awakened by the phone. I jumped up thinking it was Juan or Denie, but it was Carlos. He let me know that he had just landed and would be at my house in less than an hour. When thoughts of Juan started to overload my mind again, I went downstairs to the kitchen to make some tea. *How did my life end up this way*? I thought. My son was in jail, my daughter was nowhere to be found, and my so called husband was more interested in pussy and money than making sure his family was straight.

Since I couldn't fall back asleep, I stayed in the kitchen to wait for Carlos. I resented Carlos' ass, too. Mostly because I felt he was the cause of Rich's hanging out and the bulk of our problems. Back in the day, he would always pull Rich away from his family to handle business and I hated it. The way I saw it, Carlos needed to focus on his kids and the Bonnie and Clyde relationship with his own wife instead of the streets sometimes. Marisol was such a good person and I loved her dearly, so I always believed he didn't deserve her. Now, she was caught up. Not only with the drugs, but Carlos also had her involved in the business. She went on more moves than he did sometimes. Rich let it be known a long time ago, he never wanted me to be a part of what he did outside in the streets. Marisol's reason for being involved she once told me, was because she wanted to keep close tabs on her husband. What she failed to realize was that, when a man wanted to step out on his wife, he would definitely make a way. I lived it every day, so I knew.

All of these things were in my mind when Carlos walked in from the garage. When we made eye contact, he could see the anger written all over my face. If I couldn't talk to Rich, Carlos was going to get the blunt of it all.

"What's up, Lisa?"

"My son is in jail and my daughter is nowhere to be

found, that's what's up." My tone was dry.

"Where's Denie? What you mean she's nowhere to be found, what happened? Rich didn't mention that part."

"All you and Rich care about is Denie. You don't give a shit about Juan!"

"That's not true. I wouldn't have flown all the way out here if I didn't care about Juan. Now, tell me what's going on."

I told Carlos all that I knew and he started out the door as soon as I was done. "Where the hell do you think you're going?" I asked.

"To see what I can find out."

I still needed to vent. "I still can't believe Rich sent you instead. He ain't shit and neither are you. It's you and your father's fault why Rich is the way he is."

Carlos chuckled. "You're crazy if you believe that shit. Rich is his own man, Lisa."

"Every time you used to call back in the day, Rich would come running. Y'all played on his weakness. You and your father introduced him to the life and created a monster!"

"Man I don't have to listen to this bullshit. My focus is Juan right now."

"Oh no, you're gonna listen. I'm tired of this shit. Do you realize your family fucked up my home? I've always hated you for that. Now look, my son is turning out to be just like y'all." It felt good to vent.

"Lisa, how are you gonna blame me and my father for you and Rich's problems? It's not my fault. He's a grown ass man."

"It is your fault! Just because you and your coke sniffing ass wife thinks that the drug game is cool, I'm suppose to just accept this shit."

"Now, you're being disrespectful! This drug money you hate so much put those diamonds in your ears and this roof over your head. I ain't hear you complain when you got that X6. Don't be a hypocrite."

"Fuck you!"

"Whatever, I'm gone," Carlos replied.

"Oh, hell no, you think it's that easy? You think you can just walk the fuck away from me while I'm talking. You're going to fuckin' listen to what I've got to say!" I yelled as Carlos tried to leave. Grabbing the door before it closed, I balled up my fists and began hitting Carlos in his back. I yelled and screamed and hollered at him until I found myself hyperventilating. He tried to restrain me while I cried uncontrollably. I couldn't even catch my breath.

"Lisa, are you okay?" Carlos ran to get me some water out of the refrigerator. "Damn, I'm sorry. Here, drink this water," he said, handing me a Smart Water bottle.

"I'm sorry too, Los. I'm just stressed out," I said trying to catch my breath. I took a huge gulp. "I was completely out of line," I cried as Carlos consoled me.

I buried my head in his chest and balled while he held me on the floor of the kitchen. It had been a while since I'd been held. I missed my son and felt like I had nothing. Lifting my head, I looked at Carlos and all of a sudden I saw something in him that I'd never seen before. He always seemed emotionless as if he didn't care about anything or anyone. He looked deeply in my eyes and apologized again and kissed me on my forehead. When he wiped my tears with his shirt, I tried to kiss him on his lips, but he quickly pulled away.

"Lisa, naw, that's not cool. Rich will kill us."

"I need you, Carlos. I'm tired of Rich. He treats me like shit. All I have put up with, I deserve to be happy." When I started to cry again, Carlos held me tighter and began to rub my back. I knew he felt sorry for me. Suddenly, I raised my head and attempted to kiss him again, but this time he kissed me back deeply in my mouth, tongue and all. Carlos laid me back gently on the marble floor, got on top of me and started kissing me passionately as if these were emotions he'd always felt. I had never been sexually attracted to any other man in my life besides my husband. I couldn't believe that I was kissing Carlos in the kitchen where I once prepared meals for them both. Don't get me wrong he was very handsome, but he was always family. I was so emotional that I let my husband's cousin have me right in our kitchen. It was wrong, but it felt right.

After removing my panties, he gently began kissing my inner thighs before moving down to the lips of my vagina. He wanted to taste my love is all he kept whispering as he slowly flicked his tongue against my throbbing clitoris. He tasted me like he had something to prove. The way his tongue moved in and out of my dripping pussy, it wasn't long before I reached an orgasm.

He worked his way back up my body and kissed me on the lips before lifting me off the floor and sat me up on the island. He made love to me right there. When he entered me, I didn't have a thought in my mind of anything or anyone, at that moment, I just wanted him. His dick fit my pussy like a glove. It was perfect, like it belonged there all along. As I wrapped my legs around his waist, he picked me up and carried me all the way upstairs to the bedroom and made love to me for hours. Now, I knew why Marisol never left his ass. The sex was off the hook. He was so passionate with his love making, like it was an art. Carlos was definitely better than Rich in the bedroom. Rich was well hung, but Carlos was more passionate, taking care of any urge my body needed.

After I climaxed one final time, it was a wrap. He left my body numb, I was out of it. However, it didn't take long for reality to set in. *I just had sex with my husband's cousin,* I thought. A part of me was being vindictive, the other part of me wanted to be comforted.

"Carlos, what have we done? Juan needs me, but here I am with you." I looked deep into his eyes as we laid in the bed that Rich and I had shared over the years.

"Rich will never understand, and neither will Marisol. We can never tell anyone about this," he said in a very stern tone.

"So, are you saying it can never happen again?" I asked.

"Hell no Lisa, this shit ain't right." He bit the bottom of his lip for a second, then looked back at me. "But damn you felt so good," he said with a slight smile that displayed his small gap.

"Well, we'll cross that bridge when we get there."

"Let's cross it right now," he said as he entered me again.

It was very scary making love to him knowing what would happen if anyone found out, but I loved every minute of it. The thing that was most surprising to me was the fact that I didn't feel a bit of guilt. This was the first time since the rape that I even had an urge to have sex. I started to think, *Marisol would be devastated if she ever found out*. Her crazy-ass would definitely kill me if Rich didn't beat her to it. It was scary how much I enjoyed Carlos. When we fell asleep in each other arms, it was proof that I didn't need medication to fall asleep, but just some good dick instead.

The next morning we were awakened by Denie's voice as she came through the front door.

"Ma! Whose car is that outside? Is that a rental? Did my father come home?" Denie yelled downstairs from the foyer.

Carlos and I both hopped up. When he ran and hid in Rich's closet, I threw him his clothes just in time, right before Denie walked in.

"Where the fuck have you been, Denie? Why didn't you return any of my calls?" I placed my hands on my bare hips.

Denie stared at me then turned her head. "You told me to leave remember? And since when do you sleep naked?"

I'd completely forgotten that I didn't have any clothes on. "Don't worry about the way I sleep. Where the fuck have you been? Juan told me what happened at that club the other night. Do you know he got locked up over your ass?" I quickly grabbed my robe from the bathroom. "Where have you been?" This time my voice even pierced my ears.

"Why? How are you gonna put me out, then ask where I've been?"

"Just answer the damn question!"

"I've been over Destiny's house."

"Are you gonna sit here and lie in my fucking face? Juan told me you were with some street nigga the other night. He didn't mention anything about Destiny."

"I don't wanna talk about this. Where's my father? I talked to him this morning and he said he was coming home because he hadn't heard from Uncle Carlos."

I hoped like hell he hadn't jumped on a Red Eye.

Denie suddenly stopped and looked toward my closet. "What was that noise?"

"What noise?" I asked trying to play it off. "You're tripping."

"No, I'm positive I heard something. It sounded like it might've came from your closet or something."

I had to get her ass out of my room. "Do you need something Denie? If not, get out."

"Have you talked to Uncle Carlos, and whose car is that outside?" Denie questioned.

"The last time I checked I was your mother, so I don't have you answer to you. Now, you still haven't told me where you've been, and don't lie to me again because I know you haven't been with Destiny. I called her mother yesterday, and she said she hadn't seen you." I was ready to knock the shit of her if she lied again.

"I'm gone. I'll be back when my father comes home!"

At that point, I didn't even give a shit what Denie did. If she wanted to be a hot ass then I was going to let her. Besides, I needed her to leave so Carlos could come out of hiding anyway. "Bye!"

Carlos was completely dressed by the time he stuck his head out of the closet. "Is she gone?"

"Yeah, I heard the front door close."

"Who did she go with? Did someone come pick her up?" Carlos seemed beyond nervous as he walked toward me.

"I have no idea. I didn't hear a car, so she might've walked over one of her little girlfriend's houses. Or maybe one of her little boyfriends was parked down the street. Who knows with Denie."

"Look, I gotta go." Carlos pulled his phone out from his phone clip. "Shit, Rich called me ten times."

"Just tell him you got with some girl," I suggested. "That sounds right up your alley."

Carlos looked out my bedroom window to make sure Denie wasn't outside before he made his way downstairs. "I'll call you later. Let me try to see what's up with Juan."

"Can you give me some money?" I blurted out.

"What? How much?"

"A lot. Since Rich left, he hasn't sent me any money. I even checked his two other stash spots, but they were empty."

Carlos reached in his pocket and pulled out a stack of money. He then counted out thirty one hundred dollar bills. "This is all I can give you until I get to my house. Besides, you need to call Rich. He'll send you some cash. He's not that petty."

Since Rich always kept tabs on what I did with his money, I couldn't ask him for any this time, especially since I had plans to pay the divorce attorney I'd already talked to. Carlos would just have to be the sponsor I needed for now. Carlos made my financial problems go away for the moment, but in reality I had a feeling those problems were about to get worst.

CHAPTER FOURTEEN

Rich

After callin' Carlos' phone all night and not gettin' through, I began to worry and called Denie. She told me she hadn't spoken to Lisa, so I was immediately concerned. I let Denie know that I would be catchin' the first flight back to D.C. and for her to make sure she was at home when I got there. Juan's sloppiness had the potential of compromisin' the entire empire that I'd worked so hard to build, so I knew it was best for me to make the trip back east. Just as I was packin' my bag to leave, my phone rang. It was Carlos.

"Man, I've been callin' your damn phone all night Los, what's up?"

"Sorry man. My flight ended up getting delayed, then when I got in town, I had to calm one of my bitches down who was threatening to tell Marisol some shit, so things just got out of hand."

"So, you couldn't call to tell me that shit? Why didn't you just answer?"

"The bitch took my phone and wouldn't give it back."

"Man, why didn't you deal wit' that bitch after Juan?" I

asked.

"I know, Rich. I fucked up."

"So, what's up wit' Juan?"

"Well, I tried to go see him early this morning because I knew visiting hours start at eight o'clock, but I forgot that they go by last names over at the D.C. jail. Since his last name starts with an S, he can only get visits on Monday and Wednesday. I gotta wait until tomorrow. You might have to fly back, because the shit looks worse than I thought."

"What do you mean?"

"After talking to Lisa, it seems as if Juan got caught with 500 grams of heroin, and that shit doesn't seem right. You need to come back and talk to Juan yourself and see what's up. He might not open up to me."

"Heroin? What the fuck? We don't…" I was so pissed off, I was about to say some stupid shit over the phone. I didn't deal wit' heroin…strictly coke, so I wasn't sure what the fuck my son was into. "A'ight, man. You stayin' in D.C. or you comin' back out here?"

"I'ma chill out here for a minute to see what's good. I got some shit to take care of anyway."

"Well, I'm about to head out to the airport. My flight leaves at 8:20 a.m., so I should be in D.C. by 5:30 p.m. How was Lisa when you saw her?"

"Umm…she's cool."

"Oh, she wasn't trippin'?"

"She's always tripping, but I can understand this time. You know how she feels about Juan," Carlos replied.

"Shit, she'll be a'ight. Just come pick me up from National around 5:30 and maybe we'll be able to see what's really good. I'm about to call my lawyer in a minute to see what we can do about gettin' Juan released."

"Cool."

When I hung up wit' Carlos, Jade was sittin' on the edge of the bed, butter ball naked and ready to serve me somethin' good. She was a little upset that I was leavin', but after I gave her some of this good dick, she was back to normal. I let her know that if I had to stay longer than a week, I would fly her back to the East Coast, which seemed to satisfy her…for now. She was even in good spirits when she drove to the airport and dropped me off.

While waitin' to board my flight, I called my attorney John Leach, to see if there was anything he could do for Juan. I wanted my son to be released as soon as possible.

"Yes, John this is Rich Sanchez. How are you?"

"I'm fine. What can I do for you? Haven't heard from you in a while."

"I know, but that's a good thing. Well, it was a good thing because now I'm gonna need your services."

"Well Rich, you know I might have to refer you to my sister Sherise, because I can't represent both you and Lisa in this matter."

"In what matter? I'm callin' you about my son, Juan. He was arrested a couple of days ago. What the hell do you mean you're representin' Lisa, what's goin' on?"

"Well, Lisa came by the office 8 o'clock this morning and hired me in your divorce case, so that's what I thought you were calling about. I apologize. She didn't mention anything about Juan getting into any kind of trouble."

My blood began to boil. "What? Why didn't you call me after she left?"

"Rich, why would I call? I thought you might've been aware of this," John tried to explain. "Besides, she's my client now, so there's the aspect of confidentiality."

"Man, all the money I've given you over the years and you're goin' to work for my wife. Did you forget that I pay your ass a damn retainer fee? Is that what she used?" When John did-n't respond quick enough, I continued rantin'. "Fuck you and that confidentiality shit. You know what, I'll find someone else to take care of my son's case for me. I don't need you to do shit, and by the way, I might have your sister represent me in other ways."

When I hung up, I was beyond pissed off. Lookin' around, I noticed I had an audience of people in the airport lookin' at me, but I didn't care. *I can't believe Lisa is really tryin' to go through wit' this shit,* I thought. I was ready to get back home so I could put my foot so far up Lisa's ass she wouldn't be able to walk straight. That bitch was trippin' if she thought she could leave me that easy.

When the plane landed six hours later, I turned my phone on and dialed Carlos to let him know that I would be in baggage claim within ten minutes. Makin' my way through the airport, the gift shops were full of Valentine's Day motifs for the up-comin' holiday. I definitely wasn't in the mood for that shit at all. Valentine's Day could kiss my ass right about now.

Carlos pulled up in his rental as soon as I walked out the terminal. Opening the back door, I threw my bag inside and hopped in the passenger seat. Carlos knew me well and could tell I wasn't in the best mood.

"These punk ass police had me circle the damn airport three times," he informed.

"My bad, I was waitin' for my luggage. So, what did Lisa tell you about Denie? I forgot to ask you that earlier."

"Shit, apparently that might be the reason why Juan got locked up. Juan saw Denie and some nigga going back and forth outside a club. Juan stepped up to the dude, and pulled out the hammer on him. Denie started defending the nigga and Juan pulled off driving crazy. Got pulled over, and the rest is history."

"Who was the nigga Denie was talkin' to?"

Carlos shook his head. "I don't know."

"So, have you talked to anybody to see what's good?"

"Naw, I ain't heard shit yet."

Carlos seemed nervous for some reason. "Why you actin' all crazy, Los?"

"What do you mean?"

"I don't know. You just seem like you actin' a little weird. Like real hyper and nervous. Have you been sniffin' some of that shit? I told you about bein' around me after you fuck wit' that mess. I'm tellin' you man, you need to chill out wit' that."

"No, I haven't been doing anything. I just got some shit on my mind, but it's cool."

"You and Marisol a'ight?" I asked.

"We cool, it's all good."

Wit' so much on my mind, I didn't have time to try and pry some more information out of him. I knew somethin' was goin' on, but figured I had to deal wit' that later. I had enough bullshit goin' on. If he hadn't done anything before comin' to get me, he probably needed some shit to ease his mind. I hated that my man was into dope, but as long as it didn't affect the business, I was cool.

On the way to my house, I made a couple of phone calls and tried to get Juan released, but wit' the seriousness of his charges, a couple of folks said they would get back to me. When we pulled up to my house several minutes later, I got upset all over again. The thought of Lisa's dumb-ass usin' my retainer money toward divorcin' me, instantly set me off. I already had in my mind, when I walked in the house that I was goin' to smack the shit out of that crazy bitch for fuckin' wit' my money. She had started to really get out of hand lately, and I felt it was time to show her there were consequences for fuckin' wit' my doe.

Carlos dropped me off because he didn't feel like dealin' wit' me and Lisa's drama. As I looked around, I wondered why my truck was in the driveway instead of the garage. Nelson knew to place my shit in the garage instead of outside. Just when I was about to call Nelson, I quickly shook my head. *Hold up. If that bitch fucked up my truck, it's gonna be a problem.* Rollin' my luggage up the pavement, I became even angrier the closer I got to the door. Takin' out my key ring, I quickly slid it in the front door, but it didn't turn. I did a double take to make sure I was usin' the right key, then it dawned on me…Lisa had changed the fuckin' locks. Tryin' to keep my cool, I knocked on the door. However, no one answered. Within seconds, I was bangin' like the damn police.

"Lisa, open the fucking door!" I yelled.

"What, Rich?" Lisa shouted through the door a few seconds later.

"Open the damn door, Lisa!"

"No. Since you want to go around fucking all these other women, which got me raped, then fuck you. Not to mention, you hit me for the last damn time. It's over!"

"Lisa, stop fuckin' around!"

"Who said I was?"

"Where's my daughter?"

"She left. Call her cell."

I started bangin' on the door again. This time I was kicking it as well. "I'ma beat your ass Lisa, open this fuckin' door!"

"Now, I'm really not opening the door," she replied.

"Oh, bitch you think I'm playin' wit' you? Wait 'til I catch your ass!"

"Rich, you got ten seconds to leave. If not, I'm calling the police!"

Lisa knew all she had to say was somethin' about the police and I was out of there. "That's a'ight, bitch. I'll be back!" I yelled before pullin' my luggage toward my truck.

I gave it a quick inspection before I pulled out my spare key, jumped inside, and screeched out of my driveway. As mad as I was, I wasn't in the mood for anybody's bullshit. Lisa stood in the window of the livin' room lookin' at me wit' a huge smile as I pulled off. I couldn't believe she'd actually threatened to call the police on me. She'd stooped to a new low, and my love for her was turnin' into hate. Drivin' down the street, I thought of goin' to Baltimore to see Honey, but then an image of my mother framed my mind. Instantly, I felt guilty. I hadn't seen my mother in over a month, so I decided to go over to her house for a quick visit. *Maybe I should stay wit' her 'til I can figure some things out,* I thought. Just as I was about to call my mother, my cell phone rang, it was Denie.

"What's up, Baby Girl?"

"Hi Daddy, are you back in town?"

"Yeah, I just left the house. Your mother changed the fuckin' locks, so I'm on my way to your grandmother's house."

"What do you mean she changed the locks? I was just there this morning and my key worked fine."

"Well, I guess your mother has had a busy damn mornin'."

"I gotta see you. I'll meet you at Grandma's house."

"Okay, Baby Girl. I think she would like that. She hasn't seen either one of us in a while."

Makin' my way across town, I tried callin' my mom, but didn't get an answer. Thinkin' that she might've been takin' a late bath, I called back at least three more times, but she still didn't pick up. I immediately began to worry because she always answered the phone. It was obvious I couldn't depend on anyone to check in on her, especially not Lisa. My mother really never cared for Lisa, but they made their relationship work on the strength of me.

I pulled into her driveway twenty minutes later, and took a deep breath before I got out of my truck. Knowin' I was about to get a lecture, I really wasn't in the mood for an argument or any more drama, but I had to take this one for the team. My mother was definitely disappointed in the lifestyle I'd chosen, but more than that she always stressed to me the importance of the, *you only have one mother* rule. I cherished both my mother and my daughter, but lately my focus had been off, which had me feelin' guilty. As I used my key to try and surprise her, I opened the door and was overwhelmed by an awful stench. It smelled as if the trash hadn't been taken out in days.

"Ma! Hey, Ma!" I called for her from the foyer.

When I entered the livin' room, I breathed a sigh of relief

when I saw her asleep in her rockin' chair. Tryin' not to wake her, I crept up behind her and noticed that she'd fallen asleep holdin' her favorite picture of me and my dad. Not knowin' how long she'd been asleep, I knew it was best that she got in the bed, so I kissed her forehead to wake her. However, I didn't get a response. She was stiff and cold as ice.

"Ma, no, Ma. This can't be happenin'. No, Ma," I repeated.

I was too late. She was gone. Her heart failure must've given her a run once again. I picked her up out of the rockin' chair then laid her on the floor. As I held on to her lifeless body, tears streamed down my face. *How long has she been dead?* I thought to myself. The fact that she'd died alone had my heart achin'. I couldn't bring her back. Wit' all the money and power that I had, the things that ruled my life, there was nothin' I could do to get back the time I'd lost with my mother. I just wanted to hold her and never let her go.

"Daddy, what's going on? What's wrong? Why are you crying?" Denie asked when she finally walked in.

"She's gone. My mother is gone."

CHAPTER FIFTEEN

Lisa

I couldn't believe that Mama Sanchez was really gone, and that today was her funeral. Apparently she'd passed away in her sleep from a heart attack. I couldn't imagine how Rich must've felt when he found his mother dead. We had our differences over the years since she never saw the wrong in her son, but I still loved her. A part of me felt bad for pushing Rich away during this difficult time in his life. I hadn't even called to say I was sorry to hear about his loss. Hell, I wouldn't have even known his mother had died if Carlos hadn't told me. Everything seemed to be spinning out of control lately. With Juan being denied a bail due to his previous charges and now Rich's mother dying, our family just couldn't seem to catch a break. Even Denie had moved in with Rich at his mother's house, and wasn't talking to me either. I thought it was crazy how everyone was blaming me for trying to move on with my life, but regardless of what anybody thought, I was going through with the divorce.

Entering my closet, I struggled with what I should wear and then finally decided on a simple black Tracy Reese dress that I'd bought last month at Nordstrom. I then pulled out my black patent leather Louboutin four inch peep toe pumps to finish off the outfit. Afterwards, I went into the bathroom, placed a few curls in my hair then applied some makeup. Looking at myself in the mirror, I was quite pleased how I put it all together. When Carlos laid his eyes on me at the funeral, I wanted him to see what he was missing. Over the past week, we'd hooked up at a hotel once and had a quick sex session, but it was obvious that he didn't want anything serious with me. He wouldn't even answer my calls half the time. He feared Rich and Marisol would find out, which was understandable. However, I knew deep down inside he felt more than what he led on. I could see it in his eyes.

The services were to begin at 10:00 a.m. and I was wondering what was taking the family car so long to come and pick me up. I could've sworn that Carlos told me to be ready by 9:00 a.m. and here it is 9:30 a.m. and they still weren't here. I decided to call Denie's cell to see where they were.

"Hello," she answered unenthused.

"Denie, I'm waiting on you guys, where are you?"

"We're pulling up at the church now."

I held a confused expression. "Who is we and why didn't you all come and pick me up?"

"Me, Daddy, Uncle Carlos, Aunt Marisol, and her friend."

"What? Put your father on the phone now!" The five seconds that I had to wait was entirely too long.

"What do you want, Lisa?" Rich asked in an annoyed tone.

"I thought you all were coming to get me? I've been sitting her waiting for over thirty minutes. Shouldn't I be in the family car, too?"

"Man, I haven't heard from you since the day you changed the locks. My mother died and you didn't even have the decency to call me and see if I was okay. Your ass will fuckin' walk before I pick you up."

"But I loved your moth.."

When Rich hung up on me, it sent me over the edge. Immediately, I went into the office and got the separation papers that Mr. Leach drew up for me and stuffed them in my Valentino bag. He'd fucked with the wrong woman and I was going to show him who was boss today. No disrespect to Mama Sanchez, but I was done with Rich. Not to mention, I just wanted to be done with his ass while I still had the guts to leave. It was time I put an end to this dysfunctional marriage for good.

I got in my truck and called Marisol's phone to see how she felt about the whole situation, but she didn't answer. I was furious with Rich, but then I thought about it. He was right…for once. I was wrong for being stubborn and not reaching out to him when his mother died. I started to feel bad and decided that maybe I should play nice until the funeral service was over.

By the time I made it to the church, the parking lot was already packed. I was pissed that I even had to search for a parking space since I was supposed to be in the family car in the first place. After circling the lot at least twice, I finally got irritated and decided to just block someone in. Where could they go until the service was over anyway?

After I raced into the church, I instantly spotted Rich and Denie on the front row along with Carlos and Marisol. After making my way to the front, I motioned for Denie to move down so I could sit beside Rich, but he refused for her to move, which left me sitting between Denie and Carlos. Trying to keep my composure, I shot Rich a look, but he didn't even look in my direction. However, his frown instantly turned into a smile when he spotted some Spanish chick walking down the aisle. He stood up and gave her a kiss on the cheek before she sat beside Marisol.

Hold the fuck up. Is that the friend of Marisol's Denie was talking about who rode in the family car with them? I thought. *Who the hell is this bitch?* Shooting Marisol an evil look, I was about to say something when the Bishop called for the last viewing for the family before the service started.

Carlos, Denie, Marisol, and I walked up to the casket with Rich for support. As much as Rich tried to hold it in, he couldn't as tears poured from his face. I could see the guilt as he looked at his mom. She looked like an angel, so peaceful lying there in all white. I wanted to reach out to him, but I feared he would push me away and I didn't want to be embarrassed in front of the entire audience. Moments later, he turned to the Spanish girl who was sitting on the front row like her ass was family, for comfort.

She even had sadness in her eyes, like she could feel his pain. Like she was the fucking daughter-in-law. I was stunned at the level of disrespect Rich had portrayed and that he'd allowed her to comfort him right before my eyes. As if that wasn't enough, once we were back in our seats, Trixie sashayed her ass up to the casket in all red looking like a child of the devil. *What the fuck is she doing here*? I asked myself.

Holding her two-year old daughter in her arms, she gave the front row a quick look, then proceeded to the casket. I definitely owed that home-wrecking whore an ass whooping. Who did she think she was coming up in my mother-in-law's funeral as if she belonged?

"Say bye-bye to your grandma, Nita. Blow grandma a kiss," Trixie whispered to her daughter, but loud enough for us to hear. When the little girl did as she was told, Trixie then walked over to Rich.

"Juanita, give your daddy a kiss, and tell him everything is gonna be okay."

"Trixie, what the fuck are you doin' here?" Rich questioned. He tried to keep his voice down.

"My daughter has every right to be here. Her grandmother just died. Why have you been ignoring my calls? We need to talk."

Rich looked around. "Get the fuck outta here," he said through clenched teeth.

"So, are you saying fuck our daughter, Rich? Please don't turn your back on us," Trixie pleaded in such desperation.

"Yes, that's exactly what I'm sayin'," Rich replied.

"No, fuck that. I won't be ignored, and you're gonna take care of your fucking daughter."

Rich was stunned by her words, and I could no longer take any more of her disrespect. At that moment, I jumped up. "You home wrecking bitch. You and your bastard child need to get the fuck out of here!" I yelled.

The entire church let out a huge gasp. I knew it looked like something straight out of a Jerry Springer episode.

Rich stood up. "Lisa, lower your voice."

Moments later, two men in the same colored jacket, quickly walked down the aisle and placed both of their hands on Trixie's shoulders. It was obvious that they were there to escort her out. However, Trixie wasn't going down without a fight.

"Get your damn hands off of me!" she shouted. "Rich why are you letting them treat me like this?" As her daughter wailed, Trixie continued. "Rich don't you hear your fucking daughter crying?" Trixie's obscenities got worse and worse until we could no longer hear her voice.

"I apologize to the family and friends of Mrs. Marie Sanchez. Mr. Sanchez, are you ready to proceed with the service?" the bishop finally asked.

"Yes, bishop, I'm sorry," Rich answered and put his head down with much embarrassment.

There was so much anger in me that I could barely hold my composure. I felt so alone and wished my son could be here to comfort me. He was all I had and now, I felt like I had nothing. I knew I didn't have it in me to attend the re-pass or go to the burial. The thought of Trixie's daughter being Rich's child made my hate for him escalate to another level. My heart couldn't bear any more pain. After the funeral service was over we walked out and were all standing outside the family car. Denie had so much pain in her eyes and she wanted answers.

"Daddy, is it true?" she asked with tears in her eyes.

Rich seemed at a lost for words. "Denie, I can explain." He tried to hug her, but she pulled back and got in the car. Rich then looked at me, but luckily my pain was hidden behind my sunglasses.

I walked up to Rich and tried my best to keep my cool. "Today proved to me that whatever we had is gone. Now, I know for sure that you've stooped to a new low and I want you out of my life for good." I smacked him in his face with the papers. "I want a divorce, so please stay the fuck out of my life."

I looked over at Marisol and Carlos before they got in the family car with a look to let them both know it was definitely not over. Carlos looked as if he feared I was about to expose our affair out of anger, but that fear in his eyes did nothing but give me the upper hand. No longer did I feel bad for sleeping with Carlos. Marisol's mysterious friend who I assumed was Rich's new sex toy gave me more ammunition to get down-right dirty. Revenge was on my mind. Never fuck with a woman scorned.

CHAPTER SIXTEEN
Lisa

Waking up the next morning was easy to do, but it was still hard to get out of bed. Checking my cell phone, I saw that I had seven missed calls. Hoping that Carlos had called me while I was asleep, I felt a glimpse of hope, until I saw that all the calls were from Denie. After Mama Sanchez's funeral drained me with all the drama, I came home, popped some pills, and slept the day away. If it wasn't for someone ringing the door bell like a crazy person, I would've still been asleep. I got out of bed and threw on my robe and ran to the door to see who the hell it was.

When I looked through the peephole and realized, it was Denie, I was instantly irritated. "What's your problem?" I asked swinging the door open.

"I have to pee. I've been ringing the doorbell and calling your phone for the past ten minutes!" Denie raced past me to the downstairs bathroom. I followed her to see if I could get any information about what happened at the funeral after I left, and more importantly who the Spanish bitch was. Even though I was done with Rich, I wanted to see if my accusations were true.

"So, how do you feel about having a two year old sister?" I asked opening the door. "You always said you wanted a baby sister growing up, and now you have one."

I could tell she didn't find my joke amusing. "That's not my sister, and can I pee in peace!" Denie yelled. She stood up a little bit to try and grab the knob, but couldn't reach it.

"Why are you taking all this out on me? Your father is the one who cheated on me with my friend and had a baby? Do you ever see any wrong in what he does, Denie? When are you going to see him for the bastard that he really is?"

"He's still my father, and I love him! I'm really sorry for all he's done to hurt you, but I still love him." Denie placed her head between her hands. "You don't have to rub it in about him having another daughter. He just buried his mother and all you can think about is how he hurt you. He needs me right now, and no matter how much I'm hurt right now, it's clear I'm all he has."

Sometimes I wish she felt like that about me. "He has that Spanish bitch, right?"

"That's Aunt Marisol's friend. They're not together. She's just cool with him that's all."

"It is so sad how that man tells you anything and you believe it."

"Just like you. As a matter of fact, let me get my clothes and go back to my grandmother's house with my dad," Denie stated.

"Go ahead, and by the way have you even thought about going to see your brother yet? If it wasn't for you being all in a nigga's face that night, he wouldn't be in jail right now."

"For your information, I went to see my brother yesterday with my father, and the last time I checked, I don't believe I told him to put drugs and a gun in his car."

"Bitch, get as much of your shit that can fit in your car and get your disrespectful ass out of my house."

"I'll get out of *my father's* house, for now!"

I wanted to beat her ass so bad, but decided to get dressed and pay Trixie a visit instead. I'd been waiting to get at her for pulling that stunt at the funeral, and today was the day. I slipped on a Victoria Secret Pink sweatsuit and some Nike Airmax tennis shoes, which was the closest thing in my closet to street gear. I then pulled my hair back in a ponytail, grabbed my Gucci bag and was out the door. Jumping in my truck, I put my Beyonce CD on full blast. Cruising down Georgia Avenue, I was only five minutes away from the shop when my mind began to race. I couldn't believe that I didn't see that Nita was Rich's daughter. She looked exactly like my husband and the name was a dead giveaway, Juanita. *How could I be so blinded by love?*

When I pulled up, valet asked if I needed them to park my car. However, I quickly let them know that I wouldn't be long and my car was going to stay double parked. When I walked in, I spoke to everyone as I made my way to Trixie's station. All eyes were on me, and it wasn't hard to wonder why. I'm sure they all had heard about the drama at the funeral by now, and knew I was there to confront my former friend.

"What's up now, Trixie?" I asked with a smirk.

"Lisa, don't bring that ghetto shit up in my place of business. If you want to talk to me about Rich, we can handle this as women later on. I have clients right now. This is a bad time."

"Bitch, did you think about that when you were fucking my husband behind my back," I countered.

"Look, you can have Rich. I just want him to take care of his daughter, that's it! It's obvious he ain't worth shit anyway."

"What do you mean, I can have him? Bitch don't think you're doing me a favor. You were the side fuck, not me!"

"And now this side fuck is entitled to you and your husband's bread and you hate that shit, don't you?"

I couldn't control myself any longer and smacked the shit out of Trixie. It wasn't long before we started tussling and she slipped and fell. Searching for a weapon, I quickly grabbed some shears off her station and went straight for her face. Blood gushed everywhere. Trixie let out a horrific scream before charging at me with a pair of smoking curling irons. Trying to prevent the hot utensil from touching my skin, I started to back up. However, the next thing I knew, somebody had hit me in my head from behind with a huge blow. I fell to the ground instantly.

Trixie and a couple of her stylists ended up jumping me. I fought back as much as I could before one of Rich's boys who hung around that area came in the shop and stopped the brawl. I still wanted more of Trixie, as he picked me up and carried me outside.

"You better hope I don't catch you in the street!"

"Let her ass go!" Trixie yelled out..

"When you look in the mirror remember me bitch. You have no clue what you did to my life!"

"And when you look at your husband, remember my daughter. She ain't going anywhere!" Trixie shot back.

Her words stung, because she spoke the truth. Getting back in my truck, I looked in the mirror and saw that I had a deep scratch across my right cheek along with a few small bruises. Pissed that I'd allowed Trixie to alter my appearance in any way, I hurried and pulled off before I ended up running back into the shop for round two. Picking up my cell phone, I dialed Marisol. She was the next one on my list.

"Hey Lisa, let me call you right back, I'm in the middle of something."

"Oh, now you wanna rush me off the phone after you hooked my husband up with your friend."

"Lisa, I had no idea they were messing around. I would never do that to you."

"You expect me to believe that shit? I trusted you Marisol and you crossed me!"

"Well, Lisa you should know me better than that. If you can't control who Rich fucks, what makes you think I can?"

"Fuck you, Marisol. You and Rich need to stay the fuck out of my life!"

I hung up on her ass. My feelings were hurt, but little did

she know, her husband would be in my bed by the end of the day. I called Carlos' phone but he didn't answer. Carlos had started to really make me feel like a jump off, but I was never going to be side girl material. I was determined to pay both Marisol and Rich back and make Carlos fall in love with me, the same way Rich did. When he didn't call back, I decided to text him.

It's me. Meet me at my house right now if you know what's good for you. The extra key is under the rock on the right side of the garage.

I circled around my neighborhood at least twenty minutes to give Carlos time to meet my demands. When I finally pulled into my driveway I didn't see any sign of him, which pissed me off. Obviously, he wasn't aware that I meant business. However, as I walked in the house through the garage, Carlos was surprisingly sitting at the kitchen table, looking nervous of course.

"So, I have to threaten you in order to get your damn attention. Where's your car?" I inquired.

"What difference does it make? What the fuck is your problem, Lisa? If you want this, you have to play by my rules or we're gonna get caught."

"Carlos, you're not gonna treat me like a side piece of ass. I know my worth."

He frowned. "What the fuck happened to your face?"

"Trixie happened, but trust me this will go away, her shit is permanent."

"What happened?"

"I went to the shop, whooped her ass, then cut her, before her fucking friends jumped me. As you can see, the bitch obviously needs help to handle me."

"Why did you go up there in the first place, Lisa? What are you trying to prove? That shit is not gonna take back what Rich did."

"Because everyone thinks I'm supposed to sit back and allow people to continue to disrespect me and treat me like shit.

I'm tired, Carlos!" When I started to get emotional, he reached out and began to hold me.

"You're right, and you know what, I have something that will make you feel much better." At that moment, Carlos pulled out a vial of coke, put a little of it on his pinky, then took a huge sniff. He then put a little on his finger for me, but I declined.

"You're all I need to make me feel better, Carlos," I said in a seductive voice. "I don't need that."

"Trust me, you'll enjoy it."

When I shook my head no again, he put the coke down, picked me and put me on the counter before making love to me right where our affair began. After a passionate sex session we ended up in the family room covered in sweat and tired. I looked at him and smiled.

"Carlos, why are you fighting it? I can tell you're starting to feel something for me. Otherwise, you wouldn't have fucked me here, knowing Rich could've knocked on the door at any minute. Who takes risks like that for people they don't fuck with?"

"Lisa, don't get me wrong, being with you is fun, but I love my wife. I can't risk losing my family and my cousin over you."

"So, why did you fuck me? Why are you here? Stop acting like I don't matter. You fill a void that I've been missing for a long time. I need you, Carlos."

I felt the tears welling up in my eyes and I tried to hold it in, but couldn't. As I dabbed my eyes, he went back to the kitchen to get his vial and started to snort some more. A part of me knew that if I joined him, it would put what we had on another level.

Marisol does it from time to time and never got addicted, so why can't I, I thought to myself. *Why not allow Carlos to introduce me to another feeling I never knew*. I was already high off of his love.

"You wanna feel better baby, come on try it," Carlos said.

When he poured some of the white powder out on his finger, I sniffed it up my nose like a pro this time. I did it one more time and then slowly sucked the rest off his finger. I felt so good that I just wanted to fuck him again, but this time I wanted it to be rough. I wanted him to bang on my pussy until it was sore, that pleasurable type of pain. Carlos was my heaven on earth and little did he know he was going to be all mine.

CHAPTER SEVENTEEN
Rich

What can make a woman so foul that she gives her husband separation papers at his own mother's funeral? No matter how much I'd hurt Lisa in the past, nothin' I'd ever done was that bad in order for her to disrespect me while I was layin' my mother to rest. The shit was unforgivable. It had been almost a month since the funeral and a tough road nonetheless. If it hadn't been for the great support from Carlos, Marisol, Denie and Jade, I don't know what I would've done. I don't know how I would've made it.

I really enjoyed havin' Jade around. She was there when it really counted and I would never forget that. My mother's death made me yearn for companionship even more, and Jade had been a great support. She questioned me about Trixie and the charade that bitch had pulled, but I told her I didn't feel like discussin' it. Luckily, she understood and decided to fall back since I was still mournin'. However, I knew she would have questions later. I owed both Trixie and Lisa a beat down for what they did.

Leavin' my mother's house, I decided to go home to pick

up the rest of the money I'd stashed so Lisa couldn't get to it. I couldn't believe it was my birthday already. It was goin' to be a little different for me this year since I was definitely not spendin' it wit' Lisa. Since she wanted a divorce so bad, I was determined she was goin' to really feel how life would be without me. My mind was already made up that I would be takin' my daughter to dinner and then spendin' the rest of the evenin' wit' Jade. Since Marisol had already gone back to California, Jade and I could really enjoy each other without gettin' the evil eye.

When I walked in the house it was quiet. I figured Lisa was in the bedroom since she wasn't downstairs. Lisa would kill Denie if she knew Denie had given me her new key. I don't know why that bitch thought she was gonna keep me out my own house. After quickly gettin' my stash from the floor board in the laundry room, I put the shit in the trunk. Wonderin' why I was able to come in the house unnoticed, I doubled back and decided to see what Lisa was up to. As I walked upstairs to our bedroom, I started to miss my home a bit. It was the little things like the mural of my family that I had painted on the wall four years ago as a surprise for Lisa for Mother's Day. As I approached my bedroom, I could see Lisa in the bed wit' the covers pulled over her head. I could also hear her whisperin', and since I didn't see anyone else in the bed, I figured she was on the phone. Walkin' over to the light switch, I turned in on, which immediately startled her. Like someone caught in the act, Lisa jumped up and quickly disconnected the call.

"What the fuck were you doin' and who were you on the phone wit'?" I asked.

"None of your business. Why are you here anyway? How did you get in?"Lisa asked.

"I pay the bills here last time I checked, don't I?"

"There you go with that shit. Did you forget we're legally separated and this is not your residence anymore? You need to get the fuck out. Go fuck your Spanish bitch, or betta yet, go be a father to your new baby!"

Somethin' wasn't right and I was ready to black out on

Lisa at any moment. As I pulled the sheets back, Lisa was completely naked, wit' a vibrator layin' beside her. I had to admit though, lookin' at her made my dick hard instantly.

"Man, I know damn well you ain't up in my house havin' phone sex wit' some nigga. You disrespectful bitch!"

"Get out!" she yelled tryin' to pull the sheets back.

"Maybe the nigga you were on the phone wit' needs to be payin' your bills!" I shouted, but I wished I could retract my words so I didn't sound jealous.

"Whatever Rich. Don't look for excuses on why you shouldn't pay the bills. Carlos has been paying the bills lately anyway, not you. Have you been bringing or sending any money lately? No, he does."

"Whose money do you think is payin' your bills? Los just sends or brings it for me, dumb-ass."

"Oh, I forgot. You're too busy fucking your Spanish bitch to be a responsible man, but it's cool Juan Sanchez because karma is a muthafucka. You reap what you sow. Trust me. It's all good. We'll have our day in court. Then I'll own half your shit!"

I reached over and grabbed Lisa by the neck and started chokin' the shit out of her. There was so much anger built up inside of me that I didn't realize my own strength. Within that short amount of time, Lisa had turned red and was losin' her breath. When I let go of her, she began to cough in between cryin'. I didn't even try to console her. Now, I honestly understood when people said, it's a thin line between love and hate.

Unbuttonin' my pants, I quickly grabbed Lisa's legs as my jeans fell to the floor. "Since you wanna be up in my crib havin' phone sex wit' another nigga, I'ma take this pussy like you probably wanted him to do!"

"No...Rich please...stop," Lisa begged.

Spreadin' her legs apart, I didn't waste anytime before pullin' my dick out then rammin' it inside of her. I ignored her desperate cries as I thrust my dick in and out of her pussy at a rapid pace. Her shit was moist, which allowed my shaft to flow in and out. Lisa swung her arms frantically to try and get me off of her, but it didn't work.

"Don't act like you don't miss this dick," I taunted without missin' a stroke.

The more Lisa screamed the more that shit turned me on. Within seconds, I started to cum. It felt good to be back inside of her again.

After pullin' out, I watched as tears streamed down her face, but that shit didn't faze me. "Now, I'll bet you'll think twice before talkin' shit to me bitch. Don't you ever disrespect me again," I said before gettin' myself together and walkin' out the room.

Leavin' out of the house, I jumped in my Range and called Denie to let her know to meet me downtown at the Oceanaire restaurant. Ridin' down 16th Street, I thought about how Lisa and I were really over. I just couldn't believe that our relationship had gotten to this point. There was so much consumin' me and I couldn't wait to be wit' my daughter to get a peace of mind. An evenin' wit' seafood and my princess would get my mind off of things for sure.

Several minutes later, I pulled up to valet, handed the guy my key and let him know to keep my car out front. When I walked in, the hostess showed me to the table where Denie was already waitin' for me. She lookined so beautiful. I wasn't ready for my baby to grow up.

"Hi Daddy!" She reached over to give me a kiss.

"Hey, Baby Girl. Why are you so excited?"

"Because it's your birthday old timer."

"Shit, thirty-nine is not old. Actually, I'm lookin' better as each year passes," I boasted.

Denie laughed. "You sure are handsome."

"Thanks, Baby Girl. So, the focus is on us tonight. No drama. I just want us to catch up. What's up wit' school?"

"Listen at the concerned dad," she teased. "Well, this past semester I got all A's and one B. I'm really trying hard to get that scholarship to F.I.T. in New York. I want to pursue fashion and have my own clothing line."

"I'm so proud of you. You know I love you, right?"
Denie shook her head. "I'm sorry for disappointin' you in the
past. You know you all I got for real now since Mama is gone."

"Well, you got your new little girl."

I looked at Denie who had a disappointed expression. "I
told you before that I don't know if that little girl is mine."

"Daddy, be real with me. She looks just like you."

I paused for a second. "Regardless Denie, you will always be my Baby Girl. Ain't nothin' or nobody comin' in between my love for you."

"Daddy, everybody always blames you for everything.
They don't see the good in you that I see. I hope one day I find
somebody just like you."

"Hold up, Denie. I want better for you. I'm not perfect.
I've made so many mistakes, and I don't want you to ever experience the things that I've put your mother through. A lot of the
reasons why we're not together now is because of me. I know I
fuckcd up. I lost my family because of the bad choices that I've
made. But no matter how bad things get between me and your
mother, know that I'll always love you."

"Why do you always blame yourself? You've been good
to Ma. She doesn't deserve you," Denie stated.

"You're wrong Baby Girl, I don't deserve her. It is my
fault and you need to start showin' your mother more respect
than you do. I don't want y'all to be at war all the time."

Denie rolled her eyes. "She just makes me sick. She always has something negative to say about you and it drives me
crazy. That's why after you sell Grandma's house, I want to go
back to Cali with you for the summer. Besides, Juan is her pride
and joy and he does no wrong. Do you know she blamed me for
him being locked up? Did she forget what he does for a living?"

"Denie, that's her only boy. She loves him even more because he was there for her when I was away. He stepped up and
was the man of the house when I had to go up the road."

"You going to jail had nothing to do with why she loves

Juan more than me. I just don't like to be around her. She looks down on me about everything. It could be the smallest thing that irritates her, and to top it off, she's always saying, 'You're just like your father', and it's getting old."

"Denie, I hurt your mother. I guess she sees a lot of me in you."

"That's still no excuse," Denie said with her lips poked out.

I wanted to get off the subject. "Well, let's try to make this dinner about us now, and the time I've missed wit' you. No more talkin' about your mother. Let's enjoy our date."

"I agree, but Daddy if Ma let's you come back, would you?"

I shook my head. "I can't answer that. For now it is what it is, so let's try and deal wit' things the best way we can."

Denie agreed to try and act better toward Lisa and we enjoyed the rest of our night. She kept lookin' at her watch as if she had somewhere to be. I knew she had little guy friends, but I didn't think she had anything serious goin' on.

"Baby, you got somewhere to be, you keep checkin' your watch?"

"Umm, I kinda had plans, but I wanted to be with you Daddy, so I told my friends that I would meet up with them later."

"So, is that why you wanted to meet me down here? You had plans on ditchin' your dad, for some lil' boy."

"No, Daddy, me and my friends are going out."

"Not that little girl Kendi or that girl Shay that your mother doesn't like, I hope."

"No, not at all."

"Okay Baby Girl, don't ever mess up our trust we have for one another."

"I won't Daddy, I gotta go!"

Denie got up and gave me a kiss and a hug. I sat there and thought about how I had betrayed my family's trust for years. How could I demand trust from my daughter, but had failed at givin' trust myself. As I looked through my phone at my pictures, I came across a picture of Lisa blowin' a kiss. A picture she'd sent to me last summer. Lisa looked beautiful. I really missed what we had, but things had gotten so ugly that I decided to keep what we had in the past.

A few minutes later, the waitress brought me the check. She was cute, and even though I was an ass man, she was spillin' out of her blouse, which caught my attention. I was about to ask her why a beautiful young lady such as herself looked so sad, when my phone rang. It was Jade.

"Hello, Miss."

"I miss you, Rich. What are you doing?"

"Well, I just had dinner wit' Denie, and now I'm about to go see my man Nelson for a minute."

"When are we going to get nasty? This morning wasn't enough for me. My pussy is yearning for you."

"Damn, you're makin' me hard as shit. I'll be on my way once I wrap up wit' Nelson."

"I'll be here waiting."

By the time I hung up wit' Jade, my waitress was gone. However, after I paid the bill and started toward the door, I saw the waitress again. This time she gave me a seductive little smile and a wink. I knew what that meant, but I just smiled back and left.

Gettin' to Nelson's house as quick as possible was important so I could get back to Jade. I wanted to be inside of her so bad, but money over bitches would always be my motto. I called Nelson to let him know I was on the way. I knew I was probably interruptin' his plans, but I let him know it would be quick.

I made it to Wheaton from downtown in less than twenty minutes. After typin' in the code to get into the gate, I called Nelson to let him know I was comin' upstairs to his apartment.

When Nelson opened the door he had candles lit throughout the apartment along wit' clusters of red balloons everywhere. I even saw a few teddy bears.

"Damn am I interruptin' somethin' Lil' Cassanova?" I just had to clown him.

He smiled. "Man, go ahead. Me and my girl were trying to get it in, but like you say money over bitches, so she gonna have to wait until we finish handling our shit."

I laughed. I loved Nelson and thought it was cool how he looked up to me. He was more like me than my own son, which was crazy. See, he knew his place, whereas Juan always felt a need to compete in a game he had no win in.

After we got started, I felt bad because our initial fifteen minute meetin' turned into an hour. Right before we wrapped everything up, the bedroom door opened and a familiar voice called out.

"Baby, how long are you gonna be?" his girl asked.

"We almost done, babe. Don't come out here like that, you see my man in here. Go put some clothes on," Nelson ordered. When I took my attention off the package, I turned around to see my daughter half naked in a red negligee.

"Oh my God, Daddy!" Denie said, tryin' to cover herself up.

"What the fuck?" I turned to Nelson. "Are you fuckin' my daughter?"

"Your daughter, your daughter. This can't be.."

Before Nelson could finish his sentence I went off and tried to knock his fuckin' head off his shoulders. There was nothing Denie could do to stop me from tryin' to kill him.

"Daddy stop, get off of him, I love him, Daddy. I love him!" Denie screamed.

"Denie, get the fuck off me. I'ma kill 'em! How long were you gonna fake and play me close so you could fuck my daughter behind my back?" I asked Nelson.

"Daddy, nooo!" Denie continued to scream.

"Unc, I didn't know…I didn't know man," Nelson said as he tried to block my blows. "She never told me."

After several more body shots, I finally stopped and looked at Denie. "Get your shit on and let's go." I then looked at

Nelson. "You better not ever touch my fuckin' daughter again."

"I'm not leaving. Look at what you've done. He needs to go to the hospital," Denie said.

Nelson held up his hand. "Denie, I'm fine. Just go with your father, please."

"No, I'm not leaving you. Daddy, you need to be worrying about your wife instead of me. I saw a strange car in front of the house not to long ago, and I'm sure it belonged to another man. She's the one cheating on you. Stay out of my personal life and worry about your own. You can't tell me who to love," Denie said in a bold tone.

"Denie, get dressed and let's go now! You lied to me. You said you were goin' out wit' your friends!" I belted. "We just talked about trust."

"Look at his eye, oh my God, Nelson, are you okay?"

My daughter was gonna have to hate me because there was no way she would ever see Nelson again. Not only was he too old, but he was in the streets, and I didn't want that for her. The last thing she needed in her life was another nigga like me.

When Denie saw how serious I was, she finally ran back in the room and got herself together. After havin' to break up an emotional goodbye, we left. At that point, I decided it would be best for Denie to go back wit' her mother. Wit' Juan bein' locked up and me cuttin' Nelson off, I couldn't risk fuckin' up my money. When we got in the car Denie cried the entire time. Tired of hearin' her sob, I called Carlos to let him know what happened.

"What's up, Rich?" Carlos answered.

"Can you believe Denie's fuckin' Nelson," I blurted out. I didn't even care that she could hear my entire conversation.

"What?" Carlos replied.

"Yeah, and she sittin' in the car cryin' over the nigga and shit. I'm takin' her ass back to Lisa." I looked at Denie. "Is Nelson the nigga you were arguin' wit' outside the club that night?" When Denie didn't answer, I directed my conversation back to Carlos. "We're gonna have more shit to deal wit' now. Man, Juan bein' locked up is really fuckin' up my bread!"

"See, I knew it was a reason why I didn't trust that lil' nigga."

"Yeah, I didn't even see this shit comin'," I admitted. "That's okay because I'm cuttin' that muthafucka off."

Carlos paused. "But then again, you sure you wanna let Nelson go. Maybe he didn't know Denie was your daughter. I mean I never trusted him, but so far he's been a loyal worker. He's even been holding shit down better than Juan."

"Los, he fucked my daughter. I can't be around him anymore."

"Man, just think about what you're doing to the business. You were just saying how you fuck with slim. I think you're letting your emotions get the best of you. Anyway, he knows too much to let him go like that."

"I can't, Los." Then again, I was beginnin' to feel bad about the way I reacted to Nelson and then somethin' else dawned on me when I thought about what Denie said. *Whose car was in front of my damn house*, I thought. At that moment, I turned up the music then began whisperin' to Carlos so Denie couldn't hear me.

"Hey, I'ma need you to start keepin' an eye on Lisa. I think she fuckin' somebody, and I don't have time to be a target to no niggas. She doesn't realize that it's not about me not wanting her to move on. It's about niggas in the street always plottin'."

"Bet. We gonna find out one way or another. I got you, bro."

"I know you got me, Los. You're the only one who has ever had my back totally. I love you bro."

"You know you my nigga," Carlos responded as if he had a little bit of guilt in his voice.

CHAPTER EIGHTEEN

Lisa

Now more than ever, I was ready to pay Rich back for what he'd done. I called Carlos and told him about Rich forcing himself on me after he'd caught me having phone sex with him. Trying to avoid other one of those episodes, Carlos decided to have me come to his house in Potomac since Marisol had gone back to L.A. Apparently, their daughter was sick so she had to put her mommy hat on, which was something she rarely did. After getting off the phone, I walked into the bathroom and started my bubble bath. As the water filled the Jacuzzi, I put my I-pod on shuffle and then placed it on the Bose docking station.

Yearning for my bubble sanctuary, I immersed my body into my hot bath and thought about Carlos. My conversations and thoughts of him made me feel better whenever I started to feel depressed about what my life had turned into. The rape was always in the back of my mind no matter how many pills I popped to try and forget it. Now, the incident with Rich was making shit even worse. Carlos and I had spent countless hours on the phone discussing how I felt and he'd become a safe haven for me. This side of Carlos I'd never seen and it made me fall for him even more. No matter how much he said we could never be serious, his actions showed otherwise. I used to hate him, but it was funny how hate turned to love so fast. Sometimes I wondered if I was just vulnerable, but I hadn't felt this way in years and I loved it.

I was ready for a drama free night. I wanted to look sexy, but not over done. After my bath, I entered my closet in my pink Juicy Couture terry robe and decided on what to wear. My old housekeeper, Anna had done a great job with the organization of my closet. My boots were all organized by color and length. My handbags were organized by designer. Winter, fall, spring, and summer were all within their own sections. I decided since we were now in March I would go to the spring section of my wardrobe and picked out a sexy gold Dolce & Gabbana bustier and my leopard Dolce & Gabbana jacket I'd ordered from a Miami boutique in Bal Harbour. Next, I pulled out a pair of dark denim True Religion skinny jeans with jeweled buttons. They fit my curves just right and made me feel sexy. Since there wasn't any snow left on the ground, I decided to wear a pair of my black quilted Chanel shoes, then finished my look with some gold bangles.

When I walked in the bathroom and looked in the mirror, I couldn't wait to call Jermaine, so he could do something with my hair. I wanted any trail of Trixie gone from my life, even the weave she'd put in. When I thought back on how she was the one pressing me to get this shit, it pissed me off. She knew Rich hated weave, so more than likely, that was her motive.

"Simple bitch," I said out loud.

Ready for my date, I grabbed my black Chanel bag, and my Gucci duffle bag out of the closet. I then went to my lingerie drawer and pulled together a sexy red nighty for the nights festivities even though I knew my night would consist of as little clothes as possible. After we were interrupted by Rich in the middle of our phone sex session, it made me want to make love to Carlos even more. Somehow I had become tainted and it was scary that I liked the new me. I really wished that who I'd fallen for wasn't my husband's cousin, but the rush made it exciting in a crazy way.

After I dolled my face up, I sent Carlos a text to let him know I was leaving. As soon as I was heading out of the door Rich and Denie were coming in.

"Where the fuck you about to go wit' an overnight bag?" Rich asked, looking my attire up and down.

"Why!" I yelled, irritated at the fact that I knew their arrival was going to make me late. After what he'd done to me I didn't have shit to say to him. I even knew it was his birthday, but I refused to wish that nigga any happiness. "Get out of here, Rich."

"Oh, I'm leavin' but you're not. Whatever plans you had, you're gonna have to cancel them because I just found Denie at my man's house half-naked."

I threw up one of my hands. "So, what does that have to do with me?"

"You're her mother. It has a lot to do with you. Do you not care that your seventeen year old daughter is fuckin' an older man?" Rich asked.

"He's only twenty-one!" Denie yelled with an attitude. She then ran upstairs to her room and slammed the door.

Her eyes were so puffy, I guess from crying. I'd never seen her act out this way toward Rich, so I was taken back. She never got upset with him.

"Rich, who is this guy?" I asked like I really cared.

"He's a dude that I do business wit', but I don't want him fuckin' wit' my daughter. That's out of the question."

"So, now that you can't control your daughter, you want to bring her back here, huh? I think she's old enough to make her own decisions on who she wants to date. You were sleeping with me when I was her age, so what's the difference?" I was tired of being concerned about who Denie was fucking. Those days were over.

"That's my daughter, Lisa."

"And I was somebody's daughter, too. Denie has learned from mistakes in the past, and I'm sure that if she really likes this guy, and if you know him, it should be fine."

I was trying to think of anything I could say to just get out of the door. Rich was holding me up and I was getting quite annoyed. I could feel my phone vibrating in my purse, but I didn't want to check it in front of Rich just in case it was Carlos.

"Well, with the series of events tonight my plans have changed. Los and I have business to attend to. So, you need to keep an eye on Denie. I don't want her runnin' back to that nigga's crib."

"What do you and Carlos have to do?" I asked. *I know this bullshit with Denie is not about to fuck up my night.*

"When did my business start to be of concern to you? Just know that Denie is your priority right now. I got shit to do," Rich said as he stormed out the front door.

"Shit!" I yelled.

When I checked my phone, I noticed that Carlos had text me and said he didn't want me to meet him at his house any longer and that Rich suspected me of cheating. He let me know that he would try and duck Rich's calls, and I would have to meet him in Baltimore later on. The next text message he sent read:

Call you in 15

I was pissed, but thought I'd wait until he called to give me a new set of instructions. I wanted to be in the right mood, so I thought I'd go to the bathroom and test a little bit of the package that Carlos left me the last time he was here. I sat at my vanity desk and poured a little bit of the powder on my silver tray that I usually placed my jewelry on from time to time. I thought that it would be best if I just did one line until I got there with him. When I sniffed the one line, it was the instant boost I needed to get my night started. As I rushed to put up my stash, Denie walked in my room.

"Ma, what are you doing? Are you busy?"

"Nothing. I'm not busy, what's up?" I said startled. I hurried and dropped the bag of powder in my drawer.

"Well, I just wanted to thank you for standing up for me with my father. I know that I've been difficult to get along with lately, so I appreciate what you did."

"Denie, don't get me wrong, I want what's best for you. We've all been through a lot, but we need to start acting as a family. We're always divided, and I wasn't raised that way. It seems like there's always a divide between us and I don't like it."

"You're right, Ma, I'm sorry. Me and Daddy just had this conversation at dinner earlier and I told him I would do better. I wanna try and work on building a better relationship with you."

I couldn't help but smile. "That would mean a lot to me. How about we start looking for prom dresses next week?"

"Well, you know I'll be making my own dress, but we can go for fabrics and accessories."

"I can't wait. You just made me so happy. I love you Denie and I just want the best for you. Everything that goes wrong isn't always my fault and I want you to know that there are always two sides to every story. I just want us to be closer. And this thing with this guy and your father, he's very protective when it comes to you. The same way my dad was with me. When he calms down, let him know how you feel. He'll come around, but you have to let him feel like he's right sometimes."

"I know, but Ma I love Nelson so much. While my father is there for money, Nelson is there for encouragement and support. My dad never spends time with me like he used to before he went to jail. Things have never been the same since. Do you think he hates me deep down inside because I got pregnant while he was away?"

"No, Denie. Your father loves you very much. He just doesn't know how to show it. His father didn't show him how to be a man. Your dad didn't know how to deal with his father looking down on him the way he used to look down on Uncle Renzo and Carlos. He decided he was going to show him he could be a man with or without your grandfather and chose the life that we're living now. Our lives seem great to everyone on the outside looking in, but really this isn't what life is about. This life is filled with emptiness, loneliness, and money. It feels good to shop and have this big house and nice cars, but when you don't have someone there to hold you when you need to be held and love you, once you get to a certain age, you ask yourself is it all worth it. A life full of jewels and furs is not always the answer." My eyes began to tear as I tried to school Denie.

"That's why I want to have my own clothing line so I can be successful the right way. I don't want to live like you and Daddy. I want a better life. I'm going to be famous, but in a legit way." Denie giggled. "I always feel like I have to be secretive and not let anyone know that I'm Rich's daughter. It's embarrassing when I go to my friend's houses and their families ask me what my parents do for a living. I constantly have to make things up, and it gets old. I mean don't get me wrong, I appreciate that my father gives me the best, but I don't want this life for myself."

"Then you need to re-evaluate the boy in your life. If not, you'll be allowing history to repeat itself."

Denie began to cry and laid on my chest as we sat on the edge of my bed. I glanced up and looked at our family photo on my dresser. That's when my family was happy. When life was great and I was in the moment enjoying everything and not thinking about the what if's. I held my daughter and said a prayer to comfort her, and thought about how I missed my son.

After embracing Denie a few more minutes, my phone rang. I knew it was probably Carlos, but my daughter and I were having our first breakthrough as mother and daughter and it felt good. It made me think to myself that 2010 was going to be my year. After consoling Denie, she went to her room to lie down. When I called Carlos back, he let me know that he had to handle some business in Baltimore, and wanted us to meet at some random motel. If I had to see him in a motel then so be it. Once Denie was sound asleep, I crept out the door to meet my new man. I'm sure he didn't want that title, but I could care less.

CHAPTER NINETEEN

Rich

This was definitely a birthday to remember. I felt bad that it was almost 11 o'clock and I hadn't made it to meet Jade yet. Wit' all that had gone on wit' Nelson, my plans had changed several times. Knowin' I now had to take over a few of Nelson's responsibilities, Carlos and I decided to head to Baltimore, and split up some of the duties. While Carlos hit up the Sandtown, West Baltimore area, I had to meet my man Julio at my strip club. My mind was all over the place, but I knew that once I finally got to Jade, she would take care of me.

When I pulled up at Lace, I thought about the last time I was there and how Nelson had fucked Cream. At that moment, it dawned on me how I encouraged the nigga my daughter was fuckin' to pay for pussy from a stripper. Every time I thought about Nelson bein' wit' Denie, the shit made my head hurt. Trying to stay focused, I got out and walked into the club. Of course the first person I bumped into was Honey. Even though I was there on business, she was so hard to resist wit' that big ass spillin' out of her thong.

"What's up, Rich? You need a private dance?"

"Naw, Shorty, I'm good. You seen my man Julio from up top? He's supposed to be meetin' me here."

"Yeah, I just saw him in the back. You sure you don't want none of this good pussy tonight?"

"Naw, but here go some change," I said, passin' her a couple hundred dollar bills. I knew she probably needed it, since tonight seemed like a slow night.

Makin' my way to the back, it wasn't long before I spotted Julio gettin' a lap dance from Cream. Although I was in a rush, I let him finish since the song was almost done. However, as soon as the shit was over, we met in the back office to take care of business before he tried to get another round.

"What up, Son?" Julio asked in his thick New York accent.

"A lot of shit, but I'll live," I replied.

"So, where's Nelson? I was surprised when you called and told me that you were gonna meet me instead of him."

"He's on vacation for a while, so call me or Carlos from now on." I never wanted my business partners to ever see a divide in my organization.

"Word. Okay, bet," Julio said.

After we took care of business and headed out of the back room, Honey and Cream were on the front stage fondlin' each other; puttin' on a show, of course. Watchin' beads of sweat rollin' down Honey's thick thighs instantly made my dick hard. There was no way that I could leave Baltimore without fuckin' her. I waited 'til they finished their set and gave her the look. She knew what that look meant, it was VIP room time.

All I needed was to have Honey's ass on my lap after the night I had. Honey was such a cute girl wit' so much potential. A part of me wondered why she was a stripper. Even though we'd fucked on countless occasions, I'd never asked her about her personal life. Guess I really didn't care. Questions like that were for relationships, and the last thing I wanted that bitch to think was that I was her man.

As soon as Honey walked in, she got on her knees, unzipped my jeans, and put my entire dick in her mouth. At only the young age of twenty-five, this chic was a true pro at what she did. As her thick tongue moved up and down my shaft then across my head, I could tell I was about to cum.

"No, that's enough. Bend over," I demanded.

I couldn't wait to be inside of her as she removed her purple thongs, and exposed her manicured pussy. Extremely flexible, Honey bent over and grabbed her ankles right before I dove inside. Honey took each stroke like a stallion as I moved in and out at a rapid pace. It wasn't long before her pussy began to grip my penis and her legs began to shake uncontrollably. I knew what that meant.

"Cum for Daddy," I said. When Honey let out a seductive moan, I couldn't hold on much longer myself. "Oh shit, I'm cumin' too."

Quickly pullin' out, my eyes rolled in the back of my head as the warm liquid shot all over Honey's back. It was an instant stress reliever. Once I cleaned myself up and zipped up my pants, I gave Honey some more money for her time. Shit, I was beyond generous at that point. Right before I walked out, Honey asked if she could ask me a question.

"Yeah, what's up?"

"Rich, what do you think of me? I hope you don't think I'm some kind of whore."

Where the fuck is this comin' from? I thought. Usually I wouldn't indulge in conversation wit' a trick, but since she had just given me a treat, I decided to play Mr. Nice Guy.

"I mean you're cool. Why are you askin' me that?"

"I don't know. I've just been thinking about getting out the game lately, that's all. I wanted to know how you felt about me. I mean..."

"Look Honey, your head and pussy game is not to be fucked wit', but I ain't really tryin' to hear that. I got a lot of shit on my mind right now. I gotta roll."

I had to cut the conversation short because I felt like I was diggin' myself deeper into a situation that I didn't want to be in. Counselin' a trick wasn't on my schedule at the moment. No matter how much she might've been thinkin' about quittin', somethin' told me that she wouldn't stop. I'd seen her kind before. Money hungry bitches didn't know how to stop.

As I left out of the club, my mind was heavy. For the first time in a long time, I felt guilty for fuckin' around. I didn't know what had gotten into me, but I just couldn't stop thinkin' about Jade, and how I'd put her off all day. At that moment, I made a mental note to call her as soon as I hooked back up wit' Carlos.

When I headed onto Charles Street, my gas light popped on. Thinkin' I needed to get some gas before I got back on the highway, I pulled into the Shell station to fill up. After givin' the attendant seventy bucks, I started the pump, but got back in the truck since it was freezin' outside. Waitin' for the pump to stop, I scrolled through a few of the satellite radio stations 'til I stopped on Jamie Foxx's, Foxhole. The comedians up there were usually funny as shit, and right now I could've used a good laugh.

As soon as I heard the gas pump click, I was about to get out the car, when I saw Lisa comin' out of the gas station. She was in such a hurry she didn't even see me. *What the hell is she doin' out here*? I thought. It was obvious that neither one of us had spotted each other before.

"Hold up. Her ass is supposed to be at home wit' Denie," I said to myself.

When she got in her car, I quickly hopped out of my truck and placed the gas pump back in the cradle before hoppin' back in the driver's seat. I was so anxious to see where she was goin', I didn't even bother to put my gas cap back on.

I called Carlos to see if he'd found out anything about who she was dealin' wit' since the last time I'd talked to him, but he didn't answer. When she pulled off, I decided to follow her just to see who she was creepin' wit' on my own. I had to admit, it hurt to see her so happy and in such good spirits. I hadn't seen her smile like that in a long time. After pullin' out behind her, I made sure to stay a few cars back.

"Who the hell could she be creepin' wit' in Baltimore?" I asked myself. Questions like this, continued to bounce around in my head 'til she pulled into the parkin' lot of an old motel minutes later. I was embarrassed to see that my wife would stoop this low and allow someone to take her to such a rundown spot.

When she parked, I made sure to keep my distance so she wouldn't see me, but made sure to keep a good view so I could see what room she was goin' in. My blood began to boil as I watched her apply some lip gloss in the rearview mirror. It took all of me to lay low and be easy so I could see what she was up to. I tried callin' Carlos' phone again, but still didn't get an answer.

"What the fuck is Carlos doin'?" I asked out loud. "I need him to meet me over here so we can take care of this nigga."

My anger was at an all time high as Lisa got out of the car, opened the back door and pulled out her overnight bag. She even pulled out a plastic bag that looked as if it had come from a restaurant. I couldn't believe this bitch actually went and bought this nigga some food, too. Eyein' the car she'd parked beside, and not recognizin' it, I had no idea who the nigga could be.

Duckin' down in my seat so she wouldn't see me, I kept my eye on her as she walked into room 102. She didn't even knock, so the nigga must've known she was comin'. Furious by this point, I hit the lever in my glove compartment to open up my stash spot. Seconds later, I pulled out my .45 and waved it back and forth. This was a job that called for a silencer, so I made sure it was in place while I allowed Lisa and whoever she was wit' to get comfortable. No matter how much I cheated on Lisa, she wasn't gonna get away wit' fuckin' somebody else. I was definitely gonna send her a message tonight. Her mystery date would soon be six feet deep.

CHAPTER TWENTY
Lisa

"Damn baby, you look good," Carlos said as soon as I walked through the door.

"So, do you, handsome."

Carlos looked so damn sexy. He reminded me so much of Jim Jones, that pretty boy sexy-thug look. He had grown a shadow on his face, and I liked it. Carlos was wearing some True Religion jeans and a pair of black Gucci rugged boots with a black Burberry sweatshirt. It was crazy that both he and Rich wore the same fragrance, Creed; a smell that always made me nice and horny.

Carlos blushed as he jumped up and locked the door. "What took you so long? I've been waiting for a while."

I held up the bag of food from the restaurant, Oya. "Well, you know Rich came by the house to drop Denie off, which slowed me up, but that's a long story. Then I went to get us something to eat. Oh, and I stopped by the gas station to get the condoms you asked for, and some cough drops."

"Cough drops, for what?"

I smiled. "You'll see."

"Rich has been calling me non-stop, but I didn't answer. I'm supposed to meet back up with him, so I don't know if we can stay all night."

I displayed a huge frown. "Fuck that. I didn't go through all this for a quickie. It's bad enough you got me in this shit hole instead of something nice."

Looking around the room, it was just as bad as the outside. With only me and Carlos' cars outside, it seemed as though we were the only people who decided to creep there for the night. The comforter was a baby pink and green floral pattern that looked hard as paper. The carpet was dirty, and the bed didn't even have a headboard, but I figured I would make the best out of it. I could deal with cheap and dirty if it meant I could be with my man.

Carlos sat at the little wooden desk and continued to break down his package. I knew he mentioned that he had to get his package ready to distribute, but I was determined that he was going to get his mind off of work to give me some of his good sex. Turning the lights off and feeling quite naughty, I got on my knees, unzipped his jeans, dug into his Hugo Boss boxers and started to massage his penis. He glanced at me with shock in his eyes before putting a little bit of powder on his finger for me to sniff. Like a disciplined student, I sniffed the powder off his pinky and kissed him on his lips. Seconds later, I kissed the tip of his dick. Quickly grabbing one of the cough drops out of my purse, I inserted it into my mouth then started sucking and massaging his shaft at the same time. All he kept saying was, "Damn, Lisa," so I knew I hadn't lost myself completely. I knew the Halls cough drop would give him that extra sensation that he needed.

As he grabbed my hair with one hand, he pushed me deeper and deeper into his lap until he came. Wanting to show him that I could be a real freak, I swallowed every bit of his sperm. Carlos made me feel young again. I felt like I was back. All the things that I did sexually back in the day were finally coming back to me.

We did a couple of lines together after I sucked him off. I'd never been into drugs ever in my life, but with Carlos, I felt like I was in another world. When we got high together, it took our sex to new heights; like we were on another planet, away from our problems. Feeling good, I straddled him then gave him a big kiss on those sexy lips. Carlos always knew how to make me feel better. He laid me on the bed before kissing me all over my body. I felt numb to everything, but his touch. I let him take control of my body and my mind. With my eyes closed, I thought to myself, *I don't want to come off this mountain that I'm on.* He licked every part of my body and just before he entered me, I begged for him to let me feel his love. I wanted to be more connected to him tonight than I'd ever been. We didn't use protection the first time we had sex, but he was very clear that it couldn't happen that way again.

"Carlos, please. I want to feel you again. You feel so good inside of me. Don't use the condoms."

He was hesitant at first, then replied, "Just this last time, baby."

His dick felt so good. "I love you, Carlos."

"I love you to Lisa. Why are you crying?"

"Because I don't want this feeling to ever stop. I wish I could just love you forever. You're the best thing that has happened to me in a long time."

The more I told him my true feelings, the deeper he pushed inside of me. His love making was addictive. I couldn't do anything but just lie on my back and let him have his way with me. It just felt so good to finally feel his flesh inside of me again. I yearned for him, and couldn't imagine it being any other way. Suddenly, I could feel the pulse in Carlos' dick and I knew he could no longer hold it in.

"Let it go, baby. Cum inside of me," I moaned.

As if he was waiting for me to give him permission, Carlos released all his juices inside my walls. "Oh shit, oh shit," he said.

As his body began to jerk, I was just about to stroke his back when all of a sudden, the door flew open. Carlos immediately jumped up as silent gunshots sounded throughout the room. It was so dark and I was so high that I couldn't make out what was going on. I screamed right before I heard Rich's voice.

"Come out, muthafucka. I know I hit you. Just let me finish your bitch-ass off!" Rich yelled.

"Rich, what are you doing here?" I screamed.

When Rich turned the lights on, I looked over on the floor by the bathroom and saw Carlos lying in a pool of blood. There were two holes in his side and his chest.

"Nooooo, Rich! What have you done?" I cried.

Rich's eyes became enormous. "No… no…no, this is not fuckin' happenin'. Los no Los, not you. How could you do this to me? Man, I trusted you!" Rich wailed.

"I'm sorry, Rich," Carlos managed to say. "Lisa, help me."

"Lisa, you betta stay where the fuck you at," Rich replied. He looked at his cousin with tears in his eyes. "How could you cross me, Los?" When Carlos shook his head, Rich grabbed his gun again. "Fuck this, now you gotta go!"

"No…Rich please. I love him. Please don't do this!" I pleaded.

"I, I love you Ri…"

It was the last thing I heard before Rich fired two more shots in his chest.

"Noooo, Carlos, please no!" I screamed. It felt like my world had come to an end as I ran over and held Carlos in my arms for the last time.

"Why did you do that? You might as well kill me, too!" I screamed.

Rich seemed to be in a daze for a few seconds before he snapped out of it. "Bitch, shut the fuck up. You made me do this shit. Why were you here with him? You're already dead to me!"

It wasn't long before Rich looked at me with cold eyes then hit me with the butt of the gun, straight across my face. I could immediately taste the blood in my mouth as I dropped Carlos and crawled across the room, but couldn't get away fast enough. Out of all the times Rich had hit me, this time was different. I knew deep down inside he really wanted to kill me. As I laid on the floor and cried, Rich stomped and kicked me like I was in a gang initiation. I just balled up in a fetal position and took my beating like a man.

"How could you do this to me, Lisa? Why Los? How could y'all hurt me like this?"

"Rich, you did this. Blame yourself, you did this!" I managed to say in between kicks.

After the last kick, he made me get dressed. Rich picked up Carlos' jeans and took the keys to his car out of his pocket. He then wrapped Carlos' body up in the comforter and put it in the back of Carlos' trunk.

"Let's go," Rich said, grabbing me by my shirt. "I'll drive Carlos' car and you follow me in my car."

"What about mine?" I asked.

"Give me your keys. I'll get somebody to pick your shit up within an hour."

"But…"

"Just give me your fuckin' keys!" Rich yelled.

As we left the hotel, I was more terrified than ever. A part of me wanted to drive in another direction and get help, but I knew that Rich would kill me. He'd turned into a different person that quick, but under the circumstances, I guess I should've understood.

We drove about twenty miles to a deserted dock. After getting out, Rich got behind Carlos' car and gave it a huge shove before it finally rolled off into the water. I burst out into tears as I watched Carlos' car sink in slow motion. It was like something I'd seen in a movie, and something I thought I'd never be apart of. Now, I was an accessory to murder, and didn't know how to handle it.

Moments later, Rich made his way back to the car I was driving, but made me get in the passenger's seat. He had so much rage in his eyes as he pulled off like a professional stunt driver. He finally began to talk after driving for ten minutes in silence.

"I want you to know it's your fault that Carlos is dead. The only reason why you're not in that fuckin' car wit' him is because of my kids. Hopefully though, you'll be so devastated from this that you'll drown in your own sorrow and kill yourself, you miserable whore." Tears kept falling as Rich continued. "So, you get high now? I saw the coke on the dresser." Rich shook his head. "I can't believe you let him turn you out."

"Rich, I'm…"

"Shut the fuck up!" he yelled. "Let me say this just once. If you ever tell anyone about this, bitch, you will die. If Los' body is found and you open your mouth, I will see to it that if I don't kill you, Marisol will, and you know she don't have no problem doin' it. Now, get out!"

I looked around. "But where am I supposed to go? I don't know where I am? It's dark out here. No street lights or nothing."

"You're on BWI Parkway. Now, get the fuck out, before I change my mind about killin' you!"

When Rich pulled the car over, he reached over me to open the door. He then pushed me out like I was a stranger. After landing on the hard pavement, I quickly sat up and tried to make my way back into the car.

"Rich, please. Don't leave me," I begged.

However, he never even looked my way as he shut the door and pulled off, leaving me all alone. All I could do was cry.

CHAPTER TWENTY-ONE
Rich

How did my love for Lisa turn to hate that fast? Thinkin' about what I'd just done, I knew I could never love her again. It was her fault that I'd killed the closest thing I had to a brother. I tried to convince myself that it was an accident, as I drove from Baltimore back to D.C. If only I'd known it was Carlos in the room wit' Lisa, maybe it could've ended differently. Flashbacks appeared in my mind on how we always vowed to each other that we would never let anything or anyone come in between the bond we had. How we would never fuck each other's girl no matter what the situation was. I thought back to his last words. He loved me. How could he hurt me this way? Money over bitches was our motto. Now, I could never hear his voice again.

I hit the steerin' wheel wit' my fist. "How could Los play me like that?"

Wit' my mind heavy, I wished I had someone to talk to, but it was too risky. When I pulled up at the Gaylord Hotel where Jade was stayin' an hour later, I just sat in the garage for a minute. Feelin' completely empty inside, I felt as though I had nowhere to turn. I also felt like I was goin' crazy, especially when my conscience kept fuckin' wit' me. After sittin' in the car for at least another ten minutes, I finally decided to make my way inside the hotel.

When I entered the room, Jade tried her best to look sexy for me even though I knew she was holdin' her anger in. She looked good wit' her ass hangin' out of the boy shorts and her breasts spillin' out of her bra, but it didn't matter how good she looked. I just wanted to be alone.

"Rich, where the hell have you been? It's three o' clock in the morning. I've been waiting in this hotel room alone all damn day. I didn't sign up for this!" she ranted.

"Jade, I've had a fucked up day. Please not tonight." I sat down on the bed.

"Have you been with Lisa? Huh, is that where you've been?"

"Stop it, Jade. If you don't shut the fuck up I'm rollin' out!"

"Well, talk to me. What happened? What's wrong with you?" It looked like she wanted to cry.

"It's nothin'. Just let it go!"

"Well, since you won't talk to me, then fuck me," she demanded. "Show me you miss me. I'm sitting here practically naked and you're barely even looking at me."

Jade started to take off the sexy underwear one at a time, but little did she know I just couldn't make love to her. I had no desire. I couldn't even get hard. Lookin' around the room, I realized that she had even ordered room service, but food was definitely out of the question.

"Jade, I can't. I've been through a lot tonight. I just need some time to think about some shit."

"I knew you fucked her. I knew it. You don't have to leave, because I'm leaving. I'll get a room somewhere else and go back to New York in the morning!" Jade yelled.

I couldn't take anymore of her naggin'. I quickly jumped up and smacked Jade across her face. The blow was so hard, she instantly flew over the bed. "Didn't I fuckin' tell you to shut up?"

When Jade got up off the floor, she looked at me in a state of shock and held her face.

"You just don't know when to shut the fuck up," I continued.

"I can't believe you hit me. I'm leaving! You fucking punta!"

"Well, go. Shit I don't give a fuck…leave!"

"I bet your wife knows what's wrong with your mute-ass. I'm out of here!"

As Jade started gettin' dressed, I went to the bathroom to take a shower. I took off my clothes and put them in one of the plastic laundry bags so I could destroy them later on. I didn't need any evidence to link me to Carlos' death. There was a lack of peace and calm in my life and at that moment I felt that a shower would help me relax and get my mind right. Adjustin' the temperature to a comfortable warm settin', I closed my eyes and allowed the water to run over my face. The way I was feelin', I just wanted to get a good night's rest. I didn't care if Jade left, just so that I could be alone. However, the moment to myself didn't last long because seconds later, her ass stormed in the bathroom and pulled the shower curtain back.

"Rich, as long as you live, you better not ever put your hands on me again!" she yelled then smacked me right in my face wit' the room service metal plate cover. "I'm not Lisa. You will not disrespect me!"

Prepared to fuck Jade up, I went to grab her, but slipped and hit my head on the edge of the tub. That shit was the last thing I remembered. When I woke up, I was layin' on the bathroom floor wit' my head propped up between Jade's leg wit' an ice pack. As bad as I wanted to beat her ass, I didn't have the energy.

"What happened?" I asked.

"You hit your head on the tub, then took a really bad fall," Jade informed. "Knocked you out cold."

"Damn."

"I'm sorry, baby. Please don't be mad at me. I just had to show you that you can't be disrespecting me," Jade replied.

I had to admit, I'd never had a woman stand up to me like that. "Yeah, and I don't have the energy to fight wit' you anymore. I just need to go to sleep."

"Rich, talk to me. Tell me what's bothering you. You can trust me, I promise."

I don't know why and what made me do it, but I told her everything. After the words came out of my mouth and I couldn't take it back, I knew deep down inside it was a mistake. How could I be so fuckin' vulnerable?

"Jade, I lost one of the most important people in my life tonight. Carlos was like my brother, and now he's gone. I have so many emotions bottled up inside of me, and no one to talk to. You just don't understand what I'm goin' through, but I don't expect you to either."

"Rich, I can't believe what you're telling me. Why did you have to kill him? Why not kill your whore of a wife instead? She not only betrayed you, she betrayed Marisol. Do you know how much Marisol loves her?"

Jade's response was confirmation for me that I'd made a mistake confidin' in her wit' somethin' so detrimental. If she were to tell Marisol, my Uncle Renzo would find out and I would be a dead man. It dawned on me that I had to play nice, or had to kill her, too. I felt so alone and she was all that I really had, so I chose to play nice.

"Jade, if I've ever needed you before, I need you now. Can you promise me that I can trust you? Can you promise that you'll never betray me?"

"Rich, I loved Carlos, like a brother. What do you expect from me?"

"I'ma put it to you like this, I fuck wit' you, shit I love you, but if you ever breathe a word of this to anyone, I will not only kill you, I will kill your family. That's a promise." Jade's eyes widened before she looked away. "Look at me!" I yelled. "I mean what I'm sayin'. It was a fuckin' accident. I didn't know it was Carlos. I didn't know!"

"Okay, Rich. I won't tell anyone. I promise," Jade responded in a low tone. "Can you try and get up now? Maybe we both could use some sleep."

Damn, I hope I can trust this bitch. Maybe the lie about me lovin' her will help, I thought as I picked myself off the floor.

After tossin' and turnin' all night and goin' to sleep after the sun came up, I finally woke up around two o'clock the next day. Before I opened my eyes, I said a prayer, wishin' that the day before was just a nightmare, but it wasn't. Long before reality set in, images of my dead cousin flashed through my mind. I'd murdered my own flesh and blood, and knew one day I would have to pay for my actions.

Lookin' on the other side of the bed, I realized that I was in bed alone, so I called out for Jade. However, there was no answer. When I reached for my cell phone on the night stand to call her, I stumbled across a note.

Rich,

I don't know how to say this, but I just can't bear the sight of you anymore. What you've done is unforgivable, and I think it's best that I leave you. Do not call me, or contact me. I don't ever want to see you again. You're a fucking monster and that was proven when you told me what you did and when you hit me for the second time. I enjoyed the time we spent together, but it's over. I have my whole life ahead of me and I don't think you fit the picture of what I want. Drama, kids with drama, and a wife is a bit much for me. So, this is goodbye and good luck.

Me

P.S. Don't worry, your secret is safe as long as you just let me go in peace.

Jade's words stung. I'd never had a woman leave me before 'til now, and this was the first time that I felt alone in my life. Even when I was in prison, I always had Carlos or Lisa by my side. Nelson was fuckin' my daughter, my son was in jail, Carlos was dead, and I hated Lisa. My life was a big mess and I didn't know what to do next. Thinkin' back to what Jade said, I didn't want to kill that bitch if she opened her mouth, but I was certainly prepared.

Grabbin' my phone to see if I could at least make amends wit' Denie, I saw I had twelve missed calls, five text messages, and two voicemails. They all were from Denie, Marisol, and the one person I didn't have the balls to talk to…Uncle Renzo. After readin' my text messages from Denie and how she was upset wit' me about Nelson, I listened to my messages.

Message 1-
March 8, 4:07 a.m.
Rich, this is Marisol. I've been calling Carlos all night. Mia is in the hospital. We've been here since one o'clock this morning. They're running tests and it doesn't look good. Her fever has been at 104, and I'm scared. You and Jade both aren't answering. Call me back, please. This is important.

Message 2-
March 9, 8:47 a.m.
Rich, it's your Uncle. Give me a call. Carlos isn't answering and Marisol needs him. Also, let me know if you all are coming back this week as planned. Give me a call as soon as possible.

Both of Carlos' daughters, Mia and Carmen, were my Goddaughters, so I needed to find out what was goin' on. Marisol was usually strong and for her to reach out to Uncle Renzo, I knew that this must've been somethin' serious. After debatin' for a few minutes, I finally built up the nerve to call Marisol.

"Hey, Rich," she answered.

"Hey, Marisol I got your message. What's goin' on?"

"Rich, Mia has had a fever that's been ranging anywhere

from 102-104 for two days, and I'm scared. She's never been this sick."

"Where are you, you still haven't heard from Los?"

"I'm at Mattel Children's Hospital UCLA. They had us come here this morning. Rich, they're sending in an Oncologist. They think Mia might have Leukemia. Rich, she's only four years old. I can't believe this. Carlos is not answering my calls or calling back. This is not like him."

"Damn, Marisol. I haven't talked to him since earlier yesterday, and you're right, he would've called by now."

"Where's Jade? I left her a message too, but she hasn't called me back," Marisol advised.

"She was upset because I was wit' Lisa yesterday dealin' wit' a situation wit' Denie. Since it was my birthday and she had our day planned out, she was mad because I got in late. She left this mornin'."

"Well, I talked to her yesterday evening and let her know I was going to take Mia to the hospital, so I don't understand why she isn't calling me back, at least to check on my daughter. Something just isn't right."

"Well, let me see what I can find out. 'Til then, keep me posted on Mia."

"Okay, hold on Rich. Lorenzo wants to talk to you."

My heart instantly sunk. I wasn't prepared to talk to him.

"Yeah Rich, did you get my message," Uncle Renzo asked.

"Umm…yeah, I just got up, but when I heard Marisol's message I called her first."

"Well, find out where Carlos is and get back to me by the end of the day. His wife needs him."

"You guys are worryin' me. Where do you think Los could be?" I asked playin' dumb.

"You would know before me. Are you still coming out here this week?"

"I'm not sure, yet. I got some stuff to deal wit' concerning Denie." I had no plans on bein' around Uncle Renzo anytime soon. There was no way I could face him right now.

"Well, handle your family business, so we can get focused on what keeps our families happy. The money."

"No doubt."

A chill ran through my body. I knew it was a matter of time before Uncle Renzo and Marisol found out that Carlos was dead. Or even worse, that I was the one responsible for his death. Never in my life had I felt like I was on borrowed time 'til now. I feared my Uncle more than the Feds, but I was determined to be on top at the end of it all.

CHAPTER TWENTY-TWO

Lisa

Three and a half weeks had passed since Carlos was gone and I still had trouble getting out of bed every day. With Denie being back home, now was the time that I wished I could have my house to myself again. Even seeing her everyday, I felt so alone. I would do anything just to see Carlos again. The only thing that seemed to comfort me was the voicemail Carlos left me a while ago. A voicemail that I listened to everyday, and was supposed to erase, but I was glad I hadn't. Hearing his voice made me smile. It was times like these that I missed talking to my father. I knew he would have all the right things to say, but I just couldn't find the courage to call. I'd tried on several occasions, but hung up every time the phone started ringing.

I yearned for Carlos' touch. Luckily, the day Denie almost caught us, he'd accidentally left his tank top, so his scent put me to sleep every night. It felt like he was there with me. For the past couple of weeks, I wondered everyday if I'd made a mistake by going to see him that night. I wondered if I wasn't so persistent would he still be alive. My Aunt Lita would always tell me, *"Everything happens for a reason. God don't make no mistakes."* This time I couldn't agree with Aunt Lita because Carlos dying was a mistake; a huge one. I just wanted to know, why my life had turned upside down once again? Just when I felt like things were getting better, something always came and fucked it up for me.

As I looked at my phone, I saw that Marisol had called me again, but I still didn't want to hear her voice. I knew she was just calling me to see if I'd heard any news about Carlos. She'd left me several messages, but I hadn't bothered to listen to any of them. Even if Carlos wasn't dead, there was nothing she could say to me. She'd allowed her friend to fuck my husband, and that shit was unforgivable. Feeling depressed again, I got up, went over to my vanity and pulled my plastic baggy of powder out of my drawer. Within seconds, I'd sniffed away my problems. One line at a time, I cried as I thought of how I felt when I was with Carlos. Getting high made me feel like nothing in the world mattered but our love. After doing two more lines, my house phone rang. It was Juan.

You have a collect call from- JUAN. To accept these charges please dial one.

I accepted the call since I'd been avoiding him as well. As much as I needed him, I just didn't know what he would think of me if he knew I was sleeping with someone he called his uncle. He had a way of sensing when something was wrong with me and getting it out of me, but I knew I couldn't avoid him much longer.

"Hi, son."

"Hey Ma. What's up, you don't love me anymore?"

I managed to crack a smile. "You know I love you. How you been?"

"How you been? Shit, I haven't seen you in almost a month."

"Well, I've been just trying to get my life in order and get this divorce thing final. Rich and I have been officially seperated for seven weeks now. I gotta get my list together outlining everything that I'm gonna ask for. "

"Damn, so you really going through with this?"

"Yes."

"So, what's going on with you, Ma? Denie said you haven't been yourself."

"You're listening to Denie now."

"No, I'm just worried about you. Denie has been mad at Rich and she's been visiting me more lately, since neither of you have."

"I'm sorry, Juan. It's just a lot going on." I tried to disguise my pain, but he heard it in my voice.

"Well, they moved me over to CTF now. It's right beside the main jail so now I can hug you and all that. Can you come see me today? I have something to talk to you about."

"I need a hug from my baby, too. Is it urgent for me to come today? You can't talk to me right now?"

"Ma, why are you avoiding me?"

"I'm not. I'll be there after I get dressed."

"Okay. I love you."

"I love you, too, baby."

I hung up the phone angry with Denie. What the hell could she have told him? *Damn, has she seen me doing a line*, I thought. If she wasn't at school I would've been ready to let her have it. We had been pretty much staying out of each other's way, but I didn't appreciate her worrying my son about me.

I got dressed and made my way to the jail to see Juan. There was a photo of me, Rich, Marisol and Carlos that we'd taken years ago on vacation that I kept in my wallet. Since Carlos and I were in the middle of the picture, it worked out perfect to cut Marisol and Rich out. Every time I got in the car, I put the picture by the odometer so I could look at him whenever I wanted. This was the first time that I had been out of the house in weeks besides going to the 7-11 every so often. Since my life was getting more and more complicated, I just had no desire to live anymore. I rode down 16th Street and crossed over to U Street so I could take Florida Avenue. As I crossed over 9th

Street, I thought about the last time I made that right turn to go and get Carlos' dinner. It was crazy how everything I did reminded me of him lately.

When I finally arrived at the jail, I was dreading the conversation with Juan, but knew I had to get it over with. Wondering what Denie told him about me had me a little worried, and I hoped like hell that I was just paranoid. However, I really missed my son, so a part of me needed to see him anyway.

Before walking in to the jail, I took a deep breath to prepare myself for the long, drawn out processing procedure that I had to encounter. However, to my surprise, things ran a little more organized. The correctional officer let me know that in the future I would have to have an appointment to visit Juan, but they would allow me to come in this time. After going through the metal detector, I caught the elevator to the second floor and waited for my son to come out. After looking around the room, I spotted Juan who was at the front of line. His uniform had gone from bright orange to navy blue, but he still looked handsome. I couldn't wait to give him a hug. As soon as he walked over to me, I grabbed him and held him tight kissing him all over his cheeks.

"Damn Ma, you miss me, huh?" he laughed.

"You look so handsome, how have you been holding up?"

Juan smiled. "I've been maintaining. How you been, woman? You look like you haven't had sleep in days."

"Juan, there's so much going on between me and your father."

"I talked to him when I hung up with you earlier and he said he'd pulled some strings to move me over here since the visits are conjugal. He said that he would be here to see me by the end of the week."

"I can't believe you called him."

"Yeah and the reason why is because I'm worried about you." Juan grabbed my hand.

"Worried about me for what?"

"Well, your daughter came to visit me so she could tell me about the bag of powder she found in your vanity drawer."

My heart almost stopped. I couldn't believe Denie had gone through my shit. "I don't know what she's talking about, Juan."

"Ma, be real with me. You don't even look like yourself. What's going on with you?"

I could no longer hold back my emotions and instantly broke down. The embarrassment I felt hurt so much. I never wanted my son to look down on me, and now he probably was. "Juan, there's so much going on. I need you to come home. Now that all this stuff is going on between me and your father, I don't know if he's still trying to help you get out."

"What's going on with y'all?"

"I will let him tell you."

"Damn Ma, when did we get to this point where you don't trust me?"

"It's not that, Juan. It's just...I can't say. Just do what you can to get home. I need you now more than ever."

"Ma, be honest are you using drugs?"

"No, Juan. I'm not."

"Okay, well I trust that you wouldn't lie to me, so I'm going to leave it alone. Maybe Denie was lying," Juan replied. "I'm trying my best to get home to you and Denie."

"Well, how?"

"I got a visit from the Feds. They offered me a deal to cooperate with them to help them bring Rich and Uncle Carlos in."

My eyes bulged. Juan obviously had no idea what had happened with Carlos ."Uncle Carlos?"

"Yeah. Speaking of Carlos, Denie said, nobody has heard from him in weeks. What's up with that? Rich wouldn't tell me anything."

"Yeah, umm…he hasn't been calling anybody back. I'm sure he's fine though." I had to get Juan back on track. "So, when did all this with the Feds happen?"

"Last week. I told them I didn't have any idea what they were talking about and I couldn't help them."

"Why not Juan? I need you and if you cooperating with the man who fucked up our lives and got you in this mess will bring you home, then so be it. Fuck Rich!"

Juan looked at me sideways. "Ma, are you tripping? I ain't no snitch. I chose this life and I'm going to take responsibility for my choices."

"Juan I need you. Just think about it."

"Ma, I can't believe you. What's going on with you?"

"I need you son. I need you home. Please do whatever it takes."

"But Ma, I wasn't raised to be a snitch. I'm a man, and men handle their business in the streets."

"So, are the streets more important than your mother? You're just like your father. You keep putting the streets first!" I yelled. I couldn't remember the last time, I'd gotten mad with him.

Juan looked around the room, then back at me. "Ma, lower your voice, you too loud."

"I don't give a fuck about these people in here."

"Alright. You need to get yourself together. I'll call you later."

Juan got up from the table, gave me a kiss on my cheek and left me sitting there by myself. When I saw the disappointment in his eyes, I knew that I'd fucked up. At that point, I considered telling him about what Rich did to Carlos, hoping then he would possibly reconsider cooperating with the Feds. Watching my son walk through the door, I cried. My heart and my mind were so heavy. I left the jail feeling worse than I felt when I arrived. I should've known that he was going to lecture me about something, but I would've never guessed that Denie had told him about my drug habit. I couldn't wait to let Denie have it for going through my shit. *How did she even know*? I thought.

While I drove home, I thought about Rich and wondered how he was coping with Carlos being gone. I wondered if he felt like I did or was his Spanish bitch keeping him company. I hadn't talked him since that night and knew that he hated me, but it was nothing I could do to change what happened. As long as he took care of his responsibilities as a father, we didn't have to speak at all.

When I pulled up to the house, there was a Pepco Energy truck in my driveway, and a man with a hard hat knocking on my door. I got out of the car in slow motion, feeling drained and approached the man to see what he wanted.

"Hello sir, how can I help you?"

"Ma'am, do you live here?"

"Yes, I'm Lisa Sanchez, what do you need?"

"Well, Mrs. Sanchez, you have an outstanding bill of $1,875.62 and I'm here to disconnect service if you're not prepared to pay."

I shook my head. "My bills should have been paid. There must be a mistake."

"There's no mistake. We've sent numerous notices, and haven't received a response."

"Let me give you a credit card to take care of the balance. Wait one second."

I walked back to my car, grabbed my purse, then grabbed one of my Visa's. After giving the guy my credit card, he called it into the office to obtain payment on the spot, but it was declined. I tried giving him two more cards, but they all declined as well. Completely humiliated, I pulled out my check book and wrote a check for the amount owed and prayed that the money was in the bank. I'd never experienced such embarrassment in my entire life. Rich had always made sure the bills were paid, so I didn't understand what was going on.

Once the guy left, I went straight to the bathroom because I had to pee. However, as I attempted to flush the toilet, nothing happened. After going over to the sink and turning on a dry faucet, it was obvious that the water had been turned off.

"Shit!" I yelled out. I was positive that Rich was to blame. I called him immediately.

"What do you want, Lisa?" he asked obviously irritated.

"Rich, what have you done? The water is cut off and the electric was about to get off, until I wrote a check. What's going on?"

"You and that house are no longer my concern. Whatever money you got left, you better make that shit work. I'm done with taking care of you."

"What about your daughter? She lives here too."

"Oh, I've got that covered. I'm gonna come back and get her, so she can stay wit' me at my mother's house."

"What? How am I supposed to survive?"

"Like everybody else. Go get a fuckin' job."

"I can't believe you. Wait until that divorce is final. I'm gonna…"

Rich cut me off. "See bitch, that's where you fucked up. I'm not givin' you a divorce. Ain't no judge gonna make me give you shit either. I'm not gonna take care of you anymore, but you're pretty much stuck to me for the rest of your miser-able-ass life. You think you're gonna be able to leave and turn on me? I don't think so."

"Why are you doing this? All of the bullshit that I had to put up with. It's not my fault things turned out the way they did."

"Lisa, I'm not tryin' to hear that shit. Figure out how you're gonna pay your shit on your own. Maybe if you stop fuckin' wit' that powder you would have money to pay your bills. Don't call me anymore!"

After he hung up on me, my thoughts on cursing Denie out changed fast. I had to get her on my side so she could get Rich to pay the bills until I came up with a better plan.

CHAPTER TWENTY-THREE

Rich

I was surprised when Denie declined the invitation to stay wit' me at my mother's house, especially since I had no intentions on takin' care of Lisa anymore. I'm sure she was still mad at me about Nelson, but I was determined to build our relationship back up. That meant me payin' the bills since Denie decided to stay at home. I didn't give a shit about Lisa, but there was no way I could have my daughter goin' without.

Bein' at my mother's house alone was a bit eerie, but I made the best out of it. Not havin' Jade anymore made me turn to Honey even more for sexual pleasure, but there was still a part of me missin'. It seemed as if everyone I loved had either left me or betrayed me. This was a time I definitely wished Juan and I had a better relationship. I'd paid my son a visit a few days ago after he called me worried about Lisa. Obviously, Denie had told him about her drug problem and he wanted answers.

I pretty much let him know that his mother fucked my man without tellin' him it was Carlos. I also didn't tell him that Carlos was probably the one who'd started her doin' the shit. He kept askin' me who the dude was, but I let him know that wasn't important. It was the principle of the matter. Of course he defended Lisa and got upset wit' me for disrespectin' her, but little did he know, she was the one who'd crossed the line. I promised Juan that I would try and visit him every week, but I'd been so busy wit' tryin' to get my money back in order, I hadn't been able to keep that promise. Six weeks had passed since I murdered Carlos, and my life had gone down hill.

"Damn, I miss Los," I said to myself.

It was a known fact by now that Carlos was officially missin' and I let Uncle Renzo know that I was doing all that I could to get to the bottom of it. His birthday was today, April 17th which made it hard to even think that he wasn't around to celebrate. Feelin' down and out, I got up to get my day started when the doorbell rung. When I looked out the upstairs window, to my surprise it was Uncle Renzo.

Oh shit what is he doin' here, I thought as I scrambled to get myself together, I had no idea he was comin', and he damn sure hadn't given me any type of warnin'.

I ran downstairs, opened the door, and greeted him wit' a big hug and a fake smile. However, he seemed a bit uncomfortable when he walked inside. I tried my best to read his body language.

"Uncle Renzo, I didn't know you were comin'. How long have you been in town?" I asked. I tried my best to conceal my nervousness.

"I just got in this morning. I've been in contact with any and everybody I know on the East Coast. No one has had any problems with Carlos. I don't know what could be the reason why he's nowhere to be found.

I quickly co-signed. "Yeah, especially wit' Mia bein' sick wit' Lukemia. I can't believe they diagnosed her wit' that shit. Carlos wouldn't just leave without lettin' me know anything. Are you sure Carlos and Marisol weren't goin' through anything?"

He shook his head back and forth. "No, not to my knowledge. Why do you say that?"

"Well, I know Carlos thought at one point Marisol was fuckin' around on him. Man, Unc, I'm just tryin' to look at it from all angles. I'm worried sick about him."

"No, and you should. I don't put anything passed anybody. No one has contacted me for ransom, so I'm confused on why someone would target him."

"Me, too. I'm hurtin' because I don't know what to think."

"Well Rich, there's something that I want to talk to you about. I couldn't do it over the phone, so I thought I would come here and talk to you in person."

Immediately, I saw my life flash before me. I was definitely slippin' because I didn't position my gun before I let Uncle Renzo in. Even at the age of sixty-two, I couldn't sleep on him.

"There are a lot of things that have gone on in this family even before you and Carlos were born that I need to talk to you about."

"Okay, well let's go into the livin' room." After sittin' on the couch, I gave my uncle a serious expression. "What's up, Unc?"

"Well, when you were a little under a year old, I went to jail and I sent your Aunt Celeste to go live with your mother and father. During that time, Celeste discovered she was pregnant with Carlos after I'd been in jail for a few months. I was released and my charges were dropped before Carlos was born." He suddenly stopped. "Are you listening to me, Rich?"

"Yeah, of course I'm listenin'."

"Well, a month or two later I got a call from your mother and she was in tears. She told me that she had caught Celeste and your father in bed together while I was in prison. She thought when I came home from prison that Celeste would go on her way and she wouldn't have to worry. What upset your mother the most was the resemblance in looks that you and Carlos possessed. She thought that I should get a blood test."

I was stunned at the news that my uncle was tellin' me and I knew exactly where he was goin' wit' everything. "So, what happened?"

"I ended up getting a test. That's when I found out that Carlos wasn't my son. I never said a word to anyone, but your mother. This was a secret that we kept all of these years."

I began to scratch my head. "So, are you sayin' that Los was really my brother?"

Uncle Renzo gave me a funny look. "What the fuck do you mean was? You're talking like he's no longer here."

I needed a quick comeback. "I didn't mean anything by that Unc.' I guess all this shit you're tellin' me, got me all fucked up."

"I hate that we kept this from you and Carlos all these years, but yes, Carlos is your only brother. I'm sterile, Rich. I'd been that way for years, and I don't think your Aunt Celeste could handle that."

"Why didn't you all tell me?" My voice was a little shaky. Killin' Carlos hurt even worse now. It felt like my heart had been ripped out my chest.

"There were so many times that I wanted to say something to you. Why do you think I stayed at odds with your father all the time? He betrayed me, so my punishment to him, was to raise both his boys to be just like me, the brother that he hated so much for choosing this life."

"So, Aunt Celeste never knew that you found out before she passed away?"

"No, she never knew that I was aware. I'm sure that she always had doubts. I'm just sorry that I never gave you all the chance at a life. I was so caught up in my own insecurities and selfishness that I deprived you and your brother of a real life. Now, look at you both. Carlos is missing, and you're so deep in the game, there's no turning back. I'm sorry."

"This can't be true. Uncle Renzo, this can't be true. No…my only brother. He wasn't my brother!"

"Yes, Rich, he's your brother. That's why you have to

find him. He needs to know."

"My mother didn't tell me I had a brother. Now he's dead and I can't tell him how much I love him."

"What do you mean dead? Rich, is there something that you aren't telling me?"

"No, I mean…he's probably dead," I quickly said. "Are there any more family secrets I don't know about? I can't believe you introduced me to this life because of a vendetta you had against my father."

"Rich, dammit, I'm sorry. I want to make things right. I would do anything for you boys. Carlos is still my son no matter what."

I was stunned. Couldn't say anything else at the moment.

"Well, I'm leaving, but I do expect you back in L.A. by the weekend. Marisol needs us both by her side until we figure out what's going on with your brother."

When he said my brother, the sounds of that made my heart bleed. I let Uncle Renzo out and decided that I needed my daughter by my side. I didn't plan on tellin' her the news I learned. I felt so alone, so I decided to give her a call.

"Yes, Daddy." She didn't sound excited to hear from me.

"How are you, Baby Girl?"

"Busy, how are you?"

"Wishin' my daughter wasn't still mad at me and wasn't puttin' another nigga in front of her father."

"Oh, like you've put your way of life in front of me all these years."

Her comment hurt. "Denie, I just need you right now."

"I have an exam in the morning and I'm studying right now. I'll come to see you tomorrow."

"Okay, that's all I ask."

"Bye, Dad."

I sat on the sofa and stared at my phone. Tryin' so hard to be strong and not call Jade, I called Marisol instead to check on Mia.

"Hello Rich, any news on my husband."

"Not yet. Where are you?"

"I'm at the hospital. I don't know what to do. I've always been strong and been able to deal with anything thrown my way, but this is something I just can't handle. Where's my husband?" she cried. "I just pray that he's alive!"

"Yeah I know. I hate to think the worst," I replied.

"Oh my God, please don't. I don't wanna think that way either."

"Look, Marisol, you shouldn't be alone at a time like this. I'm here for you. I'll fly back by the weekend okay? In the meantime be strong and give those babies a kiss for me. Oh, and if Carlos calls, call me right away."

"Okay, Rich. I love you."

"I love you, too."

"Oh, Rich if you talk to Lisa, please tell her to call me. She won't return any of my calls. Maybe she has a clue that'll help us find Carlos?"

I got extremely quiet for a moment. "Will do."

CHAPTER TWENTY-FOUR

Lisa

I woke up with an upset stomach, feeling like I had to throw up. Back and forth to the bathroom all morning, finally I let it all out. It was just clear mucus, no food at all. I had Denie bring me some toast and ginger ale to settle my stomach. As I laid in bed trying to get myself together, I began to have so many evil thoughts, and my head and heart both were heavy. My mind had been working overtime on different ways to destroy Rich's life the way he'd destroyed mine. The divorce was obviously something mild and not enough to destroy Rich for good. Besides, we had to wait too long for the actual court date, so after much consideration I thought I'd hit him where it would hurt the most; with his pride and joy…Denie.

She'd been in heaven ever since I allowed her to see Nelson; something I knew Rich would never approve of. I gave Denie and Nelson my word, that it would be our secret. That was all a part of my plan to keep Denie at my house so Rich could continue to pay the bills. He'd made it very clear that Denie would be eighteen this year and as soon as she left for college, he wouldn't have to worry about doing anything else for me. Little did he know, I had a plan that was gonna change his life forever. He was gonna pay for all of the pain that he'd put me through over the years, especially taking Carlos away from me.

My phone rang and at first I thought it was Marisol. She still continued to call daily. I knew she was just calling to see if I knew anything about Carlos, so to avoid interrogation I ignored her completely. When I looked at the caller ID, I sighed. It was Rich.

"Yes."

"Why haven't you returned any of Marisol's calls?"

"What do you think, Rich? Unless you want me to tell her where her husband really is thanks to you?"

"Stop talkin' reckless on this phone, you stupid bitch. Your Goddaughter Mia is in the hospital, so that's why she's callin'. Didn't you get any of her messages?"

"I didn't listen to them. What's wrong with Mia?"

"She was diagnosed with Leukemia. I'm flyin' back to L.A in a couple of days. I don't expect you to fly out there, but Marisol really needs you right now."

"Oh my God. I didn't know."

"Well, if you answered the damn phone you would know."

"Listen, you need to calm the fuck down."

"Just call her back!" Rich yelled then hung up.

He obviously still hated me, but the feelings were mutual. Thinking about the devastating news, I felt really bad for Mia. I loved those kids and I knew it was extremely hard for Marisol since Carlos wasn't there by her side. Putting our differences aside, I decided to give her a call once I got in my car to go see my lawyer.

"Hello."

"Marisol, it's me. I just talked to Rich. How's Mia doing?"

"Lisa, she's in really bad shape. She's gonna go through her first round of chemo next week."

I could tell she'd been crying. "Damn, I really hate to hear that. How are you holding up?"

"It's a lot on me. I've lost twenty-five pounds since she first got sick. It's been tough, especially since Carlos is missing." She sounded miserable. "Have you talked to him?"

"No, I haven't. Give Mia a kiss for me and keep me posted on her condition."

"Thanks for calling me Lisa, it means a lot."

"Well, you've been there for me all these years, through my troublesome marriage. Now, it's time for me to be there for you."

"Lisa, I'm really sorry about Jade and Rich. Please believe me, I didn't know they were together," Lisa said.

"It's cool," I lied. I was still bitter about that shit, and had no plans to forgive Marisol for not telling me about the happy couple.

"Take care, and try to visit your Goddaughter whenever you get a chance."

"Okay and I'll keep her in my prayers."

I hung up the phone really feeling sorry for Mia and not really giving a damn about Marisol. If Carlos were here, he definitely would've been by her side every step of the way. I loved Mia and wished her no harm, but this would've certainly made Marisol and Carlos' marriage even stronger, so in a way I'm glad he wasn't around. We might not have been together if he'd known that night his daughter was sick. Suddenly, my evil side kicked in when I thought, *would I rather Carlos be dead without me or alive with Marisol.*

Nursing my upset stomach, I snacked on some saltine crackers and a Canada Dry, which seemed to help a bit. As I was getting in the car, Jermaine sent me a text to let me know the owner of the shop he worked in was having a huge party at Club Layla. I instantly contemplated about not going because I wasn't in the mood to be around anybody.

Then again maybe I should have a night out on the town with Jermaine. I thought about how he really knew how to cheer

me up, especially Jermaine's friend Dike. I laughed to myself
thinking about how much fun I had with them the last time I got
my hair done. After thinking for a few more minutes, I finally
replied back to Jermaine telling him that I would let him know if
I was going by eight. Even though I couldn't tell him, my deci-
sion really depended on how much I got done for the big show-
down, *Operation Destroy Rich.*

My lawyer's office was on K Street in downtown D.C.
which didn't take me long to get to at all. The only thing that
was annoying was trying to find parking. All of the lots were
full, so I had to get change at the hot dog stand and park on the
street. After feeding my meter, I entered the office building's re-
volving doors and headed toward the elevators. However, I decided to take the stairs since the elevator was taking so long.

When I walked into the office, I was greeted by the re-
ceptionist, Ginger, who was such a dingy blond white girl. She
was originally from Houston and had a sweet southern personal-
ity as well as an accent.

"Hello, Mrs. Sanchez, Mr. Leach is expecting you. I'll
buzz him right now and let him know you're here."

"Thanks, Ginger. How's your daughter doing?"

"She's fine, getting tall. Did your son get released yet?"

"No, that's one of the reasons I'm here."

"Well, I'm praying for you."

I smiled. "Thanks. I need all the prayer I can get."

When she called Mr. Leach, he was ready for me to come
inside. His office was small, but ran professionally. There were
two other lawyers who practiced at his law firm, his sister
Sherise and another lawyer Evelyn Sharpe. All of the hustlers
kept Evelyn on retainer if they couldn't afford Mr. Leach because she was known for getting all of them off. When I walked
in, Mr. Leach greeted me with a hug as usual.

"Hi, Mr. Leach," I greeted.

"Lisa, how many times do I have to tell you to call me
John?" he asked after sitting down at his desk. "So, where are
we with everything? Are you still going through with the di-

vorce?"

I thought about what Rich said about not trying to give him one, but I wasn't about to give up. "Yes, I am. Is there anyway we could rush things along? I really need to get on with my life."

"Well, D.C. law requires that you all be separated at least six months before you file. You know the whole reason for the separation is so couples can determine how assets will be split, who will get custody of the children, who's responsible for what debt, things like that."

"I don't care about any of that. He can have everything, and Denie can go live with him. I just want my divorce. Hell, we've been separated for more than six months." It didn't matter to me if John knew I was lying. I had to get rid of Rich...fast.

John pushed up his glasses. "Why didn't you tell me that in the beginning? We could've taken another route."

"Okay, so now that you know, I need you to file for my divorce asap," I replied.

"You know, Mr. Sanchez didn't sound too happy about this divorce when we spoke over the phone," John informed.

"I don't care about that. Just do what I asked!"

John quickly wrote something down on a piece of paper. "Okay. I'll see what I can do. Is that all you needed today?"

"No, I need you to get my son out of jail."

"Well, I've been working on that, but your son is facing some serious charges. We might have to look at a plea deal."

"I don't want him to spend another day in jail, so how much do I have to pay to make this go away."

"Lisa, I would do anything for you, but it's a little more complicated."

When John went on to explain the details of the case, it didn't sound good. With his charges, Juan was gonna have to take a five year plea deal at the minimum. I tried over and over to explain to Juan that his only route was to turn against Rich, but he still hadn't given me an answer. I even wrote him a letter the other day letting him know how much I needed him. Maybe the more I pressed him, he would eventually see that giving Rich up, was the best answer.

After we laid out Juan's options, I thanked John for his time and told him I would be in touch. Walking back to my car, I began to think about the paperwork from all the life insurance policies that I'd reviewed the day before. Hopefully Rich hadn't stopped paying the premiums because I was the beneficiary for him, Juan and Denie's polices. With the plan I had in mind, even if Rich didn't give me any money, I was going to be straight.

On my way home, I stopped by Home Depot off of Rhode Island Avenue to pick up some items I was going to need for my big project. Even though I wasn't feeling well, a sudden adrenaline rush came over me. I was finally standing up for myself and doing this not only for me, but for Carlos, too.

Pulling up into the Home Depot parking lot, I found a great parking spot right in front. I pulled my list out and went in the store with a huge smile. I hadn't even made it down the first aisle before some guy in a bright, orange apron walked up to me and started to flirt. However, instead of brushing him off, I used him to my advantage to let him help me with my mission.

"Okay, what's your name again?" I asked.

"Willis, and yours?"

"Lisa. I'm so happy you're helping me because I would've been lost in this huge store. Now, here's my list. I need some gray duct tape, 100 feet of rope, two razor blades, some very sturdy nails, screws, an electric drill, and a good screwdriver."

"Gosh, pretty lady. What are you planning on doing with all this?"

"My husband and I have a huge project at home."

"Well, if you weren't such a beautiful lady, I would assume you and your husband were going on some type of caper, or something."

I laughed. "You're funny. So, which way do we go?"

Willis was a great help. He helped me pick out all of my tools, but I had to listen to him flirting with me the entire time.

After the cashier rang me up, Willis helped me load my car and
I was off.

     Nobody was ready for what was about to go down. Rich
wanted to fuck with me and think he was going to ruin my life,
but that shit wasn't about to happen. With what I had up my
sleeve, it was definitely going to destroy his life forever. I was a
scorned woman out for revenge and I planned to do whatever it
took to let Rich feel all the years of pain that I felt. There was no
time for playing victim. I was ready to settle the score once and
for all.

CHAPTER TWENTY-FIVE

Lisa

When I got home, I left all of the stuff that I'd bought at Home Depot in the trunk. I then checked the mailbox, and smiled when I realized that Juan had written me back. I couldn't wait to read his letter. Walking in the house, Denie and Nelson were in the family room playing Wii. They were scared shitless when I walked in. I guess living on edge and dodging Rich was quite stressful. After teasing them, I started up the stairs toward my room. I wanted to be alone when I read the letter, but as soon as I hopped on the bed, Denie walked in.

"Ma, do you mind if I go to Atlantic City with Nelson?"

"Are you crazy…no. It's bad enough that I let you see him behind Rich's back."

"Ma, it's spring break and we want to do something fun without my father catching us."

I shook my head. "I don't know if that's a good idea, Denie. Your father has a lot of business partners in A.C. and they might see you."

"But they don't know me. Please, Ma," Denie pleaded.

I let out a heavy sigh. "You better be back in the morning. We have somewhere important to go tomorrow."

The smile Denie displayed instantly lit up the room. "Thanks, Ma. You're the best." She quickly kissed me on the cheek before running out of the room. "Nelson, she said yes!" I heard her yell out.

She was packed and out the door in less than twenty minutes. It killed me to be so nice to her after she'd snooped through my room and told Jaun I'd been using, but it was all part of the plan. I had to play her close in order for everything to work out. I didn't give a damn about what Denie did anymore. It was all about me and my son. As I laid on my bed, I turned on the T.V. and got comfortable before opening the letter.

Hello Ma,

I'm not gonna talk a hole in your head. I just wanted to tell you that I love you and whatever you're going through out there nothing is worth you stressing yourself. It hurt me when Denie told me you had a problem. I've always known you to be strong, so I've been in here wondering what finally pushed you to this point. Ma, you've been through so much more and have overcome the worse. I want you to be happy so I've been doing some thinking about what you said, and I'm just gonna say, everything is gonna work out. I'll be home sooner than you think to take care of you. I might be home before you get this letter. Those people don't play. They work fast. I'm going against everything I believe in, to be there because you need me. I love you. Give my sister a hug for me.

Juan

A huge smile spread across my face when I realized Juan had finally listened. Now, I was ready to celebrate. After texting Jermaine to tell him I was on board and to come pick me up, I decided to take a power nap to get over my nausea so I could be energized. Not having to worry about Rich's controlling ways was a good feeling. I needed to get my mind off things especially missing Carlos.

When I woke up a few hours later, I did a few lines then

hopped in the shower, ready for a night out on the town. This was the first time since Carlos died that I wanted to look sexy, even though I really wasn't the partying type. I'd gone to the Black Hole back in the day to see Rare Essence perform, but was escorted out by Rich once he found out I was there. Another time I went to a C-Bone Cabaret and before I could really begin to enjoy myself, someone had called Rich and I was embarrassed in less than thirty minutes, with him causing a scene.

I laid out my Lamb short, black dress and decided that the exposed side detailing was exactly the look I was going for. Now, it was time to pick out the right shoes to complement my look. I decided on my blue, studded Jimmy Choo peep-toe, pumps. Right when I was about to put my dress on, I felt the sudden urge to vomit again; something I'd been doing off and on for two days. The one night I was ready to go out, I was trying to get sick, which pissed me off.

Running to the toilet, I placed my head in the bowl, and let out everything I'd put in my mouth that day. I knew Jermaine was on his way to pick me up and I didn't want him to think that I was faking, so I had to hurry up. Trying to figure out what the problem was, I thought back to the seafood I had two days ago, but quickly dismissed that because I never got sick when Jerry's Seafood famous Crab Bomb was involved. *Maybe it's from the powder*, I thought to myself. After all, I had stepped up my usage ever since the incident with Carlos. I even had to go out and find my own supply. Since Rich sold the shit, I tore the house up looking for a possible stash one day, but couldn't find anything.

After I cleaned myself up, I attempted to try and straighten my hair with my Chi flat iron, then put on my clothes. I was determined to work through the sickness. Using my MAC cosmetics, I gave myself a smoky eye with a hint of purple then applied my Viva La Glam gloss. It was time to have fun, even though I still felt like shit.

When the doorbell rang minutes later, I ran downstairs. "One second!" I yelled.

"What's up, Jermaine?" I asked opening the door.

"Wow, Miss Thang, you look good...from the neck down. What's wrong? You look like a hot mess."

"I feel awful. I've been vomiting for days."

"Girl, you might want to call it a night. You know that damn Swine Flu stuff is coming back around. I seen it on the news. I can't believe them Mexicans dun brought that stuff over here. You sure you ain't been around Rich's family?"

"No, boy, you're crazy. And Rich's family is not Mexican."

"Well, maybe you and Rich are about to have a baby or something,"

"No, me and Rich aren't having shit. Oh my gosh. I hope I don't have that Swine Flu mess."

"Well, it's contagious," Jermaine said with concern, but made it clear he wasn't trying to stay around and catch anything. "So, Sista I love you and everything but I'm about to go. You need to stay in the house and take care of whatever it is you got. Call me tomorrow."

"Okay, I'm sorry for ruining your night and making you drive all the way over here."

"Girl, you're fine. Feel better," Jermaine said after he gave me two air kisses and left.

Scratching my head, Jermaine put something on my mind that I hadn't thought about. With all the drama in my life, it didn't even dawn on me that my period hadn't made an appearance this month. As much as I'd been feeling sick, I felt it was important that I went to the store to buy a pregnancy test immediately. I didn't even bother to change my clothes before I grabbed my keys and headed to the nearest 24 hour CVS.

After driving the entire way in silence, I pulled into the parking lot and began to feel butterflies in the pit of my stomach. *Could I be expecting Carlos' child?* I thought as I opened my car door. Walking into the store, I ventured down aisle seven, to the family planning section. I hadn't bought a pregnancy test since Denie's situation three years back, so I was def-

initely out of sync. Possibly having a baby inside of me was all
that I could think of as I scanned the numerous test brands. I
was scared and nervous all at the same time. After grabbing a
digital EPT, I approached the line to be rung up.

"Hi, Mrs. Sanchez," the young girl at the counter said.

I stared at her for a second. "Hello." I had no idea who
she was, and hated that anybody recognized me.

"I'm Denie's friend, Latrese from Jefferson, remember?"

"Oh, hi Latrese, how have you been?"

"I've been good, trying to keep up my grades so I can get
a scholarship this year for college."

"That's good baby, you take care."

"You do the same, nice to see you," she said as she
handed me my bag.

When I got in the car to drive home I felt so humiliated.
Suppose Denie's friend tells her what I purchased, I thought.
Shit, I don't need anymore damn drama with Rich. As soon as I
got home, I went straight to the bathroom to take the test. Putting the narrow stick into my urine stream, I prayed to God that
if it was meant for me to have a part of Carlos, then I needed his
help to get me through it all.

My mind raced with emotion while I waited for my results for the longest three minutes of my life. When time was
up, the results read, PREGNANT.

CHAPTER TWENTY-SIX
Lisa

After crying myself to sleep the night before, I finally got some rest. If Denie hadn't awakened me when she got in from Atlantic City, I would've still been asleep. It was almost one o'clock in the afternoon, and I still felt out of it. I had a big day planned and almost lost focus. Now more than ever, I had more reason to destroy Rich. *There's no way in hell he's gonna come between me and my baby*, I thought to myself as I was faced with my new reality. I looked into my full length mirror and stood sideways as I rubbed my belly and smiled. There was a part of Carlos growing inside of me. Glancing over at the entrance of my room, I saw Denie staring at me.

"What are you doing?" she asked with a confused expression.

"Nothing, what do you mean?"

"Why were you rubbing your stomach like that?"

"No reason."

"Are you pregnant?"

"No, I'm not Denie, so don't go telling Juan or your father any false information."

"Why would I do that? I have my own business to worry about."

"I doubt that, since you went into my drawer and told Juan what you found."

Denie looked as if she was trying to figure out what to say. "Ma, I'm sorry, but I had to figure out what was wrong with you. I knew you would be pissed, but I had to do something."

"Why didn't you just come to me?"

Denie shook her head. "I don't know. I just didn't know how."

I had to play it off how pissed I was. "I guess I can understand why you did it. Maybe from here on out, you can come and talk to me instead of running to your brother and father."

"I can do that," Denie assured me.

"Good. Now, go get yourself together, because I'm taking you out today, somewhere special."

"Where?"

"It's a surprise, and we're leaving in an hour."

"How should I dress?"

"Cute. Heels. Make-up. You know, how the Sanchez girls do it," I replied.

"Oh, Okay." Denie sashayed out of my room looking confused.

As I began to get myself together, Denie came back in my room all dolled up. She had on some tight True Religion jeans, a black off the shoulder top, a wide studded belt and studded caged shoes to match. I could hoola hoop with her oversized hot pink Betsey Johnson earrings. She looked cute. I laughed to myself as I could only imagine where Denie thought we were going.

"So, how do I look, and why aren't you dressed yet?" Denie twirled around.

"You look fine, and I am dressed."

"Black tights, a hoodie, and some tennis shoes? You look like you're going to the gym," Denie observed.

"Don't worry about me. Today is my special day for you.

Come here. Let me put your hair up in a ponytail. It'll be cute like this."

I went over to my jewelry box and grabbed my Tiffany diamond barrette. I hadn't worn it since that awful day in November, but this was a special date and I thought it was appropriate for Denie to wear it.

"Ma, are you serious? You've never even let me touch it before."

"Well, I want you to wear it now."

After placing the barrette in her hair, I quickly grabbed a pair of shears from my vanity drawer while Denie's back was turned then put them in my Gucci backpack. "Okay, I'll meet you downstairs."

"Hurry up. I'm excited. The suspense about where we're going is killing me," Denie said.

"Oh, I'm excited too," I replied before watching Denie walk out the room.

I wanted to do a few lines before I left to get me pumped up. Even though I knew it wasn't good for the baby, I needed something to help me get through this. After pulling out my silver jewelry tray from under the bed, I grabbed the bag of powder from one of my shoe boxes along with a crisp dollar bill. Since I was pressed for time, luckily the bill was already rolled up in the shape of a straw. After dumping some of the coke on the tray, I used my pinky finger to make three lines, held my head down then began to inhale.

Within seconds, the powerful drug entered my blood stream and gave me the rush that I desperately needed. The more time passed, I could feel my heart rate start to increase, along with a warm sensation; a sensation that instantly made me excited. I looked at the rest of the coke. "Shit, I need this feeling to last so maybe I'll take you with me," I said, placing the small bag in the front pocket of my hoody.

"Ma, let's go!" Denie called out.

"I'm coming!" Knowing we had to hurry up, I quickly put the tray and dollar bill up and headed downstairs.

Right before walking out the door, the house phone rang, but I ignored it as we headed out the door. I even turned off my cell until it was time to make the one phone call that was going to get the ball rolling. As we pulled out of the garage, Denie looked a bit uncomfortable which worried me a little. I only had one shot to pull this off, and it was important that I stayed on task. We rode through Rock Creek Park and passed over East West highway onto Jones Bridge Road. I thought it was best that we went the back way to I-495. The car was filled with an awkward silence until I turned up the radio and we started to jam to 93.9 WKYS. Denie loved go-go and turned up the radio as soon as she heard Wale's song, *Pretty Girls,* blaze through the speakers.

After a thirty-five minute ride to our destination, we pulled up to the abandoned warehouses on Ritchie Road that brought back the worst memories I'd ever encountered in my life. Pulling around to the back of the buildings, I glanced over at Denie as she began to text on her cell phone.

"What's going on? Where are we?" she asked after finally looking up.

"Does it matter? This is our day. Can you put your phone up?"

Denie held an awkward expression. "Ma, what are you up to?"

"Well Denie, there's a lot about the man you call your father that you don't know. I want to open your eyes to a lot of things and let you know why things are the way they are."

"I thought you said today was about us, not my father."

"Oh, you have no idea. Come on and get out of the car, let me show you something."

Before we got out of the car, I turned my phone back on and sent Rich a text to let him know what was about to go down.

Rich, how much is ur daughter's life worth to u? If u want to see her alive again, meet me at the warehouses on Ritchie Rd. U should know the place. U have 30 mins. Bring at least 300k to save her. This is not a joke.

When we got out of the car, Denie's face was puzzled, especially when I went to the back of the truck and put all of my tools in my backpack. As we approached the building, the door was already ajar which made it easy to get in.

Denie stopped. "I don't wanna go in."

"Stop being such a baby. Trust me, it's a surprise," I tried to assure her as we walked inside.

After closing the door behind us, luckily there was tons of light coming in from all the dusty windows so we could see. I didn't waste time surveying to the room where I was raped for hours. The smell of funk was still in the air, and everything was still in place. The iron bed, handcuffs and all. My throat started to get tight as if I was having a difficult time gasping for air. However, I was determined to go through with my plan so, it was important that I stayed focus. If I was going to get paid so me, my new baby, and my son would be okay, this was something that I had to do.

"Ma, where are we? What is this place?" Denie questioned.

"Okay, first of all call me Lisa. This Ma shit stops now."

"Why? What's wrong with you? I want to leave."

"You're not going anywhere. See, I'm about to walk you through all the pain I've experienced over the years. I want you to feel my pain. You need to understand how much your father has put me through. All these years I sacrificed taking care of you and you never showed me any respect. If you really need to know Miss Denie, this is the place where I was held for ransom while I was raped and sodomized for hours. Your father chose to fuck my friend and her man kidnapped me to get back at Rich. This is just the beginning."

As Denie stood there in shock, I started emptying my backpack on the desk then grabbed my chrome .380 and ordered Denie to get on the cum stained bed. Denie's face was filled with fear as she started crying and did as she was told. I then made her handcuff herself to the bed so she couldn't escape. She looked like she wanted to try and find a way to get out, but quickly realized I was serious and it wasn't a game. I tried my best to calm down, but felt myself getting emotional.

"I need a hit," I said pulling out my infamous bag. Dipping my index finger inside the coke, I was able to get some power inside the back of my finger nail, then led it to my nose. After inhaling, I did the same routine two more times until my nose began to run and my tongue became numb. Denie looked at me in awe. "Don't look at me like that. See, you're here because Rich needs to feel the same pain that I fucking went through a few months ago."

"Ma, what are you about to do to me. You're scaring me." I'd never seen such fear in Denie.

"I told you stop calling me, Ma! I'm not your fucking mother. Your father cheated on me when Juan was only three years old. He fucked someone else, and claimed the condom broke when she left your ass on our door step. I've had you since you were two months old." I could tell Denie was beyond floored because she never said a word. I walked over and stood in her face. "And do you know your father never even fucking apologized to me. He never said I'm sorry for having a baby by another woman!"

"Okay, now those drugs got you delusional."

"Bitch, shut the fuck up and listen to me. He made me tell everyone you were my baby. I loved you Denie, but deep down inside I looked at you every day and saw the mistake my husband made tricking on the streets. You're nothing to me, but a mistake that I should've left on that step."

"Are you fucking serious?"

"Shut up!" I yelled then hit her across the face with my fist.

I went to the backpack and grabbed the shears and the razor blade out of my bag, ready to go to work. Denie yelled for help and tried to squirm and kick, but I managed to tie both of her feet to the bed. After grabbing the scarf I'd gotten from home, I stuffed it in Denie's mouth then placed duct tape over it. Her sounds of fear were immediately muffled. At that moment, I started ripping her shirt off then took the razor blade and ran it straight down her jeans. Once her legs were exposed, I could tell I'd cut her in several places from the blood that oozed from her wounds. Denie cried and screamed, but too bad no one could hear her.

"Didn't I say shut up? Just face it, you're going to die if your father doesn't show up with that money. Hell, even if he does show up, I might kill you anyway since I got that insurance policy. That money is about to take me, my new baby, and your brother far away from this place. Since Rich loves you so much, he'll make a way. Let me see, I guess this long beautiful hair of yours that your father loves is going to be the first to go."

Denie pleaded through the tape for me to stop, but I had no mercy. I grabbed my shears and snipped off her ponytail just like my attacker had done to me. *Perfect*, I thought to myself as I looked at her new choppy look. Just when I was about to torture Denie some more, my cell phone started ringing. I knew exactly who it was.

"What?" I answered.

"Lisa, where the fuck is my daughter?" Rich screamed.

"Nigga, fuck you. If you want to see your daughter alive, I hope you got that money. You know where I am!"

I had too much on Rich for him not to oblige my demands. No matter what, it was all about revenge for all my years of suffering and pain, and I was going to end up on top. It was my turn for Rich to play by my rules.

CHAPTER TWENTY-SEVEN

Rich

After hookin' up wit' Honey in Baltimore, I was on my way to the airport to visit Marisol for a couple of days when I got a text message from Denie that concerned me.

Daddy, I think Ma is high off something. She's acting weird.

I text Denie back and asked her what was goin' on and she told me that Lisa said she was takin' her somewhere special. I told Denie to text me when they got to their destination, but when she never hit me back, I knew to worry. Lisa had definitely turned into a different person over the past few weeks, so it was no tellin' what she was up to. I started callin' Lisa soon after, but she didn't answer. My worry turned to panic when Lisa finally responded wit' a text message that made me turn my car around and head straight to the place where Lisa was kidnapped. She demanded money from me which she definitely wasn't gettin'. I didn't want to imagine Lisa harmin' Denie, but she knew that was the one way to get to me. I knew at this point, she'd finally snapped. Somethin' had pushed her to the edge. I knew I needed to act fast to rescue my daughter from whatever

Lisa was up to.

I snapped out of my daze when my phone rang. Thinkin' it was Lisa, I quickly answered without lookin' to see who it was.

"I hope you came to your fuckin' senses," I blurted out.

"What are you talking about?" Juan asked.

"Oh, Juan. I thought you were someone else," I said. I didn't want him to know what was goin' on. "What's up? You didn't call me collect. Are you on a three-way call? You know I don't like that shit."

"No, I'm calling from a pay phone. They just let me out," Juan informed.

"Just got out? How the hell did you get out?" I asked.

"It's a long story."

"Long story. What the fuck does that mean?" Before Juan could respond, I decided to deal wit' his situation later. Right now, I had to find Denie. "Never mind, son. We'll discuss that later."

"I'm calling to see what's up with Ma. Where is she?"

I decided to let him in on everything just in case he could talk some sense into Lisa's deranged-ass. "Man, she's trippin'. She took Denie to the warehouse where she was raped. I don't know what she's up to, but I can tell you now, if she hurts Denie, it's gonna be a problem. Where you at?"

"Well, I just got out, but I've been calling her all morning and she hadn't answered. Can you come get me?"

"I can't, I'm almost in Maryland. Look, catch a cab to your grandmother's house. I stored a spare key to her car under her flower pot in the front yard. There's a $100.00 bill in the glove compartment along wit' a gun under the passenger's seat just in case you need it. Grab your grandmother's car and haul ass over to Ritchie Road. There are some abandoned warehouses that you can't miss near Central Avenue. Maybe you can talk some sense into your mother before she does somethin' stupid."

"What the fuck? Alright. I'll be there as fast as I can."

Before hangin' up, I told Juan to hurry. All I could think

about was that I would kill Lisa if she brought any harm to my daughter. The thought of Denie bein' hurt made my adrenaline rush. I sped through lights and drove on the shoulder of the road to get to my daughter as fast as I could. When I finally made it to the warehouses, I drove around the back, and instantly spotted Lisa's truck. Wit' bad thoughts and memories already floodin' in my mind about the location, I grabbed my gun from under the seat, then took a deep breath before hoppin' out. I didn't want to kill Lisa, but knew if it was between her or Denie, she had to go.

Quietly, I entered the back door and looked around to make sure Lisa wasn't tryin' to sneak up on me. After walkin' around, I finally heard Lisa's voice, and walked toward that direction. Wit' my gun in my hand, I crept to the door ready to blast her ass as I listened to her talk shit to my daughter. After hearin' her slap Denie around a few times, I pushed the door open wit' the tip of my gun. However, I was surprised to see just how quickly Lisa reacted because I hadn't even taken two steps inside before she turned around and drew her gun.

"Where the fuck is my money, Rich?" Lisa asked.

I tried to play dumb. "What money?"

I looked over at my naked daughter and couldn't believe what I was seein'. My baby girl was handcuffed by both her feet and hands with blood all over her legs. Both of her eyes were black and swollen, so I didn't even know if she could see me. I was paralyzed wit' emotions of anger, but most of all pain.

"Lisa, what have you done to my baby?"

"I haven't done anything…yet. Now, where the fuck is my money, Rich?" Lisa walked over to Denie and snatched the tape from her mouth, but made sure to keep her gun pointed at me. She ordered me to sit on the floor Indian style and kick my gun to the other side of the room. I knew Lisa had snapped, but what I didn't know was what she was capable of next, so I did what she told me to do. I knew Juan was on his way, and it was only a matter of time before he would put an end to all of this.

"Daddy, help me," Denie begged.

For the first time in my life, I felt there was nothin' I could do to help my daughter. "Okay Lisa you win. Just let Denie go. I know you're upset wit' me, but damn Lisa, how could you hurt our daughter this way. What are you tryin' to prove?"

"Muthafucka that's your daughter, not mine. She knows Rich. Tell your daughter the truth for once in your life. Tell her I'm not her mother," Lisa demanded.

"Why are you doing this? Why would you tell Denie this shit? You want my daughter to hate me that much?" I couldn't believe her. "Are you doin' this shit because of Carlos? He wasn't your fuckin' husband Lisa, I am."

"You will never understand what Carlos and I shared. I loved him and you took him away from me. You have no idea what you've done to me."

I had to laugh. "You loved him? That's funny. Well, I doubt if he loved you. He really fucked you up wit' those drugs if you think that shit."

"No, Rich. You fucked me up. All the things that you did to me turned me into this person. The lying, the cheating, you turned me into this person!"

"Stop blamin' me for this shit. You chose this life, Lisa. You knew what came wit' the territory of fuckin' wit' a nigga like me. The money…the cars, you loved that shit, remember. You loved this life when you got respect in the streets for bein' my wife."

"And that same respect in the street turned around and got me raped and kidnapped." At that point, she turned to Denie. "Open your legs!"

Denie looked at me like she needed my approval first. The fear in her eyes was unbearable to look at.

"Open your legs!" Lisa ordered again. This time, Denie slowly did as she was told. Wit' one hand on her gun, Lisa grabbed a screwdriver that was layin' on the bed and held it near Denie's open vagina.

I shook my head. "Lisa, I'm not gonna sit here and watch

you rape my daughter wit' that thing," I said. "You'll have to shoot me first."

"Why not. You sat and watched me get raped. It's just her pussy. Life goes on. Isn't that what you told me after what those bastards did to me!" Lisa held the screwdriver by Denie's body that was shakin' uncontrollably.

"Lisa, I'm sorry I said all those hurtful things to you," I replied. "If it's a divorce you want, then fuck it. I'll sign the papers. You can have everything. The house...the cars. I'll even pay alimony. Just don't hurt my daughter."

"Fuck you, Rich! You had two babies on me. How much did you want me to take all these years?" Lisa asked. "But you know what, now the tables are about to turn because I'm pregnant with your cousins baby."

My eyes widened. All the nice shit that I'd just said, was no longer an option. Just thinkin' about Carlos made me angry. "You stupid bitch, Los wasn't my cousin, he was my brother. Because of you, I killed my brother!"

"Stop lying. You'll say anything to keep me from hurting your precious Denie," Lisa replied.

"I'm not lyin'. He was my brother, and because of you, he's dead!"

Not thinkin', I jumped up and ran toward Lisa. I needed to get the gun out of her hand, in order to save my daughter. As Lisa and I wrestled for the gun, I caught a glimpse of Juan standin' in the doorway wit' a smirk on his face. I didn't understand why he was smilin'. I didn't understand why he wasn't helpin'. I didn't understand what went wrong when two shots were fired through the room and everything went dark.

TO BE CONTINUED...

THE DIRTY DIVORCE PART 2
COMING SOON

2010 RELEASES

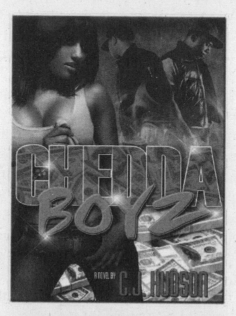

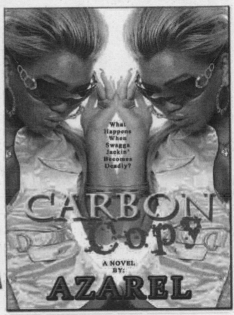

THE STREETS ARE TALKING ABOUT TRI STATE TRIANGLE 1 & 2

Meet Tamia and Sanaa, together they look for a quick fix to keep from losing Tamia's once lucrative salon. Little did they know that more money causes more problems. While keeping a secret about the true nature of their relationship these friends realize there's no easy way out of the street life!

In this explosive follow-up, Tamia finds herself plagued by drama from her past and Sanaa's fatal attraction lands her in a battle she wasn't prepared for. Meet Hutch and Juice, money is the name and beef is the game. They're fighting a war that'll endanger them both but each are determined to be the last man standing!

MAIL TO:
PO Box 423
Brandywine, MD 20613
301-362-6508

FAX TO:
301-856-4116

ORDER FORM

| Ship to: |
| Address: |
| City & State: Zip: |

Date: Phone:

Email:

Make all money orders and cashiers checks payable to: **Life Changing Books**

Qty.	ISBN	Title	Release Date	Price
	0-9741394-5-9	Nothin Personal by Tyrone Wallace	Jul-06	$ 15.00
	0-9741394-2-4	Bruised by Azarel	Jul-05	$ 15.00
	0-9741394-7-5	Bruised 2: The Ultimate Revenge by Azarel	Oct-06	$ 15.00
	0-9741394-3-2	Secrets of a Housewife by J. Tremble	Feb-06	$ 15.00
	0-9724003-5-4	I Shoulda Seen It Comin by Danette Majette	Jan-06	$ 15.00
	0-9741394-4-0	The Take Over by Tonya Ridley	Apr-06	$ 15.00
	0-9741394-6-7	The Millionaire Mistress by Tiphani	Nov-06	$ 15.00
	1-934230-99-5	More Secrets More Lies by J. Tremble	Feb-07	$ 15.00
	1-934230-98-7	Young Assassin by Mike G.	Mar-07	$ 15.00
	1-934230-95-2	A Private Affair by Mike Warren	May-07	$ 15.00
	1-934230-94-4	All That Glitters by Ericka M. Williams	Jul-07	$ 15.00
	1-934230-93-6	Deep by Danette Majette	Jul-07	$ 15.00
	1-934230-96-0	Flexin & Sexin Volume 1	Jun-07	$ 15.00
	1-934230-92-8	Talk of the Town by Tonya Ridley	Jul-07	$ 15.00
	1-934230-89-8	Still a Mistress by Tiphani	Nov-07	$ 15.00
	1-934230-91-X	Daddy's House by Azarel	Nov-07	$ 15.00
	1-934230-87-1	Reign of a Hustler by Nissa A. Showell	Jan-08	$ 15.00
	1-934230-86-3	Something He Can Feel by Marissa Monteilh	Feb-08	$ 15.00
	1-934230-88-X	Naughty Little Angel by J. Tremble	Feb-08	$ 15.00
	1-934230847	In Those Jeans by Chantel Jolie	Jun-08	$ 15.00
	1-934230855	Marked by Capone	Jul-08	$ 15.00
	1-934230820	Rich Girls by Kendall Banks	Oct-08	$ 15.00
	1-934230839	Expensive Taste by Tiphani	Nov-08	$ 15.00
	1-934230782	Brooklyn Brothel by C. Stecko	Jan-09	$ 15.00
	1-934230669	Good Girl Gone bad by Danette Majette	Mar-09	$ 15.00
	1-934230804	From Hood to Hollywood by Sasha Raye	Mar-09	$ 15.00
	1-934230707	Sweet Swagger by Mike Warren	Jun-09	$ 15.00
	1-934230677	Carbon Copy by Azarel	Jul-09	$ 15.00
	1-934230723	Millionaire Mistress 3 by Tiphani	Nov-09	$ 15.00
	1-934230715	A Woman Scorned by Ericka Williams	Nov-09	$ 15.00
	1-934230685	My Man Her Son by J. Tremble	Feb-10	$ 15.00
	1-924230731	Love Heist by Jackie D.	Mar-10	$ 15.00
	1-934230812	Flexin & Sexin Volume 2	Apr-10	$ 15.00
	1-934230748	The Dirty Divorce by Miss KP	May-10	$ 15.00

Total for Books $

Shipping Charges (add $4.25 for 1-4 books*) $

Total Enclosed (add lines) $

* Prison Orders- Please allow up to three (3) weeks for delivery.

Please Note: We are not held responsible for returned prison orders. Make sure the facility will receive books before ordering.

*Shipping and Handling of 5-10 books is $6.25, please contact us if your order is more than 10 books. (301)362-6508